Broken Pearl

Dawn Brower

Table of Contents

Acknowledgements

I AM THE FIRST TO ADMIT I can never picture what a cover should—or could look like. It amazes me when the cover artist can take the little bit of information I give them and create something fabulously breathtaking. Victoria Miller went beyond all of my expectations. She is a true genius and beyond brilliant. Thanks for making me an incredible, beautiful cover. Your creative intuition helps make this book shine brighter. I have no word to express how wonderful and generous you are—many many hugs.

To those who helped polish this story into its full glory: Leona, Amanda, and Christina, you are all marvelous, wonderful ladies. An extra special thanks to Emily, your last minute help polishing my story was very much appreciated.

Dedication

I'M DEDICATING THIS book to the most inspiring person I know, my beautiful amazing niece. She managed to overcome odds no one believed her capable of, and she not only met, but exceeded her goals. The strength and determination she held inside of her was absolutely astonishing. Alison Monaco, you are my super hero. I love you.

My only wish was you'd have been around long enough to read it. I wrote this book with you in mind—hoping you'd read the words I crafted for you. My heart breaks because I will never be able to share it with you. Now, you are one of the guardians watching out for those who need your special kind of strength. We're blessed to be engulfed in your unwavering ability to fight against all the odds. The angels are lucky to have you by their side.

Chapter One

"HAVE YOU EVER SEEN such a beautiful sight?" Rebecca O'Shea turned to her boyfriend, David Falcon, with a half smile on her face. Battleship row dotted the horizon with the commanding Pacific fleet. Turquoise waves rolled across the water and crashed into foamy white spray as it hit the beach's shallow depths. "Hawaii has to be the best place on Earth."

They were sprawled out on a red and white checker blanket, enjoying the sunrise. The sand of the beach gleamed against the sun's early morning rays. Rebecca and David were the only two souls currently occupying the secluded coastline. She leaned her head back, closed her eyes, and soaked in the warmth as she dug her toes inside the minuscule grains of sand. They fell over the top of her feet with tiny whispers of sensation as she pulled them back out. Her eyes fluttered open to take in her exquisite surroundings.

"Absolutely beautiful," David agreed.

Rebecca turned her head and gazed into David's warm chocolate-brown eyes. His onyx-black hair trimmed into short strands skimming the top of his head. The Navy's barber shaved it into the regulation buzz cut earlier in the week. She loved to run her hands across the sheared locks, absorbing the softness on her palms. He flashed her a smile, revealing dimples on each side of his mouth.

Just gazing at him stabbed her in the chest with an uncertainty she could not explain. The joy she experienced when near him surpassed any feeling she could ever explain with mere words, but it held a tinge of sadness, as if a bad omen waited to crash over them like the waves falling to shore. Rebecca hoped with all her being nothing would destroy their relationship, but her gut feelings never crossed over her without some undertone of truth. She shook off the dread and smiled back at him. No matter what happened, she intended to enjoy every moment with him. She loved him. No one else could ever make her heart soar in quite the same way.

"You're not even looking at the water." Her bubble of laughter floated across the warm breeze and faded away with the wind.

"Because nothing is more gorgeous than you."

Rebecca's lips tilted into a soft smile as her heart filled with overwhelming emotions of the warm and fuzzy variety. "You say the sweetest things. Is it any wonder I love you so much."

"What can I say? I'm lovable like that." David leaned in close to her. His nose lightly touched hers as he tilted his head to place a soft kiss on her lips. "Which brings me to why I brought you here."

"You mean you didn't want to watch the sky glow a brilliant orange-red as the sun rose in the sky?" she teased.

"No, not that it isn't a dazzling sight; however, you hold much more appeal to me."

David rolled onto his knees in front of her. He pulled both of her hands in his and stared into her eyes. "I know we have only been dating for a few months, but I feel like it's been a lifetime. I can't imagine being with anyone other than you. The first time we met, when I ran into you—literally—my world made sense for the first time. What I'm trying to say, I mean, ask you, is will you marry me? Be my wife and build a life together?"

Rebecca sat stunned for several seconds as his words washed over her. She never expected him to propose. Their courtship had been a whirlwind of nonstop activity and emotional highs. They met outside of a theater in downtown Pearl City. They both were in the process of exiting, but David forgot something, turned to go back inside, and smacked into Rebecca, knocking her to the ground. He apologized profusely for his bad manners. The encounter led to a small diner as they began to get to know each other. Not once since he asked her to accompany him to the beach a few hours ago, did she anticipate he would propose. The tiny uneasy vibe festered once again inside of her. That doubt, the niggling feeling of hesitation, told her she should back away as fast as possible. She loved and adored him and didn't see any rational reason why she should ever say no. Still, she believed she should mull it over for a few seconds, to keep him guessing. Rebecca didn't want him to think she was a sure thing.

Rebecca skimmed her fingers over the knotted blue neckerchief resting in the middle of his chest and tucked beneath the collar of his white naval uniform. Her lips tilted into a soft smile. "Yes, I will marry you."

David grabbed her and pulled her into his arms holding her tight in his embrace. He eased back and stared into her eyes. "You had me scared for a minute there. It seemed like it took forever for you to answer."

"You surprised me. It seems like a dream. I needed a moment to realize you were asking me to be your wife. I can't wait to marry you and start our life together."

"I'm glad you said that. I think we should get married after Thanksgiving. A small ceremony here on the island, and a big celebration later stateside. I'll request leave so we can have a honeymoon over Christmas and go to visit our families." He reached up and gently caressed her cheek with the tips of his fingers.

"I think it is a lovely idea. I will talk to the girls when I get back and begin planning it. I imagine we can have something small arranged in time." Enthusiasm filled her voice as she thought about the idea of her wedding. Excitement pooled in her stomach as butterflies danced around inside of her. In her dreams, she never thought she'd find someone to love and marry. Rebecca believed she was meant to remain alone. For the first time, she considered the possibility she'd been wrong in her assumption. She could see how it would all work. "It is a bit of a time crunch as Thanksgiving is only a week away, but as long as you don't want anything extravagant, it can be done. We should be able to have something set by say December sixth."

"Wonderful. As long as you are there, everything else is tiny details. Whatever you plan will be perfect as long as at the end of it all you're my wife." David rolled back over and sat down beside her. "Come here and sit in front of me so I can enjoy holding you for a little while."

BROKEN PEARL

She got up and sat between his legs making sure the skirt of her dress fell over her thighs, and leaned her head back on to his shoulder. Rebecca turned her head to study David's tilted face. He placed a soft kiss on her lips as he held her snuggly against his broad chest. She lifted her hands and rested them against his forearms with a light touch. Her heart pounded in her chest. David deepened the kiss as she opened her mouth to touch her tongue against his. Her eyes closed to allow herself to experience every new sensation without reality mucking it up. They sat in that position, kissing and holding on to each other for several minutes before David lifted his head mere inches above her face. Her eyes drifted open to meet his passion filled gaze.

"I almost forgot. I have a ring for you." David reached inside the pocket of his naval uniform and pulled out a small solitaire diamond ring. He clutched her left hand in his and slid it on her ring finger, fitting with a perfectness Rebecca couldn't help but be in awe of. After he secured it on her finger, he lifted her hand so they both could admire its sparkling brilliance, confirming they intended to spend the rest of their life together.

"As much as I'd like to stay and stare at your lovely golden red hair and emerald-green eyes, I need to get back to the ship. Unfortunately for me, I'm on duty in an hour, and there is some electrical equipment in need of repair." His left hand trailed across her shoulder and rested at the top of her head. His fingers wound through her long curly locks.

"I wish we could stay here forever, in this moment, and enjoy each other." Rebecca sighed as she continued to stare into the depths of his brown eyes.

"Me too, duty calls though. Come on; let's get up before I begin to consider a night in the brig a small price to pay to be here with you for an extra few minutes." He placed a quick kiss on the tip of her nose and released her from his arms.

"Sometimes, I wish we were not such responsible people. Reality has a sneaky way of creeping in and making us do the right thing. I'm actually on duty at the hospital in a few hours. I should go back to the cottage to change."

Rebecca stood up and grabbed her white strappy sandals from where she placed them on the blanket. David got to his feet, grabbed the red and white checkered blanket and shook the sand out of it. After he folded it and draped it across one of his arms, he reached for Rebecca's hand and led her to a nearby wooden bench. She sat down and put her shoes on so they could walk back to battleship row. David, currently stationed on the U.S.S. *Arizona*, needed to board the ship. As he needed to be there at a much earlier time than she was required to report at the naval hospital on the base near Pearl Harbor, they would say their goodbyes on the docks. The short trek only took them twenty minutes. The time flew by, and before she knew it, they stood on the docks leading to the ship he called home while stationed in Oahu, Hawaii. Pearl Harbor, home to the Navy's battleship row, was currently overflowing with boats soaking up the early morning light.

"Our time together always goes by so fast. I can't wait until I can see you again. How long are you on duty this time?"

"I don't have any free time for at least a week. I wish I could see you sooner. Maybe when we meet again, you will have some perfect plans in place for our wedding." David smiled, his stunning dimples blinding her with happiness.

"I will try my best. Now kiss me before someone comes down and drags you back onto the *Arizona*."

David complied with her request and wrapped his arms around her waist to embrace her as his lips caressed hers in a gentle, all-consuming kiss. Rebecca let the passion roll over her and accepted every ounce of love he poured into it. He let her go far quicker than she would have liked.

"I miss you already," she whispered.

"The week will fly by before you know it. We will have Thanksgiving weekend together. Maybe, we can do something special."

"No. The girls and I have an elaborate dinner planned. You should come to the cottage and bring a few of your friends. There is an intricate and detailed holiday being organized. They all miss home, and this is their way of coping. It'll be fun."

"I know a few guys who would appreciate both the dinner and the company of some lovely ladies. I will bring them along with me." David leaned in close to her and lightly kissed her again before turning to walk toward his ship. He stopped a short distance from her and turned his head back in her direction. "I'll be thinking of you each moment we are apart until I see you again." After he spoke the conviction filled words, he continued on toward his ship and boarded it.

A warm feeling spread through her. Yes, marrying David was the right decision. No matter what life had in store for them, she would not regret her decision. He made her happy in ways nothing else could. She couldn't imagine not having him in her life. Rebecca turned away from battleship row and walked to the cottage she shared with five other naval nurses. She couldn't wait to tell them her news. They would be jumping for joy at her unexpected engagement to David. All five of them would want to help her plan her wedding.

A smile of contented happiness spread across her face. She hugged herself with her arms and squeezed tight in an attempt to hold the fleeting feeling deep inside of her. Nothing could take it away from her. It would always remain a part of her even on her darkest days. With the resolution made, she walked faster toward her home away from home. Rebecca had a lot of planning to do, not just for her wedding, but also for the Thanksgiving dinner which would now include a few extra mouths to feed. She wanted to make as many memories of this cheerful time as she could. Her heart overflowed with so many emotions, she didn't know how she could be expected to contain them all.

Chapter Two

BIRDS CHIRPED A HAPPY tune as they flew across the cerulean sky, dipping and turning in sync with each other. The sun continued its ascent high into the sky. With each rise in its elevation, the warmer it became. The heat permeated the air as it blew through the palm trees and wrapped itself around Jaoel, causing tiny beads of sweat to form around the nape of his neck. He stood a small distance from the woman he'd been sent to protect and watched her walk away from battleship row.

Her red-gold hair blew in the balmy breeze, and her pink lips formed a pleased smile. A rosy glow grew across her cheeks, illuminating an already beautiful heart shaped face. She wore a white blouse securely tucked within a blue skirt floating around her hips that stopped just above her knees. Her white sandals tapped on the sidewalk as she crossed over it. Jaoel found her to be absolutely breathtaking and mesmerizing. From the first moment he spotted her, a part of him fell in love with her. It was a deep-rooted love bound in duty and honor, his only desire to ensure her safety. A notion he had to continuously remind himself—Jaoel gave up his right to an amorous relationship. Immortality didn't mix well alongside individuals with a finite lifespan.

If it meant watching from the shadows and following her in secret, he would fulfill his mission with every ounce of willingness he had inside of him. She didn't know about him, and if everything went as planned, she never would. His orders were to only reveal himself if she were in danger. So far her path continued as it was meant to. As long as nothing changed, he could remain in dark corners always observing.

"Your charge appears happy this morning."

Jaoel turned to see his commander standing behind him. His golden locks flowed around his beautifully chiseled face. A pair of icy blue eyes stared directly down at him, holding him in place. Jaoel didn't often report directly to him, but there were times he required one in person. Secondhand knowledge had a way of getting lost in translation. So every now and then, his leader popped in for an update. Other people in his unit found it unnerving to deal with, but it never bothered Jaoel. He welcomed him as he always did, with the reverence and respect his superior deserved.

"Michael." Jaoel nodded his head at him. "She had a good morning. It's why delight spills out of her movements."

Rebecca O'Shea appeared hale, hearty, and happy. The guardians couldn't ask for much else at this point. She still had no clue about her abilities. They were now beginning to surface at a stronger level. Her gift spiraled toward a point she'd no longer be able to ignore it. The onslaught of emotional chaos might cause her to unravel. She had no shield and showed no signs of developing one on her own. Jaoel would be forced to intervene soon.

"Is everything going as planned?"

"So far so good. Are you sure this is the correct path for her to be on?"

"It is. The next few weeks are crucial to us. How she handles the outcome will determine where she ends up.

Some things break people, while others thrive and grow stronger from it. We hope she isn't the sort who will be destroyed."

"I think she is a lot stronger than you realize." Jaoel shook his head and stared into Michael's eyes. "You are over thinking her situation."

"You may be right. You have to start taking a more active role. She may end up needing a solid presence in her life."

"I don't understand. I thought I was only to remain in the shadows and watching. So far, nothing has happened to constitute direct involvement. She's handling the transition well."

"Yes. We had hoped to keep to the set plan. Our advisors saw a shift in direction happen this morning. It suggested we needed to be a bit more proactive if we wanted to save her."

Jaoel jerked his head up, startled at Michael's news. Why didn't they inform him of this new direction? This was information he needed in order to do his job properly. "What shift? What caused this change? I don't understand how I could not be unaware of it."

"Nothing has changed, at least nothing we can pinpoint exactly. It's more a tremor. We don't want to take any chances if we can prevent something catastrophic from happening. Some things are inevitable and can't be changed. Her path for the most part is set, but there is a possibility she could crash and burn without aide." Michael's gaze dulled as if he could see a thousand different scenarios floating in front of him.

For all Jaoel knew, he did. After a brief pause, he shook his head and turned his attention back to Jaoel. "You know how important she is to our unit. The things she will be capable of will only benefit the world around us. We need her prepared to handle everything. When the crisis hits, how she handles it and moves forward will depend on her ability to control her emotions."

"What do you need me to do?"

Jaoel would do anything to protect her. He was a guardian, and he took his job seriously. Anything Michael needed from him it was his pleasure to give in service. He anticipated using all of his well-learned skills to make it happen. No matter what the cost may be to him, Jaoel would make sure she made it through stronger than ever.

"As I said, we need you to take a more active role. You need to arrange a meeting with her. Ingratiate yourself with her. No more shadows and watching from a distance. In order for her to survive what is to come, she will need her guardian there to guide her."

Michael turned to observe the turquoise waves floating over the Pacific. Jaoel let his words roll over him and considered what his next step might be. It shouldn't be too difficult to become a more active part in her life. She worked in the hospital on base. Accessing her would actually be simple. It was becoming a more permanent part of her life that could prove to be more difficult. Going into the hospital once would be simply explained away as a patient needing care. Stalking the halls without a reason to be there—it would be a clear way to get the local MP's calling on him for being a nuisance. It would be easier if he was around on a regular basis. He weighed all of his option and came to one conclusion. If he could be around base more often, he could run into her from time to time. Perhaps she would come to consider him a friend. An assignment at the hospital wouldn't work for him. He didn't have the necessary medical skills. Jaoel preferred a hands on approach and needed something to tinker with. While he fixed things, the human body went beyond his capabilities. Since he loved to fly, the best place for him to be was on one of the army airfields. He could tinker with the planes and make them worthy of the striking sapphire skies they coasted over.

"I see. I know exactly what I need to do. I will begin to take the necessary steps to become an active part of her life. By tomorrow morning, I will have it all in place to become a firm presence in her life."

Michael turned around and faced Jaoel. His blue eyes darkened and almost appeared black. It projected a startling difference to his normally icy blue irises. Lines formed around his eyes, and his mouth tightened into a grim line.

"I'm worried, Jaoel. There is a darkness coming. If we don't prepare well enough for it—let's just say there's a high possibility it will be here to stay. Hope is a powerful thing. We need to hold on to it and make sure it spreads. If not, well, I hate to see what becomes of this world."

"I understand. You have my solemn word that I will do everything in my power to make sure that nothing evil stays here." Jaoel stared directly into his commander's eyes.

"Good. I knew I could count on you to do what is necessary. If you need anything or run into any problems, do not hesitate to contact me. This needs to go as smoothly as possible. I trust you to see to the best interests of your charge."

"You may depend on it."

"You will have to alter your appearance of course. Your ebony locks will have to be sheared a bit shorter. I apologize for the inconvenience, but it's necessary. There will be no disguising your aquamarine eyes though. They are only slightly unusual, and maybe they won't stand out too much while you are on your assignment."

"I'm prepared to do whatever is necessary. It's only hair. It'll grow back if I wish it too." Jaoel remained stoic in his stance. He folded his arms behind his back and kept his head held high.

"You are one of my most devoted soldiers. Ever since you came into my service, you have always known your duty and have acted accordingly. It's why I gave you this particular assignment. I knew you were the only one who could handle all of its difficulties. It's perhaps one of our most complicated missions yet. It will not be easy, and it may take longer than either of us realizes. Do not fail me."

"You can count on me, Michael. I have never failed you before."

Michael's eyes glowed brighter with each word he spoke. His lips tilted into a smile, and his flawlessly chiseled cheekbones showcased his phenomenal beauty. Golden locks folded perfectly around his broad shoulders. From the pleased expression he portrayed, Jaoel knew the meeting went well. Michael believed their mission would go off without a hitch; it would not fall short of perfection or darn close to it anyway.

Jaoel hoped he wouldn't disappoint him.

"I know. Don't start now."

Michael nodded at him. For a brief moment, Jaoel turned his head away to observe the blue-green ocean. When his gaze shot upward, Michael no longer stood next to him. He always could vanish without anyone seeing him go. One day, Jaoel hoped to master the skill.

He walked away from his place in the shadows and welcomed the light. A lot needed to be accomplished before he could become involved in Rebecca's life. Her protection would always be at the forefront of his mission. She didn't have to necessarily like him as long as she survived the upcoming onslaught. Of course, it would make his job a whole lot easier if she did at least respect him. Her cooperation would go a long way in aiding his duty to guard her. Whatever darkness was approaching them, he would find a way to defeat it. No evil would be permitted to harm her.

Chapter Three

THE CHATTER FILLED the room to capacity; the acoustics making it seem louder and more animated as they talked. It took over and filled the little area with so much noise, it amazed Rebecca they could hear each other's words. There were six women sharing the cabin. The whole living space consisted of five rooms. If they all happened to be home, they scattered around the house to eat their meals. They had a small living area with wicker furniture made comfortable with pillows and blankets.

There were two bedrooms, and each housed three of the young nurses. Their single beds lined up in rows, each made up neat and tidy, except for the whirlwind of clothes often flung far and wide in each bedroom. They shared everything with each other. No secrets and a belief of what's mine is yours had become a part of their everyday philosophy.

Well, there were some minor exceptions to their rule.

No one poached another girl's beau, and any secrets shared were kept amongst themselves. Rebecca couldn't wait to share her good news with them all. Everyone gathered in the living room, the only room big enough to hold them all at once. Almost every place to sit was occupied by one of them.

"I have news," she announced to the room in general.

"Oh," Maxine said with a lift of her eyebrow. "Don't keep us waiting. Tell us what is going on in the world of Rebecca O'Shea."

Maxine Kay was boisterous and loud. She didn't stop to think before she opened her mouth, and it often showed. Her hair, a dark blond hue, curled around her neck and stopped at her shoulders. Her hazel eyes often gleamed with mischief. More often than not, she was the thrill seeker. Always looking for fun and ending up in trouble along the way.

"It's a lovely morning, don't you think?" Rebecca said as she nonchalantly ran her left hand over her hair to smooth out the curls.

"Don't be coy. You said you had something to tell us. Now don't act all shy and unwilling. Tell us already," Carolyn demanded.

Carolyn English could put a drill sergeant to shame. She was bossy, organized, and knew how to make people jump to do her bidding. Lucky for Rebecca, she had become rather used to Caro's own brand of dominance and could brush it off without a thought.

"Well, gee, if you're going to get snippy, maybe I won't share," Rebecca teased.

"As if you can keep anything in," scoffed Beatrice as she pushed her glasses back up her nose.

Beatrice Gold could make anything out of—well anything. She had a creative mind and utilized it often. As the only one in the group with that mindset, she kept herself busy by constantly crafting some project.

"She does have a point," Elizabeth agreed. She pulled an ochre strand of hair behind her ear and leaned forward resting her chin in her open palm.

Elizabeth Somers, their own personal gourmet chef. Her father studied in all the exclusive places and owned a fancy restaurant in New York. She learned how to cook while he balanced her on his knees. He expected her to take over after she married, but Elizabeth had other ideas. She wanted to help people and decided to train as a nurse. Of course, she also loved to cook, and they all took advantage of it.

Rebecca turned toward her with a cheeky smile on her face. "Oh? She does, does she?"

"You're enjoying this a tiny bit too much," Virginia piped in, a contented smile resting on her angelic face.

Virginia Hill had a soft voice and a capacity to give so much of herself it surprised them all. She was gentle and loving beyond anything they had ever experienced. Every one of them went to her when they needed to talk or seek advice because Ginny would never judge them for anything.

Rebecca contemplated her friends and admired them for each of their individual traits. It wasn't just Carolyn's rich mahogany waves, Virginia's sleek obsidian tresses, or even Beatrice's golden-blonde mane. Their physical attributes were all amazing, but those were only the superficial aspects and didn't give the full picture of who they each were. Every one of her roommates held something special inside, making them exceptional people.

"Now, Ginny, you know I'd never do any such thing." Rebecca placed her hand over her heart and blinked at her with fake sincerity.

"I don't need Caro to tell me she's lying with more conviction than a man trying to get under my skirt." Elizabeth stared up into Rebecca's eyes as the words rolled off her tongue.

Maxine stalked across the room and grabbed Rebecca's hand pulling it in front of her face to examine it. "Now what do we have here?

"Does she have a ring on her finger?" Carolyn leaped off the chair she occupied to come take a peek herself.

"I'll be, well look here. Our very own Becca managed to hook herself a man. Is it the sexy sailor you've been spending time with?" Maxine inquired.

"Well, yes. David proposed to me this morning."

"How wonderful." Virginia beamed.

"All right, now you have to give us all the details," Beatrice shouted above the growing chatter. "Everyone sit down so Becca can tell us everything. Don't leave out any details. We want to know everything."

"It was soooo romantic." Rebecca sighed.

"Yeah, yeah. Get to the good stuff. Did he kiss you?" Maxine waved her hand as she demanded more details.

"Don't interrupt her." Elizabeth got up and smacked Maxine in the shoulder with a playful tap of her hand.

"He did kiss me." Rebecca laughed. "But I'm not giving you details on it. Let's say we walked to the beach to watch the sunrise, and as soon as it glowed a bright orange, he kneeled before me and asked me to be his wife. He is the sweetest most loving man, and I couldn't be happier at the idea of spending the rest of my life with him."

"So of course he is happy you said yes, right?" Virginia inquired.

"Of course. He wouldn't have asked if he didn't want to marry me too."

"I wanted to be sure. You shouldn't marry someone unless they love you completely." Virginia's voice grew quiet as she spoke.

"He does love me, Ginny."

Virginia sat, quiet and unmoving. After several seconds ticked by, she nodded her head at Rebecca giving her stamp of approval.

"So when are you two going to get hitched?" Beatrice broke the silence

"That's where I need your help. First, I have to tell you he is coming to our Thanksgiving dinner and bringing a few of his friends. Second, we want to get married by the end of the first week in December. I think on Saturday the sixth, if we can arrange it all."

"Why so soon? Isn't it a little bit fast?" Beatrice glanced over at Rebecca with concern in her coffee-brown eyes.

"We want to start our lives together as soon as possible." Rebecca explained.

"There's no other reason?" Carolyn sat forward to study Rebecca.

"No, I promise."

They all sat, waiting, for her to interject with more information. When nothing else came from her, they nodded their heads, presumably accepting her at her word.

"Now where do we start first?" Rebecca asked.

"Thanksgiving dinner." Carolyn jumped up and walked across the room to grab a piece of paper and a pencil.

"Really? Why not the wedding?" Beatrice inquired.

"Because the wedding will be simple. Just us and the sailors David invites. Thanksgiving is going to be an all-out affair. We already have most of it planned, but it originally was just for us. We will need to plan for the extra mouths to feed, not to mention where we are going to put everyone. We don't exactly have a lot of space in the cottage." Carolyn continued to jot notes down on the paper in front of her.

"We can eat outside," Ginny suggested.

"Oh that's a lovely idea. We can take a couple tables and chairs outside. We can put some pretty tablecloths on the table. I can make a cornucopia for the centerpiece, and I also embroidered some napkins we can use," Beatrice murmured in a faraway voice.

"Good. I will add it to the list."

"I'm in charge of the main course. I could use some help with the side dishes. Who wants to help?" Elizabeth asked.

"I can help you," Maxine offered.

"Do you need any more money to help pay for everything?" Rebecca asked.

"No, we already have plenty from the original fund we created." Elizabeth shook her head as she spoke.

"Do you have any idea how many extra men we will have here?" Maxine's eyes darted toward Rebecca, her lips plumped into a coy smile.

"No, David didn't say. I would plan for say five to be on the safe side. I doubt he will bring too many though. He knows we don't have a lot of extra room here."

"That's probably a reasonable assumption to make. I'll plan for more than we think will be here. If you talk to him, please try to get a better idea of the actual number," Carolyn demanded.

"He said he is working for the next week. I don't think I will see him until Thanksgiving Day. It's going to be a long seven days." Rebecca frowned and bit her lip. It was always so hard to have so little time together; she wished he didn't have to stay locked on the *Arizona* so much. If only he could get away for a little bit and see her before Thanksgiving. They didn't get enough quality alone time.

"Okay. Well it will have to do then. I can work with what we have." Carolyn got lost in making her list.

"This is going to be so much fun." Maxine's eyes glowed with excitement.

"Can we plan the wedding now?" Beatrice asked.

"All right, fine, we can plan the wedding," Carolyn grumbled.

"You don't have to help if you don't want to," Rebecca told her.

"No, I'm steamrolling through these plans. I hate stopping in the middle of something. You know how I can get. I do want to help plan the wedding. Did you have something in mind?"

"Well, I want you all there of course. I'm open to suggestions otherwise."

"You should get married here by the cottage. We can see if Pastor Daniels can do the ceremony. I can talk to him Sunday at service if you like," Virginia interjected.

"Perfect. I will start a wedding planning list. Let me get another sheet of paper. I already filled up the one for Thanksgiving." Carolyn leaped forward to gather her supplies.

"I can help with the decorations. Oh—I can make you a beautiful bouquet. What's your favorite flower?" Beatrice asked, bubbly happiness spilling through her words.

"Oh Bea, thank you, anything you make would be lovely. I'm partial to white lilies, but I will love anything, I promise."

"I will make a cake. We can have a light lunch afterwards for everyone that attends. Maybe some tiny sandwiches and some salads for people to help themselves to when they are hungry," Elizabeth offered.

"Okay, I have Bea doing decorations, Ginny talking to Pastor Daniels, and Elizabeth making the food. Maxi you can help Lizzie and Bea wherever they need you. I'll help, too, of course. We only have one tiny detail remaining."

"What's that?" Rebecca asked.

"The wedding dress," Carolyn told her.

"Oh I hadn't thought of my dress. What should I wear?" Rebecca took a minute to visualize what the perfect dress would be—especially once David saw her in it. He'd be so awestruck as he watched her walking toward him. "I want it to be simple yet elegant, maybe some intricate beading or lace to give it a little sophistication."

"I think that calls for a shopping expedition," Maxine exclaimed.

"Definitely," Carolyn agreed.

"I do see your point, but it will have to wait. I'm on duty at the hospital in less than an hour. I need to get ready.

Let's make a trip of it sometime over the next several days."
Rebecca smiled at each of them, reassuring her roommates
how grateful she was for their help. "It's going to be fun
shopping for my dress. I'm sure you'll share your opinions
with me. Thank you so much for offering to help me pick the
perfect dress."

They all nodded their heads.

"I will make a note of it and let you know what day is
going to work for all of us," Carolyn announced.

Rebecca laughed. "Sounds like a plan. Now if you'll
excuse me, I'm going to go and change. Thank you all for
everything."

Rebecca walked away to chimes of "you're welcome"
from all five of the women. She went into the bedroom she
shared with Virginia and Carolyn and pulled out her nurse's
uniform. It took her less than ten minutes to completely
change, wave goodbye, and begin her trek to the naval
hospital. Her smile grew on her face the more she thought
about how wonderful everything in her life was. She had
five remarkable friends who were going to help make her
wedding impossibly lovely and a fiancé who loved her
completely. Nothing was going to ruin her wedding and the
life she envisioned for herself. She had a lot to look forward
to, and for the first time in her life, she snuffed out
everything that made her believe otherwise. She refused to
allow any darkness inside to ruin her happiness.

Chapter Four

REBECCA ALLOWED HERSELF to hope for one thing in her life. A fulfilling career as a nurse. She now had that and so much more. The navy trained her in various forms of physical therapy. Only a few in each class were given the opportunity.

Rebecca wrapped her arms around her waist as a wave of joy spread through her. Close to twenty-four hours ago, David asked her to marry him. She still couldn't believe she now had a wedding to plan.

"Rebecca, I require your assistance," Doctor Thorne called from across the room snapping her back to reality.

"Certainly. What do you need me to do?"

"There are a couple men being admitted with influenza. We are keeping them here, hoping to keep it contained and prevent it from spreading to the rest of the sailors on board the ship and to those working at the airplane hangars. I need you to get their beds ready in the isolation ward. Afterward, go over their charts and make sure you follow the care instructions listed."

The hospital on base wasn't enormous or even impressive. It did what it was designed to do, be functional and organized. On most days, it didn't host a lot of patients. Those that came in left after treatment had been administered.

No one stayed on any real long term basis.

Influenza, however, could be deadly. The urgency in the doctor's voice filled her with dread. Maybe this explained her feelings earlier. Could it be as simple as a possibly fatal illness giving her the doom and gloom insight? She would make sure to do everything in her power to prevent anyone else getting sick. "I will get right on it. Is it only the two patients? Is there anything else you need me to do?"

"Not until you get those things done, and yes, so far only two individuals. One is actually an army mechanic. He only arrived on the island this week. It's possible he is the one who brought it with him. They both came in together. I will get Doctor Chase to help move them to the beds once they are prepared. After they are moved, these beds need to be stripped immediately and the area cleared. I don't want an outbreak of influenza to contend with."

"Where is the other patient stationed?" Rebecca asked.

"Kenneth Blackman, he is normally on an aircraft carrier. He got grounded and is temporarily on the *Oklahoma* while he logs in some flight time to recertify. Nice fellow. Came in alongside, Joel Remak, the army mechanic. They practically carried each other in. They must have spent some time in each other's company. I'm hoping it's been limited to the two of them, and by quarantining them, it won't spread across the rest of the population on the island."

It sounded like the illness wasn't likely to spread to anyone else on the island. Rebecca hoped it didn't go any further than the hospital. If they worked fast enough, it should be limited to only those that had any contact with the two already infected.

"All right, I will start with their beds in the isolation ward. I will inform you when they are ready. Once I have completed that, I will report back to you for further instructions."

The doctor nodded his head at her. "Good. I have a few people to notify in case anyone else becomes sick. I will be back in a half hour. I'm sure you will have everything ready by then."

Rebecca watched him go for a few seconds and then turned to her own list of things. She first grabbed the necessary bedding from a nearby cabinet and carried it to the isolation room. She made up the two beds with precision, grabbed a couple pitchers filling them with water, as well as drinking cups, and placed them on the bedside table. Fluids were essential in caring for patients with influenza. Unfortunately, they couldn't always keep the fluids down. The next few days would be a constant battle while they fought off the sickness. She took a step back and surveyed the room. Everything they needed to care for the two men was in place and ready for immediate use. Rebecca grabbed the charts and read through the doctor's notes. Satisfied, she set the charts on the ends of the beds and went in search of Doctor Thorne.

She reached the ward and searched for the doctor. He was nowhere to be found. His errand must have taken longer than expected. She turned to go check another area of the hospital and ran into someone. She hit the floor with a *thud* as her backside met the linoleum tiles.

"I'm so sorry, ma'am. I thought you heard me walking up, or I would have spoken. Let me help you up."

She gazed up into the most beautiful aquamarine eyes she had ever seen. They were a combination of brilliant green and blue mixed together. Rebecca didn't think she'd ever seen eyes quite the same shade before. She remained so transfixed by the color and clarity of his eyes, she didn't move for several seconds. When she snapped out of it, she finally got a glimpse at the rest of him. His brilliant eyes were framed by long black eyelashes. The man's face was harsh and yet beautiful at the same time. Ebony locks were sheared short on the sides, but still long enough on top to fall around his forehead and hug his ears. Rebecca wanted to reach up, run her hands through it, and get lost in the depths of his sea-green eyes. Her gaze floated over him quick and efficiently. She noted he was tall with lean muscles. In her swift observation, she also noticed his skin tone dropped a few shades to become quite pale, and he wore hospital pajamas. He must be one of the patients set to take residence in the isolation room.

"Ma'am, can you hear me? Let me help you up." He waved his hands in front of her face attempting to get her attention.

"Oh, I'm sorry. I guess I got lost in my own thoughts there for a minute. It's not necessary to help me up. I'm Nurse O'Shea." Rebecca moved out of his way and stood up before him. "Do you need help?"

"I was searching for Doctor Thorne. He said we were going to be moving to another room. I thought he said he would be back a half hour ago, but it's been nearly an hour now."

"He had to notify some people about some things. I actually expected him back already. Are you Joel or Ken?"

"I'm Joel. Ken is a little too sick to move. It's partly why I went in search of Doctor Thorne. I don't know what to do to help him."

"Well, you shouldn't be out of bed either. I will go see what's going on with Mr. Blackman, and you can get back in bed too," she scolded him.

"Yes ma'am" A sheepish grin formed on his face.

"Come along now. Let's go check on your friend. Doctor Thorne said you just arrived on the island this week. You don't appear too bad, now. When did you begin to develop symptoms?"

"Yeah, I got orders to pack and move out here immediately. Not that I mind. Who wouldn't want to be stationed in paradise? I may have started to feel bad before I got here. I ignored it and kept working. I realize my mistake now."

Most of the men who enlisted believed themselves to be invincible. She noticed they didn't want to admit they could be waylaid by an illness or injury. A lot of them attempted to work through it and aggravated the injury or illness further. So his admission didn't surprise her.

"I agree on all counts. Hawaii is a perfect place to be stationed. I've been happy here. And yes, you should have come in immediately."

When they arrived in the infirmary, Ken was passed out in his bed and unmoving. Beads of sweat dripped down his forehead, and his sandy blond hair was soaking wet. Rebecca placed the back of her hand against his face and could feel the heat radiating off of him. He was burning up.

"He has to be moved immediately to the isolation room. I will get a gurney."

"Do you think he will be okay?" His sea-green eyes filled with concern as he gazed at his friend.

"I honestly don't know, but I do hope so. I will be back in a few minutes." It wouldn't do any good to have a quarantined patient roaming the halls. "Stay with him in case he wakes up. A familiar face can make worlds of difference."

"All right. I barely know him, but I like him and would hate to see anything serious happen to him."

"We will certainly do our best to get him through this. I need to get the gurney. I will be right back." Rebecca rushed away from them to get the tools necessary to move the sick man.

She found a gurney in the hallway. An odd place for it to be, but she thanked the heavens for someone's negligence. For once, it was actually a good thing. She pushed it through the swinging doors and guided it over to Kenneth Blackman's bedside. Joel jumped forward to help her lock the wheels in place.

"Now, I need to transfer him over and wheel him to the other room. If you can step aside so I can move him over by lifting the bed sheet underneath him, I will roll him over myself."

He glanced at Kenneth and back at her. Joel shook his head and asked, "Don't you think it would be easier if I helped you?"

She hated asking him for assistance. He was sick too and shouldn't be required to aide her in moving his friend. Where was Doctor Thorne? He said he would be back to help her.

"I can do it myself." Joel moved to the gurney. "I don't want you to injure yourself trying to move him. He is large man and easily outweighs you by a hundred pounds. Honestly, I'm feeling a lot better. Just allow me to do it. I wouldn't feel right if I didn't help you."

Before she could answer, Joel lifted Ken up effortlessly and placed him on the gurney. Joel Remak must be one strong individual to be able to move a two hundred pound plus grown man without breaking a sweat while sick in his own right. Rebecca was so shocked, she couldn't get any words out of her mouth. She stood there for several seconds with her mouth gaped open.

"Do we need to secure him before we move him?" Joel asked.

"Uh, yeah, there are some straps to keep him in place. Let me fasten them, and then we can be on our way."

After they were fastened, she motioned to Joel, and they started moving. Rebecca pushed open the door and held it open. She gestured Joel inside and pointed to the beds already made up for them. They were located on the opposite wall of the room; the remaining eighteen beds were still bare. Once they got to the far side of isolation ward, she unfastened the straps and once again Joel moved Ken over to his bed before she could stop him. She should have said something to him the first time, but he seemed determined to do it whether she liked it or not though.

"Joel, you really shouldn't be exerting yourself so much. I appreciate your help, but I don't want you to have a setback. You should go lay down in your own bed. There is a pitcher of water on the bedside table if you are thirsty. I am going to return this to where it belongs, and I will be back to check on you later."

"All right, I suppose I could use some rest." He nodded at her as he went to lie down on his bed.

Once his head hit his pillow, his eyes closed, and he appeared to fall asleep. Maybe the exertion did him in. Rebecca honestly didn't know for sure. All she knew for certain after spending a short amount of time in his company was she found him quite fascinating. A thousand pinpricks of confusion pierced through her heart. She couldn't find another man intriguing.

Rebecca loved David—Joel, a soldier, needed her help—nothing more.

She rubbed her palms across her skirt to remove the dampness. Her teeth rolled over her bottom lip as she studied him through a narrowed gaze. Admittedly, she did find him interesting, but that's where her curiosity ended.

She left the room so she could finish her duties, putting any fascination with her new patient out of her mind.

The first thing on her list was to locate one of the doctors for further instructions. Joel's odd behavior never far from her mind the entire time, she didn't understand him. Maybe it was part of how he'd been raised. His mother could have instilled some pretty hardcore manners into him. Since she was being forced to spend time caring for him, maybe she would find out what drove him to do the things he did.

Chapter Five

THE WARD WAS VACANT, and an irregular silence filled the room.

Not a sound could be heard anywhere in the ward which struck Rebecca as particularly odd. The doctors were nowhere to be found, and the beds were already stripped of any adornment, not even a sheet covered them. The whole room had been engulfed by darkness giving it an eerie feel. Rebecca took a few careful steps inside and to examine her surroundings.

"Doctor Thorne? Doctor Chase?" Rebecca called out as she made her way through the empty ward.

"Is anyone here?"

Rebecca walked through the doors at the other side of the room and turned the corner leading to another part of the hospital. She hit a solid form and fell...again. Apparently it was her day for walking into people and landing on her backside. She glanced up and saw the person she ran into this time was one of the doctors she'd been seeking out for further instructions.

"Doctor Chase. I'm so glad to see you. Do you know where Doctor Thorne is?"

A file tucked between his arms and a pen in his hand, he glanced at her with a dismissal expression on his face. "He left the ward a few minutes ago to take care of a few things in his office. I'm in charge for the moment. Influenza isn't something we should be taking lightly. He ensured all of the beds in the area were stripped and taken for immediate laundering."

"Oh, I agree. That's why I wanted to let you both know both patients are in the isolation ward and resting comfortably. Although, I am a bit concerned about Kenneth Blackman. He is unconscious at the moment, and his fever appears to be quite high. I've gotten him comfortable in bed and made sure to not cover him with a blanket."

Doctor Chase stared at her for several moments as her words appeared to sink in. She hoped he gave her something to go on soon. She wanted to complete her work and head home. The day had been a lot longer and much more difficult than expected. The work of a nurse was constant and never finished. What she couldn't finish herself, another nurse would be assigned the task.

"I see. Well there are a few things I need to discuss with you. The care of the patients is one of them. There is also a small matter I know will be a high inconvenience to you."

Rebecca tilted her head and stared at the doctor, confusion clouding her eyes. She expected there would be things to discuss and didn't understand why he thought anything would be a problem for her.

"I don't follow. I mean I do, but I don't understand what might be troublesome for me."

"We are making it mandatory for you to remain here until both patients are recovered. You are the only nurse exposed to the illness. Doctor Thorne stripped the remaining beds and will also be on duty for their care. He has been sequestered in his office making phone calls since they came in. We believe this is the best possible way to prevent an outbreak. We are going to have you reside in the isolation wing with the two men. Doctor Thorne will come in to check on them periodically and give you instructions, but will remain in his office most of the time unless needed," Doctor Chase explained.

"What? I can't stay here! I don't have a change of clothes, and I have plans."

"I'm sure you do, but this cannot be helped. As far as a change of clothing, we have extra nurse uniforms in one of the supply closets. I will make sure some are sent to the isolation ward for you, if they are needed."

Thanksgiving was five days away. She was supposed to help plan it. It went beyond the planning or having time off. David expected her to be there. She wanted to see him and spend time with him. It would totally ruin things if she was stuck in the hospital. They already had so little time together. Rebecca didn't want to miss another chance to see him. Her days were always brighter and happier if she got to see him, hug him, and generally just embrace the pleasure of their love.

"Are you sure I have to stay? I honestly do have a lot of other things I need to take care of. Surely, there is another option."

The doctor had a grim expression on his face as he nodded his head in the affirmative. He didn't try to explain it all to her again, simply stood there waiting for her to accept the inevitable.

She didn't like it, but it appeared like she had no choice. "What about once they start to improve? Will I be able to leave?"

"I don't know. That is our hope of course—you are going to have to be patient and see this through. It's all I can offer you right now."

All he could offer her? She wanted a little more reassurance than I don't know and the wait and see he offered her. Rebecca would have to do her best to make sure both patients had the best care possible and hope they improved fast. She didn't want to be selfish, but she really wanted to see David and spend Thanksgiving with her friends. They would need to know about her predicament, or they would worry. Yes, they were all nurses, but none of them were scheduled to be on duty for a couple of days.

"I suppose it is all I can do. Wait and see. Can I send a letter to my roommates so they don't expect me home? If they don't hear from me, they might come searching for me. They are nurses as well, so they should understand why I have to stay."

He appeared to weigh her question over as he gazed down at her. "I am not sure it is a good idea, but I can also see your point. I know how the rest of the nurses are. They might decide to come here themselves if they are not made aware of the situation. Write the letter, and I will make sure they receive it. I will retrieve some paper and a pencil, so you can jot something down quick."

Rebecca waited in the hall for Doctor Chase to retrieve the items. Once he returned, he handed them over to her and waited while she wrote her roommates a quick note.

BROKEN PEARL

My Dearest Friends,

There has been an emergency at the hospital that requires me to stay here for the next several days. Do not worry about me. I am fine. There are two patients quarantined in the isolation room to prevent an outbreak of influenza. The doctors agreed it's best to only keep one nurse exposed. And as I was the nurse who handled their admission, I am the most logical choice. If anything changes, I will let you know. Please keep going with the Thanksgiving plans as I hope to be able to attend. If for some reason I'm still unable to be there, please give my regrets to David. Tell him I miss him, love him, and hope to see him soon.

Much Love,

Rebecca

She folded the note in half and handed it over to Doctor Chase to deliver. He grabbed it and placed it in the pocket of his white coat.

"Do you need me to do anything else, or can I retire for the evening?" Rebecca asked.

"No. Get whatever you need and go ahead and make yourself comfortable in the isolation room with the other two patients. A tray of food will be sent up. Just clear liquids for them and a full meal for you. They will knock on the door, as protocol dictates, to let you know they are ready for retrieval in the hall. I will go and bring everything in at that time."

"All right. I will keep that in mind. Goodnight, Doctor."

Luck, as usual, was not on her side. At least she could make sure both men got some proper care. Not that all the nurses were not capable, but some liked to take shortcuts to get done faster. It would also give her the opportunity to get to know Joel Remak. Something about the man seemed familiar to her, but she couldn't say what. It was a mystery she meant to solve while stuck in a room over several days in his company.

He didn't appear as sick as Kenneth.

Perhaps they could keep each other company to kill the many hours they would have together. Rebecca reached the supply closet and grabbed a few extra nurse uniforms. After she had them in hand, she walked over to the bedding and grabbed several sets of sheets and blankets. One for herself and extras in case they were needed for the patients. No reason not to prepare for every possibility before heading over to the isolation ward. With the items, she strolled on over to the room.

She didn't rush. She had no reason to.

Why be in a hurry when once she got there, she'd be required to stay there for an undetermined length of time. After she arrived at the doors leading her to the room, she pushed them open and stepped inside. Both men were sound asleep on their beds. Rebecca sighed and made up one of the beds for herself on the far side of the room. She wasn't the least bit tired, but needed the bed ready for when she needed to rest.

"Is someone else sick?" a voice asked from behind her.

She glanced over to see Joel sitting up on his bed watching her.

"No. I'm making the bed up for myself," she replied.

"Are you sick?"

"Not at all. I'm going to be your nurse for the next few days, and that means I'm staying in here with you. It's a large room, twenty beds. I'm going to stay on the far side of the ward. Let me know if you need anything. Dinner should be arriving soon if you're hungry. It is only going to be liquids, but it's better than nothing."

"Not really." Joel shook his head.

"Well, you should try to eat anyway. It's only going to be a light broth and easy to digest. How is Mr. Blackman doing?"

"He hasn't woken since you left, but he appears to have calmed down a little bit. I checked his head like you did with your hand earlier, and his skin has cooled. Is that a good thing?"

"Yes, it means his fever is down. I think that bodes well for both of you."

"That's a relief. I'm a bit concerned about him." Joel's aquamarine eyes were filled with worry as he glanced over at Kenneth Blackman.

"I will do my best to make sure you are both fine at the end of this. If you both make it through the week, you can join me and the other nurses I live with for Thanksgiving dinner."

Joel smiled at her words, and her heart jolted at the sight. It made his face light up with a glow, and it made him utterly beautiful to behold. She found him attractive and fascinating. Not a good combination for a woman happily in love and engaged. These strange feelings needed to go away before she questioned her choices. No, Joel was only a patient, nothing more than that. She liked him, but she loved David. It was only human to be attracted to someone else. What you did with the attraction though made all the difference in the world. David loved her, and she would not do anything to make him question her love for him. Joel would remain exactly what he was, a patient and someone in need of her help.

"I'll take you up on that. I haven't had a decent Thanksgiving meal in ages," he replied.

"I promise it will be good. We all have certain gifts, and the nurse in charge of food is brilliant in the kitchen. Now, go lay down and rest, or you won't get the chance."

"Yes ma'am," he agreed.

Rebecca watched as he lay down and closed his eyes. Relief flooded her senses to not have his unusual eyes trained on her. She didn't understand what was going on, but she swore she could feel an energy coming off of him. Her odd perception was growing stronger and she didn't understand what it meant. Maybe something about Joel Remak was making her more aware of her gifts or perhaps he amplified them somehow. It scared her enough to keep a small distance from him.

Chapter Six

REBECCA WOKE UP AND stretched the kinks out of her muscles. The setting sun cast shadows over the room. She jolted out of bed as she remembered her current location and reason for being there. A quick scan of the room told her the two patients still rested in their beds. She walked to the door and checked outside to see if their dinner had arrived while she slept. A tray sat outside the door on a nearby table. She peeked down the hall to see if anyone was around, but it remained quiet and dark. Glancing back at the tray of food, she ambled over to check the contents and see if any of it might still be edible. She had no clue how long ago the items had been dropped off for them.

Removing the cover, she saw it had a simple sandwich underneath resting on a plate. Three cups were filled with a juice of some kind. Next to the drinks were two bowls with covers on them. Pebbles of water gathered on top of the lid over the bowls. She removed the lid and waved her hand over the top of the broth and no heat touched her skin. Either the contents were cold or cooled off, but they would not be warm.

It was probably best because it might be too difficult for the patients to eat at the broth while it was at a higher temperature. No matter either way, they still needed to eat so she picked up the tray and carried it inside the room. She made her way over to their beds and placed it on a table across from them. Turning around, she strolled over by Joel and placed a hand on his shoulder. His eyes jolted open at her touch, and he jumped up to a seated position with his arms feeling the bed to figure out his environment.

"What's wrong? What do you need?" He did a quick scan of the room, checking out his surroundings. After his eyes traveled the entire room he turned his attention back to her.

"Everything is fine. We all fell asleep and missed the dinner call. It's a bit cold, but if you're hungry, you can still eat."

"No, I don't want any food"

"You should try to eat. If you want to get better, you will need to fuel your body for the fight," Rebecca coaxed.

Joel shook his head and peeked over at Kenneth still lying asleep on the bed next to him.

"What about him. Doesn't he need to eat to?"

Rebecca pursed her lips at him in displeasure. "Yes, he does need to eat, and I plan on waking him up as well. Don't change the subject."

"Fine. Wake him up, and we can eat together," Joel conceded.

Rebecca turned toward Kenneth's bed and strolled over to his side. She placed her hand on his forehead and felt cool clammy skin. His eyes opened into tiny slits at the gesture. He blinked several times, and his eyes finally focused on her face.

"How are you doing, Mr. Blackman? You've been quite sick. I have some cool broth. Do you think you can attempt to eat some of it?" Rebecca inquired.

"I'll try." Kenneth's voice cracked and came out more of a croak with each word.

"Do you think you can feed yourself or would you like my help?"

He cleared his throat and stared up into her eyes. "Thirsty."

Rebecca walked over to the side table and filled some water half way into a glass. She turned back to Kenneth and tilted it up at his mouth. He swallowed the water with quick movements. He drank every drop in the glass and smiled up at her.

"Thank you. My throat was quite dry. The cool water felt amazing going down," he whispered.

"You're welcome. Would you like to attempt the broth now?"

"Yes. If you will help me sit up, I want to try to eat it myself."

Rebecca set the empty cup on the table and twisted back around to help him sit up. When she rotated back into position, she noticed Joel standing by Kenneth's side. How had he gotten over there so fast? She thought he was still in bed while she talked to the other patient, but Joel seemed determined to do more than he should.

"Mr. Remak you should be in bed"

He ignored her, his attention remaining on Kenneth. "Hey, buddy, how are you feeling? You had me worried for a minute there. Let me help you sit up."

"Joel, Mr. Remak, I must insist you get back in bed. It's my job to help Mr. Blackman sit up, not yours."

He continued to ignore her words and reached down to lift Kenneth up onto a sitting position. Rebecca could feel her ears begin to burn with anger. She clenched her fists in a tight ball at her sides to physically restrain herself from lashing out at him. The blasted man tried her patience like no one she knew. She had known him less than half a day, and he already did things that made her want to smack him. Unfortunately for her, she couldn't act on those impulses. She needed to remain professional and attempt to reason with him. While she reined in her anger, he finished lifting Kenneth up into the sitting position and stood back up at his side.

"I'm not going to repeat myself again, Mr. Remak. Please return to your bed. I will bring you both your broth once you are sitting comfortably."

She turned her back to him and walked over to the tray. She grabbed two spoons and both bowls of soup and carried them over to their bedsides. At the table between their beds, she placed the items and gave them her full attention.

"Who wants their broth first?" she asked.

"I can feed myself, ma'am, if you want to hand it to me," Kenneth replied.

Rebecca took the lid off the soup and placed the spoon inside letting the handle rest on the lid of the bowl. With care, she walked over to him and handed him the bowl. With shaky hands, he took it from her and balanced the bowl in his left hand. He picked up the spoon with his right hand, and with a slow pace, brought it up to his mouth. The liquid managed to stay in place, not a drop spilling, as he began to feed himself. Satisfied he could manage on his own, she turned her attention back to Joel and was shocked to see him already eating his broth.

"What are you doing?"

"I'm eating. You said I needed to if I wanted to get better."

"You're correct." Rebecca fought the urge to roll her eyes. "I did say that. However, you are also doing way more than you should. I need you to stop and consider what your actions are going to do for your overall health. If you keep overtaxing yourself, you might set yourself back. I'd like to leave this hospital at some point, and you are contradicting me at every turn. You should have waited for me to bring you the soup instead of taking it yourself."

Rebecca couldn't help thinking of David. She was stuck in this room with an obstinate patient when she'd rather be with the man she adored. Normally, she enjoyed her job, but dealing with her current circumstances was trying. What she wanted to do was feel David's arms wrapped around hers, engulfing her with the warmth of his love. No, she had to stay at the hospital and do her duty as a nurse. With a sigh, she turned her attention back to her patients.

Joel's eyes lit up with humor as she scolded him for his actions. The corners of his mouth twitched as he appeared to fight a smile from forming.

"This isn't funny," she exclaimed.

"Of course not, it's way more than that."

"I fail to see your point."

"I can see that." He gave into his urge to smile, and it lit up his face.

Butterflies invaded her stomach, and she placed a hand over it to try to quiet them. "Why are you doing that?"

"Doing what?" he asked.

"Smiling like that"

"I can't help it. You make me want to smile." He flashed her another heart-stopping grin.

"Well stop it." Rebecca's belly flip flopped and filled with a weird feeling. Something about Joel—made here want things she shouldn't. The little swirls, dips, and highs...each one a new sensation, she needed for them to go away. Whatever Joel was doing, she wanted him to just stop already.

"Sorry, Becs. You'll just have to accept it; I can't help how I feel."

"Don't call me that. I don't have to accept any such thing."

A boisterous laugh floated through the isolation ward, ricocheting across the walls and making it louder as it bounced around them. Surely he didn't know what his smile did to her insides. She thought she had better control over her tumultuous emotions. Apparently, he sensed something inside of her. Her gift blossomed, and she could feel a warmth begin to grow inside of her. The sensation reminded her of amusement. Maybe she could feel the mirth growing in him, and that was why she had these fluttering deep inside when he smiled. That didn't give him the right to say things like that to her.

"Honestly, I'm feeling much better. I promise you, I won't have any setbacks, and we will get out of here in time for that Thanksgiving dinner you promised."

She forgot she invited him over for dinner if they got better in time. Rebecca was starting to regret extending the invitation. Nothing she could do about it now. It would be rude to back out and say he couldn't go. It didn't matter anyway. She planned on devoting all her time to David.

"Absolutely. So keep that in mind when you are starting to do too much. I'm going to go eat my own meal now. When you are both done, let me know, and I will come retrieve your bowls. You should both rest afterwards. It will go a long way in helping you to heal."

Rebecca turned her back to them both and strolled over to the tray. Picking up the plate with the sandwich and a cup of juice, she carried them over to a nearby chair and sat down. After she made herself comfortable, she ate in silence. She chewed without thought and didn't taste any of it.

Her thoughts were too absorbed on the feelings Joel Remak caused inside of her. She didn't know what any of it meant. It could be her intuition kicking in to full gear around him. Maybe her gift was growing into something more and those feelings he invoked were actually something coming from him. She truly hoped so, because she didn't like it one bit. There was nothing she could do about it, so she tried to let it go as she finished her meal.

If the patients needed her, they knew where to find her. She needed to absorb all the new sensations growing inside her and didn't need her unusual reactions to Joel to cloud them. So she kept her distance from him for the rest of the night.

Chapter Seven

AFTER SPENDING THREE days in a hospital ward with two men she barely knew, Rebecca needed to go home. She was becoming stir crazy only having Joel and Kenneth for company. As soon as she could, she planned to leave the hospital. If she had to spend any more time with them, she might lose her mind. Yes, Doctor Thorne occasionally stepped in to check on them, but for the most part, it was just the three of them.

The more time she spent with them, the weirder her gut feelings became. Sometimes a feeling would creep in she didn't recognize. An emotion that did not belong to her, but one radiating off one of the other two men—they became a part of her to the point she didn't know if the sensations actually belonged to her or not. She separated herself from the overwhelming feelings and tried to pinpoint their root. Joel's amusement flooded her system, and something she couldn't yet recognize, but mainly because one tiny bit of emotion, she believed might possibly be hers. Sadness fell off Kenneth in waves. So when the three of them sat down to talk, opposite emotions ruled inside of her. If she sat with them much longer, she could face a system overload. It wouldn't take long before she'd to have to get up and gain a little distance from the two men. Insanity—the ordeal would soon be driving her over the edge, and she couldn't find anything to hold onto to prevent herself from falling over it.

The whole thing left her confused. She didn't understand any of it. All she wanted was her friends and to see David. She missed them and being away from them hammered it home.

"Hey, Becs. Any idea when the doctor is going to let us out of this joint?" Joel brought her out of her own thoughts with his question.

"I'm thinking if we're all lucky, tomorrow. You both have shown signs of incredible improvement, and you are definitely past the contagious stage." She turned to glance up into his aquamarine eyes. No matter how many times she saw them, they always caught her by surprise. Such unusual and ancient depths staring back at her, she didn't know what to make of them.

"Good, the room is starting to feel a bit stifling," Joel replied.

"How are you feeling today, Kenneth?" Rebecca asked.

"I'm doing all right. I think I share Joel's sentiments. It's time to leave and rest someplace else."

"You think you can manage to take care of yourself in the barracks?" she asked.

"No need. I already requested permission to stay with Joel here in the room attached to the airfields. He stays there by himself and said he could use the company. Being close to the planes will give me more opportunities to log in some flight time. He's on one of the smaller airfields and fixes a lot of the planes in need of repair. It's a perfect solution for both of us."

Rebecca turned her attention back to Joel. He sat on his bed watching them talk. Not once did he stop to interject his own thoughts.

"You work on the airfield alone?" she asked.

"It's a tiny one. They don't need more than me on it. It's been abandoned for a while now. If I ever leave, they will probably no longer use it. With me here, no one has been there to take care of the planes. They take the overflow to me, and these days there isn't much." Joel got up off his bed and walked to a nearby window to glance outside.

"You are not a prisoner. This is just until you are well. If you are the only one that takes care of the airfield, what happens to it when you're not there? Wait, didn't you say you just arrived on the island this week?" Rebecca stared at Joel waiting for him to reply.

"Exactly right. I received transfer orders and took over the position at the airfield the day before I arrived at the hospital. It's small. I repair the planes, and Kenneth here has been testing their flight readiness. So it only needs to be the two of us. When the planes are ready for use, they send pilots over to fly them back to the larger air bases," Joel explained.

"I don't understand how Kenneth got so much sicker than you did. You didn't even spend a lot of time together. Doctor Thorne's theory doesn't seem accurate now that I've had some time to think about it."

"Do you really need to figure it out? Can't you accept sometimes different things effect different people in different ways?" Joel asked.

"He does have a point. We're getting better. That's all you should be concerned about," Kenneth interjected.

They were both right. The status of their health should be all that was important to her. It seemed a bit odd Doctor Thorne thought Joel brought the influenza over with him and spread it to Kenneth. Joel was already on the mend when they both arrived, barely sick. He only stayed because the doctor ordered him to. When she had more time to think about it, she'd have to figure out what it all meant. For now, though, she would concede to them both as right because they were indeed correct. Their continued improvement would remain all she deemed important.

"All right, I won't push it. So when will you know if your transfer request was approved?" Her attention directed at Kenneth as she spoke.

"It's already been accepted. I received my answer the day I got ill. All my belongings have been moved into my new quarters. I don't suppose anyone informed the captain of the *Oklahoma* of my new housing yet," Kenneth replied.

"Why do you believe that?" she asked.

"Because the doctor believes I'm still residing on the *Oklahoma*. It's part of the reason he kept us quarantined here. He didn't want to spread it to anyone aboard the ship. If he bothered to ask, we would have told him the only ones we have contact with are each other. Of course, I didn't say a whole lot when we arrived. I think I passed out as he examined me. Still doesn't explain why Joel didn't correct his assumptions."

"I didn't know what his assumptions were. He didn't exactly get chatty with me. He checked us over and left, saying he would return soon. Although he never did. If not for Becs here, I don't know what would have happened with us. I went in search of the good doctor and found her instead."

"What a mess. Well, not much we can do about it now. We will all be out of here tomorrow, and I'm due for a break. I have essentially been on duty for several days. They will have to give me some extended time off. I'm looking forward to that with the holiday weekend coming up."

"We're still invited to your Thanksgiving feast right?" Joel inquired.

"Absolutely. I don't break my promises. I'm sure the girls won't mind. We are already planning on some of David's friends joining us."

"Who is David?" Kenneth asked.

"He's my fiancé. We're getting married on December sixth. I have a bit of wedding plans to finish too. I can't wait to get out of here just as much as you two do."

Kenneth frowned at her as he said, "Is David on base?"

"Kind of. I mean, yes. He is on the *Arizona*."

"I see. I guess I'm wondering why he hasn't been by to check up on you. If my fiancée was cooped up in a hospital, I'd be here to see her," Kenneth replied.

"Oh well, he probably doesn't know. He's on duty all week and told me he wouldn't be able to see me until Thanksgiving. I'm sure he'd be here if he knew. I only told my roommates to let him know what was going on if I didn't make it to Thanksgiving dinner."

"I'm sure you're right." Kenneth closed his eyes and lay his head down on his pillow.

"Of course I am. Why wouldn't I be?" A wave of misery hit her. Something troubled Kenneth Blackman, and she meant to find out exactly what it was.

"Kenneth," she began.

"Leave it be. He will open up when he's ready." Joel stopped her from finishing her question and pulled her away from his bedside. With a firm grasp of her hand, he led her over to the bed she occupied on the other side of the room.

"Why did you stop me?" she asked. "He is so sad. I just want to help him."

"You're not ready to dig in too deep. Don't take on more than you can handle."

"I don't know what you're talking about."

"Don't you?" His eyebrow lifted up.

He knew far more than he let on. One day soon, she would begin to delve into what all of it meant. Once again though, the blasted man was right. She wasn't ready to find out. If she poked too much at it, she might not like what she discovered. So she would let it all go for now.

"Maybe I do," she replied. "More importantly, I think you do too. So you're aware, you and I are going to have a conversation posthaste—and you are going to share with me everything you know."

"When you are ready, I will be more than happy to explain it all to you. It will be a necessity. That day isn't here yet. When it builds up inside of you to the point you cannot hear yourself anymore, come find me. No matter what else, remember that, because you will need my help."

She nodded and turned her back to him. Such cryptic words, but those were an admission in itself. He knew what was happening to her, sensed it somehow. Maybe he had gifts similar to hers and could get an impression of the things around him. If true, maybe she would need him to understand and get a grasp of the changes in her gift. For now, she didn't want to talk about it or even think what it might mean for her. All she wanted to do was finish what she started and get through the rest of the day. If at all possible, she wanted to have a wonderful Thanksgiving with her friends and David. She refused to let this thing inside of her dictate her life.

"Fine. For now, can you leave me be. I have much to think about."

He nodded at her and walked back to his own bed giving her the space she requested. The man acted considerate and appeared concerned for her. The whole thing confused her. She would follow his lead, for now, and let herself experience everything before diving in. Once she was ready to accept what was happening, she would seek him out and make him explain everything. With that decision made she let her mind wander to more pleasant musings, like her upcoming wedding. No reason to raise her stress levels over something she couldn't control.

Chapter Eight

THE AIRFIELD HAD ONE small hangar and a tiny ammunition shed. In the hangar, a plane could be stored while in the midst of repairs. The planes usually parked along the runway until they could be flown to a much larger airbase. Sleeping quarters were housed inside the hangar with enough room for two people, two single cots, and a storage chest. Jaoel peered over the landscape and counted three planes in need of attention. Each plane's engine housed a tiny malfunction making them unsafe for flight. He watched as Kenneth Blackman entered the hangar by the side door and walked inside. After a few moments, the main door slid open wide enough for a plane to pass through. No planes were inside the hangar as it awaited its first patient of the day. Jaoel laughed at the image it projected. The hospital mended people, and this particular hangar repaired planes. It amused him in many ways to think of it as an airplane hospital. If only the planes could talk, what interesting tales they would weave.

"Did everything go as planned?"

Jaoel turned to see Michael standing next to him. It never failed to surprise him how easily he sneaked in without anyone the wiser. If his leader hadn't wanted him to know he was around, he would not have revealed himself. He glanced up at Michael and saw his hair was tied back in a leather band and his ice blue eyes held concern as he surveyed the same area Jaoel just finished observing.

"Yes. Everything went flawlessly." Jaoel folded his arms around his chest and a half smile tilted up at the corner of his mouth.

"This amused you?"

Jaoel turned to stare at Michael. A perplexed expression filled his face. His head was tilted to one side as he studied him trying to figure out why he appeared entertained by how smooth the plans went.

"Rebecca O'Shea is a bit different in person. I don't know how to explain it. I've been observing her for a while now, but it's unlike anything else in my experience—to be in her sphere. She burns brighter than the sun. It's possible to get roasted if you push too hard," Jaoel explained.

"I fail to see why this is funny in any way."

"If I were in your shoes, I probably wouldn't either. I can't describe it in any other way. In all my time as a guardian, I have never met anyone like her. She breathes life into this old soul of mine."

"Ah, I suppose that explains everything. We are tasked with a lot, and after a while, we forget who we are. The duty is always there. We do what is asked of us, but what makes us individuals is misplaced. For some reason, she is reminding you of something you lost a long time ago. I understand why you are smiling. She's a gift in ways beyond our comprehension."

Jaoel let his news sink in. He wouldn't have been able to put into words what happened when he spoke with Rebecca for the first time. She filled him with light and energy just being in her presence. When her full powers hit her, she would be breathtaking. Knowing she helped him find something of himself again truly amazed him. What other surprises would he have in store for him when he got better acquainted with her?

"Yes. She does fill a hole in me I didn't know I'd lost. I didn't realize I even missed anything until now. I wouldn't have even known why I was drawn to her until you explained it all. Have you experienced this before?" Jaoel asked.

Jaoel never knew any of it was possible or existed within the world of the guardians. When you lose a part of yourself and fail to take notice—how are you expected to realize its returning to you? Something about Rebecca called to him. What exactly that could be, he did not know. He did need to understand it all, though, so he would be able to deal with it. Surprises—at least those not of his own making—couldn't be surrounding him when he needed to be ready for anything.

"No. I personally have not. I am much older than you are, and perhaps it's not in my destiny to find that missing piece again. I know my duty, and from the moments I first pledged my vows, I knew this was the correct path for me. I'm content with the path I've taken, as most of the guardians are. Sometimes, though, we are meant for even more than this. Our fate is determined to alter its course and set a new one. My friend, I believe you may be heading down a different path. Time will tell, and you will know when it's upon you. You know if it is supposed to happen it will. Don't stress over what can't be changed."

"I don't understand. I chose to be a guardian. Are you saying sometime in the future I will no longer be one or that I won't want to be?" Jaoel demanded.

"I don't know. I can't answer questions about something that hasn't yet come to pass. I'm not a seer, Jaoel. You know as much as I do. I'm only speaking from experience."

His words were no comfort to him. Jaoel wanted answers, and he wanted them now. If only he knew a way to find out what it all meant, but he knew Michael spoke the truth. He could sense the changes growing inside of him. No one would be able to help him. The only person who could help him was himself. Jaoel needed to wait and see what his destiny had in store for him. Just because he chose to be a guardian didn't mean he had all the answers.

"All right. I will let it go for now. Let's get back to business. Why are you here? I thought we discussed everything we needed to several days ago."

"I sensed a change. I know now it was within you," Michael revealed.

"Is this going to make the mission more difficult?"

"I don't know—it's too soon to say. We'll have to take it one day at a time. The darkness is getting closer. Nothing can be done to stop it. All we can do is ride through the storm and hope to make it to the end in one piece."

"Her powers are starting to grow. She senses emotions already. I thought she wasn't supposed to start feeling them for several more weeks."

"There is a force out there making the time table push up. It's going to test everything she has inside of her. She knows she is different, has always known. What she doesn't know is how different she actually is. It will be up to you as her guardian to make sure she understands the gravity of it all."

Jaoel held his fists tight by his side. His eyes darkened as he glanced over at Michael. Doubt flooded his depths threatening to overflow and spread to those around him. He didn't think Michael fully understood what he asked. He didn't want to be a detriment to the mission. His inclusion could make it all explode into something unrecognizable. His blunders shouldn't be the reason chaos surrounded them. Jaoel would not be the guardian responsible for Rebecca O'Shea's possible downfall. He didn't know why, but she did something to him deep inside. Something like that didn't bode well for a guardian who prized their self-control and ability to handle any situation. The fiery redhead made his system go a bit crazy inside. Something he never experienced in his entire life, even before his guardian days.

"I know, but if she is changing me, it could have a negative effect on her to be around me. Maybe you should assign someone else to take over."

"No, and my answer is final. You are the one we handpicked for this mission. It is you who must see her through. No one else will be able to handle it. I'm not going to explain it all to you again." A firm expression took over Michael's face as his icy blue eyes held him in place.

Jaoel realized Michael refused to let him give in to his darker demons. He was making him continue on. In a way, this was a test. He needed to know Jaoel would be able to handle anything and see this through to the end. In normal circumstances, it wouldn't be an issue, but with his own soul going through some unforeseen changes, it made things a bit more difficult. Something he would need to keep close to his heart as he made his next step. It would be a reminder of what he could lose should he fail. Not only would Rebecca pay the price, but every guardian in existence would be changed. All he could do was believe Michael made the right decision for him, Rebecca, and all the guardians.

"I will trust you know what's best. I'll remain here and keep watch over my assignment. I only have one question. Do you have any idea what the timeline is for the darkness? I know you said it's coming, but I would like some idea of when to expect it."

"I'm sorry, but I don't know. All we know is what we feel. This place and time is writhing with so much pain and suffering. It's hard to pinpoint the exact time it will find its way here. If I were forced to guess, I would say anywhere from two weeks to three months. Keep in mind it is just a guess, and it's probably not even a very good one. I'm sorry. It isn't much to go on," Michael explained.

A couple of weeks? It could happen that early? Jaoel needed to start working faster. Rebecca might need him far sooner than he realized. There was a lot happening over the next several weeks. Thanksgiving dinner the next day, her wedding, and so many other things—he didn't know where to even begin with it all.

How was he to protect her when he had so much working against him? Before he got into panic mode, he took a deep breath and exhaled. He let the exercise calm and focus him on what needed to be done. No way would he allow anything to happen. He needed to gain control, and the breathing allowed him to see what his first steps should be. Any information was good information. He could use it to his advantage.

"It is a lot more than I had a few minutes ago. It gives me at least something to work on. She is getting married in a few weeks. Perhaps it has something to do with that. Should I prevent it or let it go forward?"

"We shouldn't interfere with her life in drastic ways. It is her decision to make as far as who she takes for a husband. Let the wedding go on. It is probably what happens far past her wedding that will matter," Michael explained.

"Sometimes our jobs are too difficult. We are tasked with protecting certain individuals and given limited information. Whoever devised this method of doing things didn't think things through. They should have gifted us with all the knowledge we need to do our jobs. It's so frustrating to know something is happening, but not the who, why, or even when. I..." Jaoel glanced over to see Michael staring at him. His ice blue eyes were filled with sadness and concern.

"The coming days will be the most difficult ones you have ever lived through. I can't express that enough. We can't change anything. The reasons do not matter. Can I trust you, or do I need to stay and help you with this assignment?"

Jaoel realized he acted like a fool, ranting and raving like a child. Michael was right, as usual. They needed to be as vigilant as possible. The rest didn't matter.

"I can handle it. You can go. If anything changes, I will send you a message."

"Good. Remember everything happens for a reason and don't try to question the whys of it all. It won't help you or her." Michael turned to leave, and Jaoel didn't attempt to watch him go. He needed to get things into perspective.

Jaoel studied the airplane hangar, the possible last resting place for the mechanical birds of the sky. They came to this place to be fixed and possibly find flight once again. His job, his duty, was to make sure his charges didn't find their final resting place. As a guardian, he guided them on their path so they could help others. He knew the reason he became a guardian and it was time he remembered that. He took a deep breath and let himself think of all the reasons he needed to regain control of his emotions. If he let them spill out, it could cause damage which couldn't be undone. After he leashed his power, he geared himself up to begin fighting the upcoming darkness. Rebecca needed him to be at his best, and he refused let her down.

Chapter Nine

DUSK WAS UPON THEM. After spending her nights at the hospital without a chance to leave, Rebecca appreciated the sight before her. She wrapped her arms around her waist and hugged herself as she watched the brightness of the sun's rays fade away into darkness, leaving room for the stars to light up the night sky. A warm breeze floated around her, so she closed her eyes to absorb its affectionate embrace. Home, this place filled with love and laughter, she missed it so much the past several days. Tomorrow was Thanksgiving, and she truly had much to be thankful for this year.

"I'm so glad you are home where you belong."

Rebecca opened her eyes and turned to see Virginia standing next to her, her angelic face surrounded by obsidian curls. Blue eyes narrowed with concern as they fell on Rebecca's face.

"It feels good to be home. I'm sorry I couldn't be here to help with the Thanksgiving plans. Did David ever send a note by? I'm wondering if we know who he is bringing with him."

Rebecca didn't expect him to have sent a note. He would have no reason to, but it didn't stop her from wanting to hear from him. She'd been cooped up in the hospital for days and missed him. The sooner she was able to see him, the better off she'd feel.

"No, we didn't get any word from David. We went ahead with the plans we have in place." Virginia reached out and placed a hand on her arm. "What happened at the hospital? We all found it strange they wanted you to stay with no relief."

"Two patients sick with influenza. Doctor Thorne became firmly adamant they needed to keep it contained. I found it odd, I admit, because they were not very sick. The one patient got better almost immediately and the other one only a day after him. It almost appeared as if something withdrew the illness from them, making it possible for them to heal quicker than normal."

"But you didn't get ill yourself?" Virginia inquired.

"No. I'm fine. I suppose we are lucky it didn't get more serious. I'm glad I wasn't stuck there through Thanksgiving. Which reminds me; I invited the two of them to dinner tomorrow. I hope it's all right."

"Of course it is. They should be somewhere where they can get some good food in them. Elizabeth has been planning and cooking for the past few days. I think she may have gone a bit over board. Did you see all the desserts, breads, and appetizers she already had made up for tomorrow? I wonder who she thinks is going to eat it all?"

Rebecca laughed at Virginia's description of all the food in their tiny kitchen. "She doesn't get to cook like this often. Let her have her fun. I'm sure it comes from missing her family. I bet they went all out like this on Thanksgiving."

"You are probably right. We will get to partake in part of her family tradition no doubt." Virginia's lips tilted into a knowing smile.

"Is there anything left for me to do?"

"Not tonight. Perhaps you can ask Elizabeth or Beatrice tomorrow what needs to be done. They are the ones who will need help. I know we will need to set up the tables outside and put all the decorations Bea has made up. Another one who has been all too happy with their task this week. I have to wonder if they were channeling their concerns into the things they could control."

Rebecca stopped to stare over at Virginia. Her lips were in a flat, grim line, across her face. Her eyes sparked with worry and concern, while her arms were folded across her chest trying to hold something inside. Rebecca decided to try and figure out what was going on inside of her friend. She flexed her building power and reached out to decipher the sentiment on Virginia's face. An emotion, almost unidentifiable filled Rebecca. Pain, an oh so agonizing pain, filled her. It made her stumble and fall to the ground with a hard *thud*. She gasped for breaths as she clawed at the ground. Grass and dirt jammed underneath her fingernails with each swipe of her fingers across the lawn. Rebecca tried to figure out what it all meant as shrieks of agony filled her head.

Virginia called her name, but it seemed so distant, like an echo floating through the breeze. More screams filled the void. She wasn't sure if they were hers, Ginny's, or the resonance of what's yet to come. She had the sensation of someone's arms grabbing her and pulling them inside their embrace, holding on to her like she could to fall to pieces.

Oh, maybe she could. That would explain the feelings exploding through her. Then just as sudden as they overtook her, the sensations left. Deep inside, she could still feel them all, a residual of their invasion, but they no longer filled her. She once again could hear the world around her and recognize her own emotions. Her breathing tapered off and calmness took root inside.

"Becca. Speak to me. What happened?" Virginia demanded.

All of Rebecca's limbs were weak and tired from the onslaught. With a feeble attempt, she tried to sit up, but only collapsed back into Ginny's arms. "I don't know. The pain became so strong and unmanageable. I couldn't stop it. It had been too much and so very close."

"Does this have to do with you being in the hospital? Are you getting sick? Maybe we should take you to the hospital and have the doctor look at you." Virginia rattled off words so fast they were almost unrecognizable. Rebecca understood most of what she said. Two words stuck out plain and clear, hospital and doctor. No way was she going back there. She escaped and was able to breathe fresh air again.

"No. I'm not going there until I'm scheduled for duty. I need a break from there. I just left the hospital and have no desire to return. Help me inside so I can get some rest. I'll be fine, Ginny. I promise this has nothing to do with the influenza. I had to help two patients get through it. I'm not sick. It's an entirely different matter I cannot explain."

"I don't know. Are you sure? I don't want something to happen to you. I was so concerned when your note arrived. Caro had to talk me out of going to check on you. She is always so reasonable and stated you would never want us to take that kind of risk."

"She's right. You were much better off here instead of being stuck in the hospital with me. I'm fine. I had a little emotional overload," Rebecca reassured her.

"Did we hear screaming?"

They both turned to see Maxine and Carolyn standing by the front door of their cottage. Maxine walked over to them with Carolyn not far behind.

"Do I need to repeat myself?" Caro demanded.

"No. I mean, yes, there was a bit of screaming, but no you don't need to repeat yourself."

"So are you going to explain what it was all about?" Maxine asked.

"I'd rather not. I'm a bit tired and could use some help getting inside."

"She's right. It is rather complicated. I apologize if we disturbed you, but I'm glad you're here. Can you help me get Becca inside? She is feeling rather weak at the moment." Virginia turned toward them, pleading with her eyes.

"Oh, all right. I expect some sort of explanation at some point though." Carolyn kneeled down and wrapped her arms around Rebecca's waist to help lift her up. Once they had her standing, one of Rebecca's arms slung over Carolyn's shoulder and the other over Virginia's.

"Maxi, go get the door so we can help her inside," Caro demanded.

They took slow agonizing steps to the front of the cottage. Caro pushed them forward at a steady pace, and Maxi held the door wide open for them. Maxine stayed in the living room as they helped Rebecca to the bedroom they shared. They escorted her inside and set her on her bed. Rebecca leaned back, but left her legs over the side of her bed. It was more energy than she could muster to lift them on the bed with the rest of her. Virginia checked over at her, and with gentleness, lifted her legs onto the bed for her.

"I still think you should see a doctor. I can call them to see if they will come here." Virginia suggested.

"No doctors, Ginny, you promised."

"I know, but I'm worried."

"I still don't know what happened," Caro stated.

"Nothing happened."

Carolyn stared into Rebecca's eyes. Saying without words she didn't believe for one minute nothing happened as Rebecca had stated.

"Oh all right, something happened. I don't know how to explain it without sounding crazy."

"Why don't you start at the beginning," Virginia suggested.

"The beginning is hard to pinpoint. Maybe there is no real beginning. Maybe it's always been there, dormant, and waiting for me to try to understand it."

They both stared at her waiting for her to expand on what she said. She wasn't sure how to explain to them what happened deep inside of her. Taking a big breath, she closed her eyes and sought the right words to make them understand.

"Sometimes, I get these feelings. I've always considered them intuition or a gut feeling, but they are so much more than that. Sometimes I know things, and I can't explain it.

What happened outside was so much bigger and confusing. Feelings of thousands of people filled and crushed me so thoroughly, I couldn't breathe." Rebecca rubbed her hands over her face.

The energy sapped out of her, but she needed to try to explain a little bit to her friends. "I don't know what is happening to me. It started several weeks ago, and I kept brushing it aside. It grew more in the hospital. Nothing this extreme has ever happened before. Whatever it is doing to me, it's far more than I've ever experienced before."

"How is that even possible?" Caro asked.

"I don't know, Caro. It's worse than that, though."

"I don't understand. How can it be worse?" Ginny sat forward with the question spilling from her eyes.

"Because it hasn't happened yet. I mean the pain and suffering. It was an echo from the future," Rebecca whispered.

They both stared at her for several seconds before Caro spoke. "You're right"

"Right about what?" Rebecca asked confusion filling her face.

"You can't see a doctor and tell him any of this. They will lock you up in a mental ward for insanity. You are not insane. I can see what's happened to you. The toll it's taken on your body. That is not something to mess with. I will be the first to say I don't understand it, but I know you, and I also know what this world is willing to accept. They are not going to believe you can sense some future tragedy that is going to affect thousands of people."

"She does have a point," Virginia agreed.

"I know she does. It's why I said no when you suggested the doctor. I don't understand any of this myself. He said I wasn't ready, and yet I tried anyway. I should have listened."

"Who said you were not ready?" Caro asked.

"Joel, one of the patients with influenza. I think he's like me. He sensed what I had been about to do, in the hospital with the other patient, and stopped me. He said I wasn't ready and shouldn't attempt it yet."

"Didn't you say you invited them to Thanksgiving dinner?" Virginia asked.

"Yes, I did."

"Do you think they will actually come?" Carolyn's eyebrow rose with her question.

"I don't know, probably. They seemed keen on coming."

"Good, we can pick his brain when he gets here. For now, let's keep this all between the three of us until we know more," Carolyn suggested.

"I don't have a problem with that. There is so much I don't understand. This thing, what's going to cause so much hurt, I can't pinpoint when it will happen, and I know it will. That doesn't give us much to go on or a way to even prepare.

"Don't worry about it right now. Rest. Let Caro and I take care of you. When this Joel comes by tomorrow, the three of us will sit down and have a nice chat with him in private."

Rebecca nodded her head in agreement. She couldn't think past the next few moments anyway. Tomorrow was soon enough to leave it be for now. While she didn't know when it would happen, she also sensed it wasn't immediate.

BROKEN PEARL

Tired, so tired, her eyes were refusing to remain open. She let her eyelids slide closed and allowed sleep to come claim her.

Chapter Ten

"WAKE UP! RISE AND SHINE. It's a brand new day for fun, friends, and lots and lots of food." Carolyn shook Rebecca awake, her excitement filling the room with a swirl of movement.

Rebecca opened her eyes into tiny slits to watch her roommate flutter through the room. How did Caro have such an abundance energy? If given the choice, she would much rather stay in bed and sleep the day away. Carolyn already had her hands filled with lists of things they needed to do.

"Why are you not moving yet? Everyone else has been up for hours, but you kept on sleeping. Everything is under way, and I have to say, the smells coming from the kitchen are marvelous. You have to get up and at least appreciate that."

Rebecca rolled over and stared at her. Her eyes were open wide, and she could get a better look at her friend. She was dressed in a white dress with mint green polka dots in various sizes all over the dress. It wouldn't be her first choice, but Caro had odd taste in clothing—she only required them to be functional.

"I'm really tired, Caro. I can't seem to find the energy or motivation to get out of bed."

Carolyn's firm expression softened into one of concern. She rushed over to sit on the bed and placed the back of her hand on Rebecca's forehead.

"You are not running a fever. You're actually quite cool to the touch. At least we don't have to worry about you being sick. I know whatever happened last night drained you, but if you don't get up, everyone else is going to question things. Yes, I remember our rule is no secrets, but this is a bit different. We need to control the situation until we understand more."

"I know, and when Joel gets here, I will need to talk to him. He has the answers to so many of my questions. It's time he shared what he knows."

"Are you certain he knows what is going on with you," Carolyn asked.

"Yes. It isn't so much what he said, but how he said it. He knew what I was about to do. I was way too shocked to question him at the time. I wanted time to absorb it and analyze what it might all mean. I should have listened to him, though, and maybe I wouldn't feel so weak right now."

Carolyn smiled down at her and tapped her on the shoulder. "Well not much you can do to change it now. Get up and start moving. Maybe once you get in motion, you will find some energy."

"I certainly hope so. What time is it anyway? I am so out of the loop; I don't even know what time we are having dinner. I told a bunch of people to come and didn't give them any specific information. I'm a terrible host."

Carolyn's laugher filled the room as she walked toward the door. "No worries, it is what I do best. I sent an official invite with all the information to David. He knows when to be here. I sent a special message to be hand delivered to Joel this morning. I wanted to do what I could to make sure he arrives on time. You are not the only one who wants to grill him for information. I'm very curious about this airplane mechanic."

"Good. I have one less thing to worry about. Now go do what you do best and order everyone around." Rebecca flashed her a reassuring smile. "I'm going to get up and take a shower. It might do wonders to make me feel better. I will find you for my assignment when I'm done."

"All right. If there is anything left that needs done, I will get you started on it when you are finished. Oh, to answer your question, it will be noon in fifteen minutes. Dinner is scheduled for four. I instructed our guests to arrive around three. It gives you three hours to start functioning at a more active level." With those words, Carolyn shut the door as she left the room leaving Rebecca stunned at her words.

How could it already be almost noon? How could she have slept so long? She jumped out of bed and pulled on her robe to go take her shower. She pulled out her favorite blue dress and set it on her bed. Her shoes were already sitting on the floor waiting to be put on after she dressed. She left the room and walked to the bathroom.

"Oh, you're awake. Good. I was beginning to worry."

Rebecca stopped and turned to see Virginia walking out of the kitchen.

"Yeah, I'm going to go take a quick shower. I should be ready to help with everything in less than an hour. I promise."

"No, take your time. I don't want you to overextend yourself. It's why we allowed you to sleep. You spent days working in the hospital and while you probably got rest, no doubt it wasn't good rest. Everything is getting taken care of."

"Are you sure? No, I don't feel right leaving it all to you guys and not helping at all. I will still try to get done as fast as possible."

Virginia gazed at her with a serene smile gracing her angelic face. After a moment, she nodded her head in agreement. "Go take your shower, Becca. Come find us when you are done, and we will find something for you to do."

She pretty much echoed Carolyn's earlier words. Rebecca believed they were only placating her. She couldn't do much else about it. They probably had most of the work for Thanksgiving done anyway. Carolyn had her lists, and her main focus centered around making sure everyone did their part. If she needed to, she would reassign a task so that it got done. Efficiency was a skill Caro formed into an intrinsic ability.

"Caro will know what needs to be done. I will locate her after I'm done getting ready for the day. Thank you for looking after me. Sometimes I try to do too much and don't know my own limitations. I'm going to find out what it all means today."

"Yes, the airplane mechanic. I hope he comes so we get some answers. I'm going to go see if Bea needs any more help outside. Go on and start getting ready. We will speak more later."

Virginia walked through their living room and exited the cottage. After Ginny went outside, Rebecca turned to go into the bathroom and take her shower. Once she finished, she rushed back to her room and dressed herself in the clothes she set out. Her hair would have to air dry before she could do anything with it. Any other method would leave it a frazzled mess of epic proportions.

After careful consideration, she weaved it into a braid and wrapped it around into a bun at the nape of her neck. Her creation had the effect of being both stylish and elegant. Satisfied with the results, she walked out of the room in search of Carolyn. She would see David soon, and Joel. She needed to see Joel so he could tell her what was going on with her. Maybe he knew what all the pain she experienced the night before meant and if it could be changed. Perhaps he even got a taste of it as well. The day may have started later than she expected it to, but she still had a lot to get done.

She missed David so much and couldn't wait to see him again. Their week apart seemed like forever, and she couldn't wait to feel his arms wrapped around her again. Of course, very little plans had been made for their wedding, but she could share with him some of what they already worked through. The date, place, and time were set and ready for them to say their vows. On December 6, 1941 she would marry the man she loved. Nothing could detract from her happiness. A frown formed on her face as she realized something actually could. Something catastrophic was coming, and it could make an impact on her life with David. No, she wouldn't allow it. She would find out what it all meant and find a way to prevent the devastation. There had to be a way to make sure no one would ever feel that much misery and pain. With hope filling her, she let the dark thoughts float away because if anyone held the capabilities to prevent the darkness from finding root, Rebecca believed she might. She trusted her new capabilities, because if she didn't, she would have to admit she might lose the person who made her euphoric for the first time in her life. David was her future, and she rejected anything and everything which stood in her way.

Chapter Eleven

THE TABLECLOTHS WERE all pearly white with coffee colored embroidering depicting an original Thanksgiving harvest weaved through the sides. The two unique creations hung on each of the tables set outside for their holiday dinner. A fruit-filled centerpiece sat on each table. The cornucopias Beatrice made for the meal were distinctive as well as stunning. At every place setting sat fine china and silverware. In front of each plate, a napkin matching the tablecloth rested, waiting to be unfolded with dinner. Rebecca scanned everything to make sure not a single piece was out of place. Satisfied with the results, she turned to go inside to make sure no one else needed her help.

"Everything appears great."

Rebecca glanced over her shoulder to see her fiancé, David, standing behind her. His chocolate-brown eyes made her insides melt. Turning on her heels, she wrapped her arms around his waist and rested her head in the crook of his arm. His arms tightened hugging her closer to him.

"I'm so glad to see you," she mumbled against his broad shoulder.

"I don't know about you, but the days started to feel like they took forever. I began to think I'd never hold you in my arms again."

She couldn't have said it better herself. Leaning back in his arms, she stared up into his eyes. The past week didn't rate high on her list of possible favorites. Staying at the hospital for days had been some of the most agonizing of her life. Rebecca didn't want to repeat the experience ever again.

"I agree. Soon, we will be married, and the separation won't have to be quite so lengthy. This reminds me, we need to discuss where we are going to live once we are married. We will need a place all our own. It might take some time to get settled. We might have to live a few weeks as a married couple in separate places."

"Once we are married, we can apply for different housing, but I will probably still be required to be on the *Arizona* more than I am at home. I still like the idea of having our own house, and you there for me to come home to." David leaned down and placed a quick kiss on her lips.

"It does sound lovely. The girls and I made some plans. The date is set, and we are going to get married right here outside the cottage. Bea is going to handle the decorations, Lizzie the food, and Caro has it all organized. They are just as excited as we are."

"I'm sure it will be wonderful." David pressed his lips to her forehead in a light kiss. "What day did you pick?"

"Saturday, December sixth, at three o'clock, will that work for you?"

She watched as David tilted his head as he appeared to be deep in thought. His onyx-black hair gleamed underneath the sun's bright rays. After a few seconds, he turned his attention back on Rebecca.

"I think it will be perfect. I need to make sure, but I believe I'm on duty for the night shift that weekend. If something changes or I'm wrong I will let you know. Worst case scenario, we will have to adjust the time. No matter what, I'm going to be here to marry you. There is nothing I want more."

Her lips tilted upward into a smile as she stared up at David. She couldn't believe how much she loved him. It filled her to the brim, spilled over, and absorbed back into her soul each time she stared into his eyes. Nothing had ever lighted up her life as much as loving him did. Her inner radar told her his feelings mirrored hers. An affectionate flush fluttered inside of her every time she found herself near him.

"Good. I will let Caro know to move forward with the planning."

"Did I hear my name?"

Rebecca twisted out of David's arms and saw Caro walking out of their cottage. She carried a tray of food and placed it on one of the tables.

"I told David about the plans we have made so far. He says it sounds perfect, and we should go ahead with it all. He will make sure to show up on time." Rebecca's face beamed with delight.

"Good, because I've have too many lists made for him to object now. I'd rather not have to start all over again."

David laughed at her statement. He didn't know how true it actually was though. Carolyn meant every word she said. She did have a bunch of lists made and hated having to start over from scratch.

"I'm serious." Carolyn stared at him with a determined expression. Her eyes narrowed in on him, and her lips pursed up into a firm line.

"I know you are. David doesn't know how you operate yet. Give him time. He will fall in line."

"You don't have to make me sound so controlling..."

Rebecca gave her a piercing glare and tapped her foot.

"All right, fine. You're right I can be a bit demanding," Carolyn agreed. "Which reminds me, where are these friends you planned on bringing with you? I planned for extra people, and so far, I only see you."

"Doug and Keith needed to do a few things before they came. They're on a different ship, the U.S.S. *Oklahoma*. They will probably be here soon, I told them to meet me here when they got off duty. I couldn't wait any longer to see Rebecca. I missed her too much to wait another second."

"I think you might be too good to be true." Carolyn's voice filled with disbelief.

"I'm a man in love. We say and do whatever is necessary to keep the girl." David stared at Carolyn and winked. "It also helps I mean every word."

"David, you there?"

They all glanced to see two men begin their approach toward the cottage. One of them had brown hair and the other's a blond so pale it almost appeared white. They kept walking until they reached them and came to stop next to David.

"Glad you both could make it. You didn't have any trouble locating the place?" David asked.

"No man, we do know how to follow directions. Now introduce us to your friends," the man with light brown hair demanded.

"Sorry. This is my fiancée Rebecca and one of her roommates, Carolyn." He gestured to the two women. "Ladies these are my two best friends, Doug and Keith."

Doug's olive green eyes complimented his light brown hair. A smattering of freckles dusted his cheeks and nose. The smile on his face was infectious. Rebecca couldn't help returning it as she shook his hand and then turned her attention to Keith.

"Thank you for inviting us." Dark grey eyes stared back at them as Keith nodded his head. His pale blond hair contrasted the color of his eyes.

"It's our pleasure. Any friend of David's is always welcome. Dinner is going to be ready soon," Rebecca explained.

"When I left the kitchen, Lizzie said everything was right on schedule. She sent me out with a platter of food. Pretty soon, she will be sending the rest out with Maxi, Bea, and Ginny."

"Perhaps one of us should go in and see if she needs any help."

"I will go. Stay here and keep the men company. Besides, our other guests should be arriving soon, and one of us should be out here to greet them." Caro moved away from them and entered the cottage.

"You're expecting someone else?" David asked.

"Yes. It's a long story. I'll make it short and say they were a couple of patients at the hospital I took care of this week. I invited them to come to dinner. They both should be here. I don't know why they haven't arrived already."

"Could that be them coming now?" Keith gestured toward two men walking up the path to the cottage.

Rebecca blinked and noticed the two men Keith pointed at. Joel ambled along with Kenneth by his side. They appeared to be having a jovial conversation as they made their way to the cottage. They kept talking right up until the point they reached Rebecca.

"So, not too long afterwards, I ended up here." Joel finished his story and turned toward Rebecca. "Hey Becs, we're not late are we?"

"My name is Rebecca. Please use it." Rebecca didn't like him calling her by that awful nickname. He needed to stop, but so far, he ignored her wishes. "No, you're not too late. You're in luck. Dinner has not been served yet. I hope you'll enjoy everything we have planned."

Joel studied the tables as the rest of Rebecca's roommates exited the cottage with their arms filled with platters of food. He rushed over to their side and offered to help. "Please let me carry those for you."

Maxi flashed him her most gamine smile. "You can carry me if you want. I don't mind."

"Ma'am, I don't know if I could handle you. I'll leave the privilege to one of these other guys." He took the tray out of her hand and walked toward the tables. "Is there a certain table this needs to go on?"

"Set it on either one. We are going to have an informal dinner. I'm Caro, what's your name?"

"Joel Remak, it's a pleasure to meet you."

"Oh the pleasure is all mine. Don't leave right away after dinner. I want to pick your brain. I have a few questions for you."

With those cryptic words, Caro walked away and back into the cottage. Joel stared at Rebecca with a confused expression. "What did your friend mean?"

Rebecca shrugged her shoulders. "I'm not sure, but I think she just wants to talk to you. I wouldn't worry about it for now. She said she would ask you after dinner. I'm sure you'll find out once she's ready to explain."

After she finished speaking, Lizzie walked out with a platter of carved turkey with Carolyn right behind her with a duplicate. They each placed a platter on one of the tables and then turned their attention to all of their guests.

"I hope everyone is ready to eat," Lizzie called out.

"If everyone will take a seat we will bow our heads to say a prayer of thanks." Ginny motioned for everyone toward the tables.

Rebecca grabbed David's hand and led him over to one of the tables. He pulled out her chair and helped her take her seat before sitting down himself. She placed her hands together to get ready for Virginia's prayer and noticed Joel sat across the table from her. His aquamarine eyes would be on her during the entire dinner, unnerving her with every glance.

"Now if everyone would bow their heads to pray. These are the words of Ralph Waldo Emerson. I think they are duly appropriate for today and make a good prayer and blessing," she explained as she bowed her head. Her words were firm and clear as she spoke. "'Lord, we thank you, for each new morning with its light, for rest and shelter of the night, for health and food, for love and friends, for everything thy goodness sends.'"

"Amen," everyone said in unison.

"Help yourself. Let's eat." Lizzie gestured to all the food on the table.

No one needed to be told twice. Soon platters were being passed around and plates were filled with food. The meal passed by with laughter and good conversation. Thanksgiving had always been one of Rebecca's favorite holidays even when she didn't have much to be thankful for. It gave her an opportunity to appreciate the things good in her life. This year, she had something to be thankful for and for once she didn't have to think too hard to come up with a reason. Her heart was filled with so much gratitude for all of her blessings she didn't know how to express them all. On this third Thursday of November, in the year of 1941, she realized she had so much to live for. Rebecca made a promise to herself as she glanced over at her friends and her fiancé. Not for one moment would she take any one of them for granted.

Chapter Twelve

DUSK FELL OVER THE yard as they finished cleaning up from Thanksgiving dinner. All the food eaten or stored in the kitchen and every table stripped of the tablecloths and already carried back inside. The men were grateful for being invited, so each pitched in and helped with the extensive cleanup. Rebecca didn't want the day to end, but it came to a close far too soon.

"There you are. I've been searching for you." David stood behind her and wrapped his arms around her waist.

"Lucky you, finding me here all alone."

"Where is everyone?" he asked.

"Your friends left a few minutes ago. All the girls are inside with Joel and Kenneth. I'm sure they will have to leave soon too, but for now, they are entertaining them with stories."

"So what are you doing out here all alone?"

How to explain to him she needed a few minutes alone? The energy inside the house became stifling. The longer she stayed inside, the harder it became to filter it out. This gift of hers, if she could consider it a blessing, was growing at an alarming rate. So much so, blocking out everyone's emotions proved almost impossible. They leaked through and were trying to find a home inside of her. Physically pushing them out and releasing them took all of the energy inside of her. As wonderful as this day had been, it also drained her. So she escaped for a few minutes to try to recharge and regain her equilibrium.

"I wanted to make sure we didn't forget anything out here."

"Looks like we did a thorough job. Although I can't complain. I admire your diligence. It gives me the opportunity to spend a few minutes alone with you before I leave."

"You have to leave already?"

"I'm sorry, I do. I'm on shift early in the morning, and I need to get back." David's lips touched her forehead with a quick, gentle kiss. "Besides, we have a curfew. If' I'm not back on board soon, I'll end up in the brig."

Rebecca pulled at the sleeves of his uniform and pouted. "I wish the navy didn't take up so much of your time. I don't get to see you nearly enough."

"There might come a time you wish I didn't hang around so much." He laughed.

"Never. I will always want you to be with me. I hate anything that takes you away." Rebecca wrapped her arms around his waist and gazed up into his eyes. "How much time do we have left?"

"I need to leave now."

"Really? You can't spare more than a few minutes." Rebecca leaned in closer and ran her hands up his back. Her smile cajoled and teased.

David pulled her close and placed his lips on hers. A kiss filled with sweetness and desire. Their tongues danced together to a rhythm unique to them. A hum of pleasure filled the air as Rebecca squeezed him tight against her. A mix of emotions swirled inside of her. A blend of hers and David's. They were in sync and at odds with each other at the same time, a conundrum of emotional chaos. A push and pull for dominance, each wanting to gain control. A punch in her gut had her gasping for breath and pulling away from David. Her breathing became ragged and harsh. Rebecca held onto her stomach trying to find her center of gravity. The world spun around her, and she collapsed to the ground.

"Rebecca what's wrong." David's voice was desperate with worry.

Rebecca stared up at him and blinked several times. The sensations within her tapered off, and her breathing evened out. This thing inside of her needed to get itself under control. She would not live the rest of her life in fear of kissing the man she loved. If she couldn't have the joy of showing David how much she loved him, then what was the point of it all?

"I'm all right," she whispered.

"You are not all right, Rebecca. You had trouble breathing and fell down. That is as far from all right as you can get. Maybe we should take you to the hospital."

Not another person wanting to take her to the hospital. Didn't they understand she couldn't go there? No, David wouldn't know that. He wanted to make sure she would be all right. He didn't know that going there might be detrimental to her well-being.

"No, I am not going to the hospital. I promise I'm fine. I got a little overwhelmed and had trouble coping."

"That doesn't leave me with a good feeling. Are you scared? Did you panic and that's why you had trouble breathing. Talk to me. I need to understand what is going on in your head."

How could she explain something she didn't get herself? If she was going to get David to let it go, she'd have to give him something he found acceptable. A reassurance nothing serious was wrong with her.

"I don't know. Maybe I did panic a little bit. I can't explain it because I don't understand it. I do know it's not you. It is something I have to work out myself. I'm going to be fine." Rebecca talked to him with soothing tones. She didn't want him to be afraid for her. "I promise, if you need to go back to the *Arizona*, everything will be all right with me. I don't want you to get in any trouble."

"I don't feel right leaving you like this. Do you want me to help you inside? It's the least I can do. I will come by in a few days, so we can talk and make sure you are okay."

Rebecca was glad he was going to back to the *Arizona*. Yes, she missed him, but she needed to understand what was going on inside of her. Once she had a firm grip on everything, she would explain it all to him. He would need to have a firm comprehension of her ability if he was going to be her husband. The only problem was she couldn't give him details she didn't have herself yet. David loved her—he would want to help her.

Rebecca gave him a reassuring smile. "It's probably best. I can manage to get myself back inside. I'm not too weak to move. I need to process this all myself. I will see you in a few days."

David got up and stared down at her sitting on the ground, his expression perplexed and uncertain. His eyes filled with worry and his mouth in a grim line on his face. Rebecca knew he wanted to ask questions, but now really was not the time for them. Mainly because she didn't have any of the answers he sought. She didn't understand any of it herself. To her knowledge, only one person might have an explanation for what happened to her—what continued to plague her now on a daily basis. Once David left, she planned to seek him out. Joel better be prepared to give her all the information she wanted. Her life as she knew it depended on his ability to help her.

"I love you, Rebecca." David kissed her lightly on the lips. "I'll see you soon."

"I love you, too."

With a final glimpse, David turned and walked away from the cottage, and from her. Maybe the next time she saw him she would be able to explain everything better. She sure hoped so at least.

"I thought he would never leave."

Rebecca turned startled at the sound of Joel's voice. How had he sneaked out without her or David realizing it? Had he listened to their entire conversation? Did he watch while David kissed her? He had no right to spy on her, on them.

"Take it easy. I have only been out here for a few minutes. Well long enough to see you collapse. Want to tell me what that was all about?"

"Don't you know?" she asked.

"If I did, I wouldn't be asking you."

She raised her eyebrow, questioning the veracity of his answer. He did appear to not know why she collapsed. Maybe he didn't have a clue what was broiling within her.

"I had an emotional overload."

"I thought I told you not to take on too much. You are far from ready, and your shields are nonexistent."

His eyes flashed daggers at David's retreating form, and then he turned them on her. Why was he angry? What right did he have to be irritated about something she did to herself?

"Yes, you did, but here's the thing. I don't have to listen to you. You're not my father, brother, or even my husband. You are nothing to me."

"Little girl, you are walking a very fine line. Don't push me. Now tell me what you did."

"I didn't do a damn thing, and I don't have to explain myself to you."

"Now that's where you are wrong. If you want to survive, you need to tell me everything. I am the only one who can help you. Fighting with me will get you nowhere. Now let's try this again. Tell me what you did."

Blasted man did have a point. He very well could be the only person capable of helping her. She didn't know anyone else with any clue about her gift. Rebecca might as well give in and explain the whole thing to him now.

"Just now? I didn't do anything. It kind of, well, happened, and I couldn't control it."

"Something tells me there is more you are not saying. You didn't do anything *just now*. It implies you did another time. Don't leave anything out, Becs. If I'm to help you, I need all of the information."

He folded his arms across his chest and stared at her, waiting for her to expand on what she already said. If only he hadn't used that infernal nickname, she might have given him the information much quicker. Instead, she wanted to hold onto it as long as possible. Something about him made her want to push back and make demands. She didn't like a domineering person, but on him it looked good. Rebecca didn't want to like anything about him, and that alone unnerved her.

"I may have tried to..." she muttered.

"I didn't hear you. Speak up," Joel demanded.

"I reached into Ginny last night. It broke through something inside of me and wiped me out."

"You did exactly what I told you not to do. What else happened?"

"I don't know what you mean." Rebecca bit her lip as she stared at him.

"Are we trying something new?"

"Excuse me?" She gave him a puzzled expression. Her eyebrows crinkled up as she tilted her head.

"Sexy Becs, are you trying to distract me so you don't have to tell me everything."

"What? No, I'd never—how dare you imply such a thing."

His heated gaze roamed over her body, and she could feel a blush begin to heat her cheeks at his perusal. "You're stalling—and then you go and bite your lip—what else am I to think."

"Not that, did you ever consider this isn't something I find easy to talk about."

"I guess not. Why don't you ease up a bit? I'm here to help you."

"I know." She sighed and bit her lip again.

Joel groaned and wiped his hands across his face. "You really need to stop doing that."

"You are acting like I'm doing it on purpose. I'm not trying to flirt with you. I'm engaged to David. We are getting married in a two weeks. Getting fresh with you is the last thing on my mind. I have some real problems here, and unfortunately for me, you're the only one around who can help me."

"You're right, of course you are. This is my problem. I'll deal with it."

"Good, I'm glad you can admit when you're wrong."

"I'm not wrong. Never mind. I'm not going to argue with you. We have bigger issues to deal with," he exclaimed.

"Fine."

She didn't want to argue with him. If she could avoid talking to him, her life would be so much better. As she couldn't exercise that option, she would keep reminding herself to breathe.

"Now tell me what happened," he demanded.

"A darkness is coming."

At her words, Joel stood still as shock rolled over his face. He grew pale, and his face went blank. Not a good sign in her estimation.

"You know what it means don't you?"

"Not exactly, no one does. It's something being sensed by those with special gifts. What it means for you is we need to start working to build your shields. We will have to meet every day."

"I don't know..."

"Every day, Becs. If you don't, you won't be able to handle the shadows when they get here. It will destroy you."

Rebecca didn't have much choice. Not if she wanted to live and have an actual chance of a life with David. If this guaranteed she would get to spend a happy life with David, then she needed to comply with Joel's demands.

"Do you really need to make it all sound so ominous," she asked.

"Yes, I do. I think it's the only way to get you to take it serious."

"I don't like this or you," she told him.

"You don't have to like me. But you do need to do everything I say. If you're all right with doing so, we can start working tomorrow."

"Why not tonight?" she asked.

"Because you will need rest. Your strength is too low to begin work right now. What happened to you a few minutes ago drained too much out of you."

"Yes, I suppose it did. I don't work at the hospital, so my whole day is free. What time do you want to start working?" she asked.

"After the sun rises. It's best to start at the brink of a new day. I will explain more when I arrive. I'm going to go get Kenneth and leave now. You need to go in and rest." He turned to leave, stopped, and stared over his shoulder. "Oh and one more thing Becs."

At this rate, she was going to slap him before she learned anything. "What?"

"Wear something comfortable, I suggest pants. Unless you want me to get a peek under your skirt." Heat filled his aquamarine eyes as they traveled a slow sensual path downward stopping at the edge of her blue dress.

Such an irritating male. Message accepted, but she refused to give him the kind of response his blatant statement had been geared toward. If only she could get through this without his help. Rebecca nodded her head in agreement and followed him inside. He said his goodbyes to everyone and left with Kenneth. She went into her room and prepared for bed setting out clothes to wear the next day. Not long afterward, she fell asleep with thoughts about what she hoped to learn the next day.

Chapter Thirteen

REBECCA WOKE TO A SHADOWY room. Not even moonlight streamed through the bedroom window. She couldn't sleep anymore, so she decided to get up for the day. Glancing over to make sure Carolyn and Virginia still slept, she lowered her feet to the floor. On her tiptoes, she grabbed the clothes she set out for the day and crept out of the room. The she used the tips of her fingers to guide her way to the bathroom in the dark.

Once inside, she shut the door and flipped on the light. She picked up her watch, checked the time, and noted it was half past six. The sun should begin rising soon, and that meant Joel could arrive at any moment. She needed to get ready and be outside well before he arrived. She took off her nightgown and placed it on a hook on the back of the door. Soon afterward, she was dressed in a white blouse with lace weaved through the sleeves and charcoal-gray pleated slacks. Shutting off the light in the bathroom, she moved her way through the living room and toward the front door. Her black flats were sitting by the door for her to slip on and step outside to wait for Joel.

"Good, I don't have to come in and wake you up."

"Don't be absurd, or creepy. I do have roommates who wouldn't appreciate your perversions."

A small chuckle rolled through his lips. "You say it like it's a bad thing. I promise I don't have any strange obsessions you need to be concerned with. Everything we do is necessary. You might not like it much."

"You are not building a solid reason for me to continue on with this farce. Keep talking, and I will turn back around to go inside. I'll leave my fate to chance."

"Bad call, Becs. But it is yours to make. I'm heading out now. If you still want my help, then follow me. I have several ideas where you can begin to gain some control over your gift."

Rebecca wanted to smack him on the head. She doubted the reason she hit him would actually register. No use bothering to do something when it would prove futile. The arrogant jerk did have a bad habit of being right. She did need his help. Hating to admit it aloud, she kept her mouth shut and forced herself to walk after him.

They walked for several minutes until they reached a secluded beach. As she inspected her surroundings, she realized they were standing next to a breathtaking lagoon. There were rocky cliffs with over hanging vegetation on the far end. Red coral creepers twisted in thick green vines across the cliffs. A coral reef skimmed around the edge, separating it into a separate body of water, a clear blue crystal sparkling beneath the bright sun. Orchids, blushing purple and pink, grew along the edge. Their perfume, a sweet and clean aroma, tickled her nose.

"Is that a coral reef? It's hard to be certain gazing across the lagoon. The water is clear enough, though. I think it is one shining from the bottom. I would love to go swimming in there and see all the underwater structures and sea creatures. I love places like this." Rebecca stared out across the water with her hand resting on her forehead, shading the sun from her eyes.

"I believe it is. I haven't had the satisfaction of checking it out myself yet. I chose this place to work because it's secluded and no one should disturb us."

Rebecca lowered her hand and glanced at Joel. His gaze seized by the beauty of the paradise before him, his eyes mirroring the color of the water. He shook his head and turned to her. The easy smile once again on his face.

"Maybe we both can explore it someday. Right now, I would like to ask you some questions."

"I will answer what I can," he replied.

"No you will tell me everything I want and need to know"

"You're so feisty today. It looks good on you, Becs"

Rebecca had to get control over this situation. The first step was to make sure he stopped calling her by the nickname he created for her. She didn't like it when anyone failed to respect her wishes.

"Don't distract me, and for the last time, quit calling me that. It is not my name."

"I'm not, and no, I won't. It suits you."

Rebecca rolled her eyes. "Explain what is happening to me."

"You're an empath."

"Pretend like I have no idea what you are talking about and explain it like I'm an idiot." She slanted her hand waving it in a flippant gesture.

His mouth twitched as he fought a smile. "I doubt anyone would ever mistake you for a fool."

"Which is why I told you to pretend." Rebecca folded her arms across her chest and tapped her foot. "I'm waiting."

"You know how you get a feeling, but you can't explain it?" he asked.

"I've always considered it a gut-feeling."

Joel nodded his head. "Yes, but you know it isn't as simple as that."

"I do now—after what happened the other night. I've never experienced anything like it. I don't even know if I could describe the sensation."

"The darkness?" he asked.

"Yes, so much pain coursing through me. A physical ache compounded by emotional chaos. I could feel myself being ripped apart from the inside out."

"Tell me what you know about it."

"I don't know what you mean. I explained how it made me feel." Her eyes crunched up filling with confusion.

"Fixate on something beyond the sensations, the pain, to the message you received."

"Message? You think someone tried to tell me something?"

"Not someone, not even something. An empath is more than the feelings they filter through them. They know things, and understand what is going on around them at a level that defies reality. So whatever you sensed, you are one of the rare people that can decipher what it means. You have to, for lack of a better word, translate it."

"Can't you do it?" she asked.

"No, I'm not an empath. My gifts are different than yours."

"So how did you know what I planned on doing with Kenneth?"

"I can sense energy, or more fitting, psychic resonance. Each one has a different reaction, and I can decipher what ability is being used."

Rebecca let his words absorb inside of her as she paced around the sandy beach. Her arms wrapped around her waist, she stopped and stared at him. "So when I reached out and get a feeling about what bothered Kenneth, you were able to tell I had this empathic ability."

"The simple answer is yes," he replied.

"So how can you help me if you're not an empath?"

"I can help you to build shields so that you won't be struck down every time the emotions get to be too much. I can feel your power growing and getting stronger. Do you understand what that means?"

"I think so. I used to sense things before, but the level is much more intense now. Sometimes it feels like I'm an open wound, never healing, but continuously ripping apart."

"I hate to tell you this, but it will only get worse if you don't build strong shields and learn how to control it."

"I get it. You don't need to keep saying how bad it will end up for me. What do we need to do first?"

"Sit."

She tilted her head, startled, her eyes widened with uncertainty. "What?"

"Sit down in the sand and cross your legs. We are going to do some mental exercises."

Not sure if what he suggested would work or not, but willing to give it a try, she sat down on the sand as he instructed. Once she crossed her legs, she leaned back resting her hands against the warm sand. "Are you going to stand towering over me the whole time?"

"No, I'm going to sit a short distance away from you." He sat down in a similar position as her with a few feet separating them. "Place your hands on your knees and close your eyes."

Rebecca moved her hands into the position he told her to and closed her eyes. "What now, oh wise one."

"This isn't the time for jokes."

She crunched up her nose and pursed her lips. "Sorry, but this feels weird. What do we need to do next?"

"I'm going to project an emotion at you. You need to concentrate on it and force it out of you. The point is for you to recognize a feeling, so you know how to block it when you need to, and vice versa when you don't."

"All right, I'm ready."

She sat in silence for several minutes. The time ticked by in slow measures, and she began to think the exercise was an ineffective endeavor. As the idea formed in her mind, a wash of pleasure lit up within to replace the doubt; it warmed her and gave her an intense feeling of happiness. She liked it so much she wanted to wrap it up and keep it there forever, something to lean back on when her days spiraled down into horrible uncontrollable turmoil.

What had Joel told her to do? Recognize it and push it out so she could build a shield to protect herself. Why would she ever want to deny herself such a wonderful feeling?

It grew more powerful and overwhelming the more she drew it inside. It burned so bright, it blinded her as it took over. An uneasy feeling developed as she realized her mistake. He said to push it out, and she acted the fool, refusing to listen. She thought she knew everything when she knew nothing.

She came here to learn and forgot the first rule. Push it out, remove it, block it, yes she could do this, the chant repeating over and over inside her head. In her mind, she pictured the joy and built it into an enormous ball of energy. Focusing all her power on it, she created something her mind could work with. Once all of the bliss filled the ball, she took it and threw it out, far into the void. It glowed in the darkness, a large distance separating it from her center, easily retrievable if she wanted to have it again, but in a place far enough away it wouldn't cause her harm.

Her eyes flew open and found twin aquamarine pools focused on her face.

"You're simply amazing, Becs."

"Of course I am, but why do you think so?"

"I was starting to believe you wouldn't be able to control it, but you proved me wrong. You managed to cast it aside and build a small shield. Happiness, joy, love, anything that gives us pleasure are the easier emotions to accept, but are the hardest to control. They feel so nice sitting inside of us, it's hard to let them go. I started with those because I believe we may be short on time. When we get to hatred, pain, and envy, our tasks will get a bit difficult because it will physically hurt you. It is also harder to project something you are not feeling. We've made a good amount of progress in a short time. I will walk you back to the cottage now. We will meet again tomorrow at the same time and work more."

"Is it really necessary to work at this each day?" she asked.

"Yes, because while you did a great job, it's only a small step in the right direction. The shield you built would be smashed to pieces at anything heavier."

"I guess you're right. I'm so new at this."

"You're going to be fine, Becs. It's my job to make sure of it. I'm going to make sure you are prepared for whatever the fates decide to throw your way."

Rebecca didn't want to know why Joel believed he needed to prepare her. He seemed like a nice enough guy, when he wasn't on a mission to annoy her. No matter what he thought, his job did not include preparing her for emotional chaos. Still, she couldn't help being grateful for his help. After their morning together, she believed she might be able to handle her growing power and also gained some insight into her gift. They walked back to the cottage. The sun filled the sky, and the warm breeze blew through them. A smile grew on her face, and she let her own joy fill her. A few minutes later, the cottage came in sight, and Rebecca stopped to gaze at Joel.

"Thank you for helping me and seeing me back to the cottage. I think we should go our separate ways here."

"Afraid to be seen in my company?"

"No, I don't want to explain to my friends where I went. They can be a bit smothering at times."

"I understand I don't mind leaving from here. I'll see you tomorrow."

Joel turned and strolled away in the opposite direction. Rebecca watched him for several minutes to make sure he kept on the reverse path. Satisfied with his progress, she turned back toward the cottage and ambled toward it. Her pace slow and easy, enjoying the alone time. The morning had gone well, and she hoped the day continued on in the same way.

Chapter Fourteen

AS REBECCA APPROACHED the cottage, she could see a flutter of activity. Carolyn and Virginia stood just outside the door, deep in conversation. Checking her watch, she realized she had been with Joel for three hours. She didn't realize how much time had passed. Her friends were probably worried about her. Quickening her pace, she strolled over to where they stood.

"What are you two up to?"

Carolyn raised her eyebrow and stared Rebecca. "We could ask you the same thing. Where did you disappear to so early this morning?"

"I didn't go anywhere special. I woke up early and couldn't sleep, so I went for a walk, watched the sunrise."

Everything she told them was the absolute truth. She did wake up early and couldn't have gone back to sleep if she wanted to. Rebecca also went for a walk and saw the sunrise. What she left out in that statement told a different story. No reason to tell them she spent the morning with Joel learning to control her gift. They already worried too much about her.

"Oh I get it. You went to meet your fiancé for some alone time." A knowing smile grew on Carolyn's face. "No need to say more."

"But..."

Virginia held up her hand to stop her from speaking further. "We understand if you want to see David. Actually, he is the reason we were going to come searching for you."

"Oh? What does David have to do with anything?"

"You are marrying him, right?" Carolyn asked.

"Of course, I'm looking forward to it."

What were they up to? Did they know she spent the morning working with Joel? No, they couldn't possibly have found out about any of it. She made sure she was very careful when she left the cottage. It had been quiet in the house and everyone still asleep. Whatever they sought her out for had nothing to do with Joel or her morning activities. Something else had them all stirred up and waiting to pounce on her. She had to wait and see what they wanted.

"Good because we want to go over some of the wedding plans with you. We are going to go inside now, because we have a surprise for you," Virginia exclaimed.

Rebecca stared at Carolyn and after a few seconds turned her gaze to Virginia. She didn't know what the surprise could be or if she liked the idea of it. Her friends meant well so she would just go with it. Even if she hated everything about it, she would pretend to love it. So she nodded and followed them inside. Bea and Lizzie were sitting on the wicker furniture sipping on a hot beverage.

"Oh good, you found her." Beatrice set her drink down on the table and rushed to her side. "I've been a little bit impatient and driving them mad waiting for you."

"I'm sure they didn't mind." Rebecca reached out to reassure Beatrice. "What do you need me for?"

"We have a few things to discuss about your wedding," Lizzie explained.

"Caro and Ginny did mention that outside. I thought everything was already set."

"It is, but you are again forgetting one small detail." An amused smile grew on Carolyn's face.

"I am? What?" As far as she knew she hadn't forgotten anything. What were they talking about?

"Your dress, silly." Bea jumped in place clapping her hands with excitement. "I did something, and I hope you don't mind. I got a bit carried away with you being stuck in the hospital."

"What did you do?"

"Do you remember a few months back when I took your measurements?" Bea asked.

"Yes, so you could alter my nurse's uniform."

"Since I already had them, I decided to make your dress."

Rebecca stood there stunned at her friend's words. Getting a bit carried away took things to a whole new level. How did Bea know for sure she would even like the dress? She had no words to express the shock filling her. Glancing around the room revealed each one of their faces displayed huge grins. They were so happy with this outcome how could she destroy that?

"You made me a dress? For my wedding?"

"Not exactly. I have a shell of a dress made. The basic outline. I will modify it and add embellishments once you tell me what you want."

"All right, so what do you need from me?"

"I need you to try it on so I can make sure I got everything right, and we can also determine how to make it into a fabulous wedding dress. I will go get it so you can try it on." Bea rushed out of the room to go get the dress.

"I think she might be more excited for my wedding than I am. Something I didn't believe possible."

"We're all excited. You're the first one of us getting married. It means something for each of us to have part in it," Carolyn explained.

"Which reminds me, I need to know what kind of cake you want," Lizzie jumped into the conversation.

"What kind? Any kind you feel like making works for me. It's cake, and I will eat it, because I don't often get to indulge in sweet stuff."

"If you're sure, I think I will make it a simple yellow cake with butter cream frosting."

"I'm sure. Any cake is a good cake as far as I'm concerned. In fact, all this talk about cake is making me want some." A bubble of laugher exploded through the room as Rebecca allowed herself to feel happy.

"Here it is. I hope you like it. I know it's not finished, but this is my first wedding dress..."

"I'm sure it's lovely," Rebecca reassured Beatrice.

Beatrice handed the dress to Rebecca. She took it into her bedroom and changed into it. The lines of the dress were exquisite. It had a simple bodice, sleeves capped in chiffon, and a swing skirt that fell below her knees. She couldn't have done better if she picked the dress herself, simplicity with classic silk and chiffon, not one embellishment anywhere on the gown. As she studied it, she understood what Bea meant by describing it as a shell. Rebecca left her bedroom and went to model the dress for her friends.

"This dress is beautiful, Bea." Rebecca twirled for them to get the full look.

"Oh, it fits you too. All I need to do is sew on some pretty beads or embroidery to make it special."

"Bea, you outdid yourself with that dress," Carolyn's voice filled with awe.

"Do you want me to do anything specific with it, Becca?"

"I don't know. I honestly didn't think far enough ahead to imagine what my dress would look like. This is already way past my expectations, and it's perfect. Maybe you could keep it elegant and simple when you finish it? I don't need anything elaborate."

"I can't wait to finish it. Once I add the rest of the details, I will have you try it on again to make sure everything works for you." Beatrice ran her fingers across the skirt of the dress. "You can take it off and give it back to me whenever you're ready."

"I'll go remove it now. I don't want to ruin it before the wedding."

Rebecca went back into her bedroom and changed out of the dress. She put her original clothes back on and carried it out to give back to Beatrice. Once Beatrice had the dress in her hands, she went and put it away to work her magic on another day.

"Are you getting excited?" Virginia asked.

"I am. It's starting to feel real now." Rebecca turned to stare into Ginny's eyes. "I have a dress, a beautiful, unique, and remarkable wedding dress. Bea is amazing. I am so glad she decided to do this. It saves time searching for one. She knows me so well and made something for me so very special. My heart is filled with such love for all of you. No one else has friends as brilliant as you all are. Thank you so much for helping me plan my wedding."

Virginia picked up Rebecca's hands and held them within her own. "We are equally thankful to have you as part of our lives. We wouldn't have it any other way. Each one of us is excited to be a part of your wedding. Don't you know how much you mean to us?"

"I expect as much as you mean to me. We have only known each other a short time, but you all have become more my family than my own ever could be. They were not very caring and left me to my own devices. It's a miracle I survived with such neglectful parents."

Rebecca didn't like to think about her parents and where she grew up. They both lived in a community of poor Irish-Americans in New York. There were days her stomach growled with hunger because they never had enough to eat. Her mother meant well, but she died the year Rebecca turned six. Her father had to work two jobs to make ends meet. She stayed with a neighboring family and almost never saw him.

Was it neglect if he couldn't even take care of himself let alone a small child? He did the best he could with the circumstances life thrust upon him. It was for that reason she wanted to do more with her life. As soon as she turned eighteen, she enlisted in the naval nursing program. A decision that proved to be the best one she ever made.

"Don't dwell on the past. It's not something you can change, and even if you could, you shouldn't want to. It made you the person you are. It's that girl we all love and respect." Virginia's face shined with a serene smile.

"I don't want to change who I am. This is who I am, and this woman I've grown into is remarkable in her own right. It took me a long time to realize that and to appreciate the circumstances that allowed me to become her. No, I don't plan on living in the past. I have a bright future ahead of me. One that is filled with love and lots of happiness."

"Good. I'm glad you know how wonderful you are."

"I hate to interrupt such a beautiful moment, but there are a few other things we need to discuss." Carolyn came in carrying one of her lists.

"I thought everything was set," Rebecca exclaimed.

"It is. I want to go over everything one last time to ensure we thought of every detail."

Carolyn took perfectionism up to a whole different level. Rebecca was willing to humor her a bit and go over everything once more. She sat down on one of the wicker chairs and prepared to go over every aspect of her wedding one more time. The time passed by a lot faster than she realized, and before she knew it, Maxine came home from her shift at the hospital. It reminded them all they missed lunch, and Lizzie offered to make everyone a sandwich. That was how they spent the rest of their day. Planning, eating, and enjoying each other's company. Rebecca gazed at all of her friend's with a contented smile. She had a lot of amazing things in her life, not the least of which was these five incredible women.

Chapter Fifteen

"KEEP CONCENTRATING, visualize the shield. Check every area to make sure there are no weak spots."

Rebecca did as he demanded inside of her mind. They had been meeting every morning for two weeks. With each meeting, she began to feel herself growing stronger and more in control. Still, she believed she had a lot to learn before she mastered it. Today, Joel wanted her to build a shield, one that would remain in place unless she needed to drop it to use her gift. He'd said it was time to close the complete openness and prevent unwanted emotions from seeking refuge inside of her.

"I think it's solid all the way around."

"Good, then it's time to open your eyes. Our work here is done."

Rebecca smiled as her eyes flew open. Joel stood a few feet away from her with his arms folded across his chest.

"I can't meet tomorrow morning."

"Why not?" he asked.

"It's my wedding day. I'm not focusing on anything else. I will meet you Sunday morning before my shift at the hospital."

Joel frowned and raised an eyebrow. "You're new husband won't mind you traipsing off to meet another man?"

"He won't know. He has to work all night, so after he gets off duty, he is going to bed for some much needed sleep."

"Not much of wedding night."

"It's enough we can get married. The rest can wait until we have time to enjoy it."

Joel shook his head and frowned. "Sweetheart, if I were in David's shoes, nothing would prevent me from spending the night with you. He's too wrapped up in his duty to appreciate what he has."

"He needs his sleep so he can be at his best. I don't want him to make a mistake because of me. No, we can wait to have our night together."

"Suit yourself, but you are wrong. Even if he made a mistake, it wouldn't be your fault." He shrugged his shoulders and turned to walk away from the lagoon. "I think we're done for today. Come on. I'll walk you back to the cottage."

Rebecca was startled at his abrupt mood change. She hurried to catch up to him. "You're mad?"

"Not at all, maybe a bit frustrated. It's not your fault, Becs. Don't start to drop your defensive shield when you just built it. I can work through my own demons."

They didn't get more than a few steps when a voice called from behind them.

"Jaoel, we need to speak."

Rebecca turned around to see an extraordinary and beautiful male. He had golden blond hair that shimmered as it floated in the wind. Becca tried not to let her gaze fall on him directly. Just a tiny glimpse of him hurt a little bit, his male beauty both wondrous and unique. She didn't usually use such words to describe a man, but nothing else even came close to expressing the vision before her. His harshness only added to how exquisite he appeared to be.

"Who are you?" she asked.

He didn't even glance at her or acknowledge she existed. His eyes stayed fixed on Joel. Wait a minute, what had he called him? It almost sounded like he said Yah-el. It sure didn't sound like he called him Joel. Did that mean Joel lied to her about his name?

Joel stopped and stared at the man. "Michael, what are you doing here?"

"I needed to warn you. Others sensed something new and threatening coming."

"Is it new, or are they sensing the same darkness?"

Rebecca waved her hands in front of Joel, attempting to get his attention. "Hello, are you going to answer me? Who is this guy, and what did he just call you?" Rebecca demanded.

"It's hard to tell. It could be the same one. We only know one thing for certain. It's a scarier, more evil version coming."

"Do we have a timeline yet?"

If they continued to pretend like she didn't exist, she would have no choice but to beat them on the head with a stick. This talking over and around her had surpassed irritating Rebecca and instead angered her.

"Hello, I'm still here, but if you don't start talking to me, I'm going to walk away. I have a wedding to be ready for tomorrow. Not that it appears like the two of you even care..." Rebecca crossed her arms over her chest, her eyebrows puckered, and her lips turned down into a scowl. When they continued to ignore her, Rebecca kept her promise and turned on her heels to walk away from them stomping her feet with each step she made.

"Becs, wait," Joel called.

Rebecca didn't have time to stop and placate him any longer. She gave him every opportunity to answer her questions—and she had quite a few of them too. The strange man who popped out of nowhere for one, followed by a close second, the name the man called him. She could hear him running to catch up to her. It didn't take long before his hand grabbed her shoulders to prevent her from walking further.

"I asked you to wait." Joel leaned over to catch his breath.

"I didn't see the point. You seemed to have everything under control with your friend."

"I'm sorry if your feelings got hurt, but what occurred back there happened to be important. Michael needed to tell me about the approaching darkness."

"Honestly? You mean the one I sensed myself? I'm sure I didn't understand what he talked about." Rebecca did a good impression of studying her fingernails and acting blasé.

"No need to be sarcastic, Becs. Although, I find this look on you to be quite attractive. You should do it more often." His chin rested between his thumb and forefinger and then his tongue rolled over his teeth.

Rebecca placed her hands on her hips and stared into Joel's eyes. "Don't even try to change the subject. I want answers. Let's start with Michael. Who is he, and why did he come to see you?"

"The simple answer is Michael is my boss."

"Is that all you're going to tell me? He is your boss? What do you do, and here's a bigger question, what are you really? Michael, he's so frighteningly beautiful. Just a small glimpse at him terrifies me and makes me want to reach out and touch him. I don't know what to make of that."

"Michael is...he's very old. It has changed him."

"What is he?"

"He's a guardian, but it's more complicated than that. Michael is our leader, the one that organizes everything and corrals us when necessary. His word is law."

"So are you're a guardian then? Is Joel your real name?" she asked.

"Joel is a nickname of sorts. My real name is Jaoel," he replied.

"Yah-el? So Michael said you're name when he appeared out of nowhere?"

"Yes, it's actually spelled similarly to Joel, you just add an A in-between the J and O. When I wanted a more modern name, I removed the A. Not too many people have a name as odd as I do."

Rebecca gave herself a few minutes to take in this new development. She had more questions. There were so many questions in her mind, she couldn't process them all. So her tutor also worked as a guardian. She didn't have a clue what being a guardian entailed. One day, she would take the time to interrogate him with more thoroughness, but right now, it took everything she had to process his name change. Not to mention the approaching darkness. She needed to move past the little things and find out what the reason Michael came to see Joel or Yah-el, whatever the heck he wanted to call himself.

"I don't know. I kind of like it. Now that I know you're real name, why don't you explain to me what Michael came to tell you."

"Either the darkness is changing, growing, or so close, they can feel it stronger than ever before. Those with more control over their gifts than you can't seem to tell. Their best guess is it will be here as soon as today and as late as next week."

"No, it can't come today. I refuse to let it." Rebecca took several steps back—putting distance between them. She sliced her head once to the left, then right, in a concise firm movement. Her lips pursed as her eyes poured into him. "Tomorrow is my wedding day, and nothing is going to prevent it from going forward."

Joel laughed so loud, she jumped from the sound. "So let me understand what you're saying. You don't care if it comes, as long as it doesn't have the bad behavior of interrupting your wedding?"

Rebecca crunched up her nose. "I see your point. It's selfish of me to think of my own life and not how this is all going to affect everyone around me. I don't care though. I have a right to my feelings, as much as the next person. I want to get married. The darkness be damned."

"Be careful what you wish for, Becs. You might get it. Don't tempt fate." Joel shook his head, cautioning her.

"I'm not going to think about fate or bad omens. I'm going to think good thoughts and pray nothing goes wrong.

Maybe we will get lucky, and this darkness we sense is nothing more than the war spreading through Europe."

"You're not that naïve. Don't pretend you are. I'm sure the darkness has a lot to do with the war, but it's coming this way. America won't be able to stay out of it"

"Fine, so some bad evil thing is heading in our direction. I'm still not going to worry about it. I'm going home to let my roommates pamper me the day before my wedding."

Rebecca turned and stormed away from Joel. She believed in the evil force. How could she deny it when it decimated her a few weeks ago? Perhaps ignoring it was stupid, but she meant what she said. Nothing and no one would prevent her from becoming Mrs. David Falcon tomorrow afternoon. If anyone stood in her way, she would make them rue the day they ever tried.

"Fine, Becs. Go concentrate on your wedding. If it makes you happy to pretend this darkness does not exist, who am I to stop you."

Rebecca stopped in her tracks and turned around to face Joel. "Exactly, its time you realized you can't stop me. I love him, and I will marry him tomorrow."

"Good, I'm glad you love him and want to spend the rest of your life with him. However long that might be. Are you going to be happy if you don't do everything in your power to stop this? Can you sit by and let other people get hurt because you are only thinking about yourself?"

"Yes, because I don't believe it is going to happen as soon as Michael says it will. When the time comes I will help."

"But only if it doesn't interrupt your wedding right? Because it's more important than other people's lives."

Oh, he infuriated her. She wanted to walk over and punch him in the stomach. Maybe she should and see how he liked it. Every word out of his mouth made her stomach roll with unease. She wanted to return the favor in some small way.

"You're not going to guilt trip me into calling off my wedding, so you can quit while you are ahead."

"I'm not trying to make you feel guilty. I promise you are doing it all on your own."

"I don't believe you."

"I don't expect you would," he replied.

"I guess this means you won't be at my wedding tomorrow."

"No, I believe I will have better things to do. Have a beautiful wedding, Becs. I hope it lives up to all of your expectations."

With those words, he spun around and strolled away. Rebecca didn't like how their conversation ended. She didn't want to think about his words and how much they hurt her deep inside. Each one cut like a knife through her heart, piercing it, making it sting with pain. He sure knew how to make her doubt her decisions. What if it all went down tomorrow, and it ruined her wedding? But what if it didn't? She refused to think about it. As far as she saw it, the wedding should continue on as planned. If she saw any signs tomorrow indicating it should be postponed, she would do so. In the meantime, she would carry on as usual, go home, and spend the rest of the day with her friends. She wouldn't let the possibility of any darkness get her down. Rebecca had more things to concentrate on than the fate of the world.

David was the love of her life, and she planned on being with him forever. That had to mean something, or why bother?

Chapter Sixteen

JAOEL KICKED A ROCK in his path, sending it spiraling in the distance. The disagreement with Rebecca weighed on his mind. He wanted her to understand the gravity of her actions, but nothing he said made a difference. What little he got out of Michael suggested the darkness could arrive at any moment. Everything they knew to be true regarding the shadows pointed straight at Hawaii. Whenever it chose to strike, the devastation would hit the islands the hardest.

"I gather she didn't want to listen to what you had to say."

Jaoel turned to stare at Michael. His arms were folded against his chest as he stared off into the distance. He didn't want to have another useless conversation and wished his leader had gone home. The sad, unfortunate truth was Michael did what he wanted, and Jaoel had no control over his actions. If he wanted him to leave, he would need to hear him out. Nothing would stop Michael from saying or doing anything.

"No, she is being unusually selfish at the moment. All she sees is her wedding looming in the distance. It's like she has forgotten everything she experienced when the dark seeped into her a couple of weeks ago. She wants to concentrate on a happy time. That does not include a possible tragic event."

"Can you blame her?" Michael asked.

"Yes," he exclaimed.

Michael didn't say anything. He stared at him with a hard expression on his face and shook his head. Not saying a word said everything to Jaoel. Michael wanted to shame him into seeing reason.

"You think I'm being unreasonable, don't you," Jaoel asked.

"I see both sides, and I understand why each of you feel the way you do. It's not an easy thing to decipher who is right and who is wrong. It's a gray area, Jaoel. Neither one of you is wrong, just as both of you are also right. If it makes you feel any better, I don't believe anything is going to happen tomorrow. It looks like it will be a lovely day for a wedding. You should be there for her, support her in her decision."

Jaoel cocked his head to the side with disbelief. Michael expected him to go to Rebecca's wedding? No, not a good idea. He would not give her his blessing in this.

"I'd rather not attend her nuptials. I don't see the point in encouraging her down the wrong path."

"You believe her decision to marry is the wrong path. Is it the wrong path for her or for you?"

"I don't know what you're talking about," Jaoel replied.

But he did know. He could feel the change inside of him. The time he spent with Rebecca opened him up to something, and he kept pushing it aside not wanting to acknowledge it. He wanted her to see him, to love him, but she didn't. His feelings didn't matter to her. She didn't even appear to like him much most days. So if she wanted to marry her fiancé and plan a life with him, he wouldn't stop her, but he also wouldn't stand by and watch it happen.

"I think you do know, so I won't push it. I will push you to attend the wedding though."

"What? Why would you do that?" Jaoel asked.

"Because it's important for you to be there and mend fences, or have you forgotten what your assignment is?"

"What does any of that have to do with her wedding?" Jaoel inquired.

"I don't believe anything will happen tomorrow. Have you considered I may be wrong? What if some dark shadows are preparing now as we speak to spread their evil, and you are not there to stop it? I'm not saying it can be stopped, because we don't even know what we are dealing with, but you could be there to save her. She is the key. We have said this all along. You can't abandon her now when she may need you the most. This isn't about you or your feelings. It's time to set those aside and do what's best for the greater good."

Michael could be long winded and also very right. Jaoel didn't want to admit it aloud how much he had a point, so he nodded his head in agreement. His feelings didn't matter right now because Rebecca needed him. He took a sworn oath to protect her. Michael assigned him as her guardian, and he would make sure not one thing caused her any kind of permanent harm.

"Fine, I will go to her wedding. I refuse to attend it as a guest though. I will remain in the shadows, so if she needs me, I can be there. I cannot give her my blessing."

"Fair enough, although I think you are making a grave mistake, Jaoel. It would go a long way for her to know you support her no matter what you feel."

"Possibly, but it's too much to ask of me."

"Very well, if I hear anything else, I will be in touch."

Jaoel turned away from Michael and continued on his path to the airfield. He would go check on his friend Kenneth. Maybe he could talk him into going to the wedding with him. At least he would have someone to talk to about everything. Someone on his side. Kenneth guessed at Jaoel's feelings for Rebecca. He remarked on it after Thanksgiving dinner, but didn't push for confirmation. The man respected his privacy, and any one that did that, earned his respect. After several minutes of a steady pace, Jaoel reached the hangar and entered it from the side door.

"Kenneth are you here?" he called out.

Kenneth's head peeked out of their tiny barracks at the sound of Jaoel's voice.

"Hey Joel, did you just get back?"

"Yeah, I saw Rebecca. Tomorrow is her wedding."

"Oh man, I'm sorry. Are you going?"

"I told her I couldn't go, but maybe I should. You feel like going with me?"

Kenneth appeared to ponder over his words for several seconds. His eyes clouded over, and he had a dreamy expression on his face. He didn't have feelings for Rebecca, too, did he?

"If you don't mind, I think I would like to go. I like her friend, Carolyn. I'd like to have a chance to get to know her better."

He liked Carolyn? It was a very interesting development. One he didn't mind taking advantage of. It would give him a ready excuse for attending when he said he wouldn't. One he would have no problem sharing with Rebecca if she asked.

Jaoel would even help Kenneth out if he could. The man had been a mountain of sadness for the past couple of weeks. He didn't know why he had been so unhappy, but it would help him a lot to open himself up to something good.

"I didn't realize you had a thing for her, and if I minded, I wouldn't have asked if you wanted to go to the wedding with me. I didn't want to go alone, and you are the only other person I talk to on this island."

"What time is the wedding?"

"It's at three, I think. I will double check and let you know. We should probably plan on being there at least a half hour early. I don't know how they are setting everything up. I know they plan on having it all at the cottage, the ceremony and a light dinner afterwards for everyone."

Kenneth nodded his head and smiled. "It works for me. I can take a plane up in the morning to log in some flight times. You know I won't be around here much longer. Next week, I meet with the admiral about putting me back on an aircraft carrier. If it goes as well as I hope it does, I'll be leaving Hawaii and sailing somewhere in the Pacific."

"Then I hope it everything goes well for you. I know you've been a little sad for a while. You never did tell me what happened to get you grounded."

Kenneth grew quiet and turned his back to Jaoel. The silence consumed the hangar, and he wondered if he should not have mentioned his gloomy disposition. He didn't want to bring up something that possibly hurt him. Now he couldn't take it back. He should not have mentioned anything, but sometimes things happened for a reason. Maybe he would shake it off and let it go. Kenneth turned back around and fidgeted. He appeared as if he wanted to say something, but had trouble finding the right words. Then everything spilled out and told Jaoel everything he kept bottled up inside of him.

"My best friend got killed in some practice drills. We couldn't do anything to save him. His plane burst into a ball of fire. He was trapped inside. We were stuck watching him burn with a feeling of helplessness. I didn't take it well and blew up at the injustice of it all. I, well, took out my anger on my commanding officer. Stripping me of my wings and sending me here gave me the opportunity to reevaluate everything. As far as disciplinary actions, it could have been a lot worse. I'm grateful they are allowing me a chance to prove myself again."

Jaoel knew something caused Kenneth pain, but he hadn't known exactly what it had been. His friend's loss resulted in a lot of justifiable agony. If Jaoel could take away his loss he would, but reviving the dead happened to be way beyond his capabilities.

"I'm sorry about your friend. It's hard to lose someone you care about. I've been told that, over time, it gets easier to deal with. You never forget, but the pain eases."

"No, I will never forget him. We grew up together, and he is the reason I joined the navy to begin with. He wanted to see the world, and I wanted to fly over it. So we both trained as pilots. I can't help to think sometimes he might still be alive if he hadn't followed me toward flying. He could have done anything, but he wanted to do it with me." Kenneth's face lost color the more he talked.

"You can't blame yourself. We are only responsible for our own decisions. Your friend made the best decision he could for himself. I'm sure he didn't regret one moment he spent flying or being with you. He wouldn't want you blaming yourself."

Kenneth was quiet for several minutes. He clenched his fists at his side and then eased them open rubbing them against the side of his pants. "You're right of course. He wouldn't want me to blame myself. It's still not easy to let go of. I'm working on it. Thank you for listening to me."

"No, thank you for trusting me enough to open yourself up to me. I know how hard it can be. Now I'm going to go get some work done. These planes are not going to fix themselves."

Jaoel left Kenneth alone and strolled over to a nearby plane. His toolbox lay underneath waiting for him to pick up what he needed. He glanced at the engine and prodded it and played with its inner workings. After several minutes, he found the problem and a huge grin formed on his face. He loved fixing things, and he couldn't wait to hear the plane's engine purr once again. One thing he knew for certain, it was far easier to fix a machine than patch up someone's aches and pains. He hoped Rebecca could forgive him for acting so harsh earlier. Michael spoke the truth; she would be more willing to let him be a part of her life if he actually went to the wedding. So he would go with Kenneth and ease his way back into her life. If she wanted to marry David, who was he to stand in her way? He would support and encourage her like the good friend she considered him to be. A guardian needed to put all feelings aside in order to protect their charges. Jaoel would try his best to do that, even if it killed him on the inside.

Chapter Seventeen

REBECCA WOKE UP TO a brilliant light shining through the window of her bedroom. The need to stretch overwhelmed her as she kicked her blankets off. Her arms flew above her head, reaching for the wall, and she could feel her muscles elongate as she pointed her feet toward the foot of her bed. Relaxing her muscles, she curled up into a ball and sighed. She lay on her bed in the fetal position for several minutes before deciding to begin her day.

Rolling out of bed, her feet landed on the floor with a soft *thud*. She stood up to her full height and reached for her robe. Today, she would become Mrs. David Falcon. In a few short hours she would begin preparing for her wedding. No one would make her feel less than happy with the events scheduled for today. She couldn't wait to stand before the minister and say *I do*. Still, excitement filled her as anxiety rolled through her stomach. Rebecca rubbed her arms as tiny goose bumps began to spread across them from an unexpected chill.

"I see someone is ready to get a jump on today's activities."

Rebecca turned to see her roommate Carolyn rolled on her side staring at her. A knowing grin fell across her face as she leaned her head against the palm of her hand.

"I have every reason to. I'm getting married today after all."

"That you are and it's my pleasure to help make it memorable as well as beautiful. What do you want to do first?"

Rebecca stopped to think about it, and nothing came to mind. "I don't know. The wedding doesn't start for several hours. I hadn't thought that far ahead. I suppose I could go for a walk and enjoy the morning."

"You don't want to eat something?" Carolyn asked.

"I couldn't possibly put anything in my stomach. With the constant fluttering, I doubt I could keep much down. I think a walk would help a lot to calm my nerves. I need some serenity before I say my vows.

Carolyn shrugged her shoulders and asked, "Do you want company?"

Rebecca didn't want any company along because she wanted the peace and quiet to think. Joel made some valid points the day before, and she wanted to consider what he said with care. Plus, there was always a chance he would show up unannounced. There were plenty of times he would appear without warning. She didn't want company along if she happened to run into him.

"I think I would rather be alone."

"If that is your wish, I will respect it. Make sure you get back here at a reasonable time. You will want to have time to bathe and make yourself beautiful for your groom."

"Where is Ginny? Did she get up already?"

Carolyn nodded her head. "I think so. I didn't hear her though. She could be anywhere."

"I am going to get dressed and see if I can find her before I leave."

Rebecca walked over to her chest of drawers and pulled it open. She pulled out some slacks and a simple blouse, not wanting anything elaborate to wear before donning her wedding dress later. With quick sure movements, she took off her nightgown and dressed in the clothes she selected. She scanned the room to locate her shoes and remembered she left them in the living room. She grabbed something to pull her hair back and walked out to find her shoes. Once she entered the room, she located them next to one of the wicker chairs. She slipped them on and searched for Virginia. She found her sitting outside on the porch swing talking with Beatrice.

"Good morning, did you sleep well?" Virginia gazed up at her with a serene smile gracing her face.

"I did. I'm going to take a walk, but wanted to come talk to you before I left."

"You're not going to be long are you?" Beatrice asked in a panicked voice.

"No, of course not. I don't expect to be gone longer than an hour. Why?" Rebecca responded.

"I want you to try on your dress one last time to make sure I don't need to make any changes."

Rebecca tilted her head in thought and glanced over at Beatrice. "Do you think it's necessary? I think it should be fine with whatever alterations you have already made. I don't want you to be working on my dress up until the last minute."

"I can't help it." Beatrice pushed her glasses up onto the bridge of her nose. "I need to make sure it's perfect, or I won't be able to relax."

Rebecca's heart warmed in appreciation. She was grateful beyond words for everything her friends did to make her wedding day extra special. No matter how much she tried, Rebecca knew she would never be able to repay them for their kindness.

"I promise you, it will be perfect. Everything you all have done for me has made this day extraordinary. Today is going to be exceptional because of all of the love you guys have put into it. I am blessed to have so many wonderful people in my life."

Beatrice wiped a tear from the corner of her eye. "Now look at what you've done. Making me cry when I swore I wouldn't. I'm going to go inside before I make a bigger fool of myself."

Rebecca shook her head in disagreement. "You are not a fool, Beatrice Gold. You are a beautiful person, inside and out. Don't ever think less of yourself. Now if you want be alone to get yourself together, I understand. Go on inside, and I will talk with Ginny."

Beatrice stood up and wrapped her arms around Rebecca in a fierce hug. "We like doing things for you. I have never met anyone who appreciated a kind gesture more than you. It makes me feel so good to do something for you because you enjoy it so very much. Trust me when I say, the pleasure is all mine."

Rebecca choked up as emotions flooded her. She couldn't express all of the feelings spreading through her brimming over the top. They were all hers, the shield she built with Joel the day before still intact. Beatrice's lips trembled into a small smile and she turned to walk inside.

"What did you need to talk to me about, Becca?" Virginia asked.

"It's a tiny thing. I wanted to ask you to do something for me."

"Anything"

Rebecca tilted her head in surprise. "You don't even know what I want, and you're already agreeing. Don't you want to know what the favor is before you agree."

"It doesn't matter what you need me for. I'm happy to help," Virginia replied. "Now tell me what you need."

"It's a minor thing, but it's important to me. I didn't bring it up in the planning because it didn't occur to me until this morning." Rebecca stopped and bit her lip a moment of indecision entering her mind. "Could you lead us in prayer before we say our vows? I feel like it's important we take a moment to thank God for bringing us all together."

Virginia placed a hand over her heart, and her face lit up into a pleased smile. "I'd be honored to lead us in prayer. I'm so happy you asked me to. Now go on your walk. Rest assured I will make sure everything goes well."

"Thank you so much. I knew you were the right person to ask. I'm going to go take some time to myself. Reassure Bea I will be back in time to try on the dress for her. I don't want her fretting about something she has no control over."

Virginia waved her hands encouraging Rebecca on her way. "I will, don't worry about anything here. We have everything under control. Go, enjoy your walk. I know how much pleasure your daily exercise has given you."

With a laugh, Rebecca left the porch and strolled along the path leading away from the cottage. The morning sunshine warming her each step she took. Soon, she would be at the secluded lagoon where she practiced building her shields with Joel. She secretly wished and hoped he would be there once she arrived. Rebecca didn't know why, but she had an uneasy feeling resting inside of her. She needed to see Joel and set things right with him. If she could do it before she married David, she would feel a lot better about the situation. She gazed up at the bright sky and couldn't see how anything bad could possibly happen on such a fine day. Whatever darkness was heading in their direction, it wouldn't show up anytime soon. Well, at least not today, not when it was such a glorious and gorgeous day. Only one thing stood in her way from having an exquisite day, Joel and his anger at her reluctance to cancel her wedding. He thought her actions selfish and unreasonable. Just because she refused to let some elusive darkness ruin her happy day did not mean she was in any way selfish. She wanted what every bride did, an unforgettable wedding day.

Turning the corner and rounding the bend, she found herself at the lagoon. The crystal blue pool gleamed in invitation, and the sand sparkled under the sun's bright rays. She scanned the area and did not find the person she wanted to see. Joel either hadn't come to the lagoon, or he had already left. Either way, she couldn't speak to him before her wedding.

She didn't believe he planned on coming. She twisted her hands up in front of her and rolled her lips between her teeth. Nothing she could do about it now. She would talk to him tomorrow if she could find him. If he happened to come to the wedding, even better. Rebecca turned around and left the lagoon behind. She promised Bea she wouldn't be gone long. Her wedding dress awaited her, and she couldn't wait to try it on. Joel and his misgivings would have to wait for a day when she had more time to give.

A resolution made, Rebecca continued on with her trek back to the cottage. At least at home she had several individuals that would always be on her side. They wouldn't judge her to be self-serving and only thinking about her needs. They expected her to be excited about her wedding. Still she couldn't get Joel off of her mind. Maybe once she started getting ready for the wedding, she would be able to let it go. Until then, she would do the best she could to move forward.

Chapter Eighteen

THE DRESS BEATRICE held in her arms couldn't be any more perfect. She had done such a wonderful job creating something beautiful. Rebecca ran her fingers over the soft silk and chiffon. The simple dress became a vision in ivory. The waist now displayed an intricate belt of beads swirling through. In the middle of the belt, a pattern formed, a miniature crystal lily surrounded by a string of petite pearls creating a vine of leaves around to the back of the dress. At the edges of the skirt, the same pattern of leaves were sown in on a smaller scale. Delicate lace graced the center of the chiffon capped sleeves.

Rebecca held a hand over her heart, and a tiny tear fell from the corner of her eye. "Oh Bea, I don't know what to say."

"Say you like it," Beatrice pleaded.

Rebecca hung the dress on a hook on her bedroom door and walked over to Beatrice, pulling her into an affectionate hug. "Like it? I can honestly say I like it, but what I feel when I stare at this dress goes way beyond liking. I adore it, and I'm so honored to wear it. Thank you for making me the best wedding dress a girl could ever imagine."

"Are you sure? I mean, you don't hate it?" Beatrice stepped back and wrung her fingers together. With an anxious expression on her face, she glanced from the dress back to Rebecca. A small frown formed on her face.

Rebecca lightly smacked Beatrice's shoulder. "Stop it. You did a beautiful job. Now I'm going to go put on my exquisite dress and get ready to marry the man I love. Are you up to helping me?"

Beatrice wiped the tears from her eyes and laughed. "Of course I am. I can't wait to see how it looks on you."

Rebecca pulled the dress off of the hanger and stepped into it. She turned her back to Beatrice, so she could fasten the multitude of pearl buttons she sewed into the back of the dress. After the last button slipped through its tiny slit, Rebecca twirled around so Beatrice could get the full view of how she looked in the dress.

"I love how I feel wearing this dress. It's so pretty, it gives me brilliant vibes. You are a genius, Bea." Rebecca ran the palms of her hands down the dress and over the design resting at the waist of the dress.

"I managed to find a white few lilies for you to wear in your hair. Have you decided how you want to style it yet?" Beatrice asked.

Rebecca ran her hand over her hair and grabbed a piece, running it between two of her fingers stopping with a tip resting between them. "I think I want to wear it down. Maybe we can put some of it up and pin the lilies in the back to accentuate my curls."

"I love how your hair is weaved with shades of copper and gold. The lilies will be a nice contrast against it. Do you want me to try to do your hair how you described it?" Beatrice asked.

"How much time do we have before the wedding?"

Beatrice glanced at her watch. "It's a quarter to two now. The wedding is a little over an hour away. Are you starting to get excited?"

"I am my stomach is a flutter of nerves. I'm going to go sit down and attempt to sit still so you can help me with my hair."

Rebecca sat down with her back toward Beatrice. With gentle hands, she pinned her hair on top so her curls cascaded down her back. She picked up a white box and opened the lid. Inside sat three delicate white lilies. She pulled one out and pinned it toward the top at the back of her head, the next one on the opposite side an inch down, and the last one another inch down on the opposite side, underneath the first one. A zigzag pattern of flowers suspended through the curls floating down her back.

"I'm done. It looks so elegant, Becca. Do you want me to get a small mirror so you can see?" Beatrice asked.

"Yes, please."

Beatrice grabbed a hand mirror and handed it to Rebecca. She held it up and turned her back to the large vanity mirror. She could see the flowers pinned in her hair. Beatrice was right; they were elegant against her red-gold curls. She turned around and set the mirror on the vanity table. A serene smile stared back at her from the large mirror. Everything had such a surreal feeling to it, but she knew it all to be real. In less than an hour, she would become someone's wife.

"Is David here?"

"I'm not sure. Would you like me to check?" Beatrice asked.

"It doesn't matter. I'm nervous."

"I'll go check for you. I'm sure if he isn't, though, he will be soon."

Rebecca nodded her head in agreement. "I know."

Beatrice left the room, giving Rebecca time alone. She stared at herself in the mirror for several minutes lost in her own world. Her image blurred before her, and her shield dropped. Pain stabbed her in the chest, and she gasped for breath. She choked as she struggled to get air into her lungs. Just when she thought she might pass out, she managed to put her protective barrier up and could breathe once again. A knock on her door had her swinging her head in its direction.

"Come in," she called out.

A muffled voice asked, "Are you dressed?"

"Of course."

The door opened a little bit, and Joel's head slipped through. "I want to make sure it's all right for me to enter. I hope you don't mind me coming to see you. Carolyn told me where to find you."

The sight of him made her smile. "Yes, please come in. I'd like to talk to you."

"Good, because I think we need to clear up a few things. I'd like to get it out of the way before your wedding." He walked into the room and shut the door with a soft click behind him.

"I went to the lagoon earlier hoping to see you there."

Joel came over to stand by her. His arms folded across his chest no emotion showing on his face. His ancient aquamarine eyes softened as he gazed down at her. "I needed time to think by myself. I didn't get a chance to go out there. Michael came by to see me, and we went over everything in more detail. He pointed out a few things to me and gave me a lot to think about. I owe you an apology. My feelings about your wedding don't matter. I'm here if you need me to be. I'm a guardian and only here to help you, not make passing judgments."

"Of course your feelings matter. You're right I need to be concerned about the darkness. I had another feeling seep through." Rebecca stood up and placed her hands on his arm. "Just before you knocked on the door, it broke through my shell."

Joel's eyes filled with shock. "Wait a minute, what?"

"I don't know what happened. It set upon me without any warning. One minute I studied my reflection in the mirror, the next sharp needles poked through piercing me with uncontrollable pain. My throat began to close up—it scared me.

"Were you able to get your shield back up? Are you all right?"

"I'm fine, I promise. Although, I have to think, in light of this, Michael is right."

Joel's lips twitched into a smirk. "He usually is. It can be rather annoying from time to time"

"I want to get married. It's just, well I'm not so sure I should now." Rebecca fidgeted, twisting her fingers in front of her.

"If marrying David makes you happy, then yes, absolutely, you should marry him. Don't let anyone or anything stand in your way."

Tears welled up in her eyes. Why did he have to be so nice to her? If he came back with sarcasm or flirted, she would have been able to brush it all aside. All the little doubts that kept creeping in. She raised her hands and wiped the wet droplets falling down her face in a quick sweeping motion. "I don't understand why I'm crying."

"Come here." Joel pulled her into his arms and hugged her. She rested her head against his shoulder and sniffled. He rubbed her back soothing her. With his arms wrapped around her, she believed everything would be all right, and he would make sure she remained safe from any harm. His voice calmed her nerves and helped to ease her tears. "It's probably some aftershocks from what happened a few moments ago. I wouldn't let it worry you. You're wedding is starting soon. It's all right to be a little overemotional."

Rebecca pulled herself out of his arms and took a step back. "I'm sure you're right. It will all be fine."

"Of course it will. I'm glad we had this time to talk. I'm going to go outside and wait for the wedding to start. We will speak more later."

Rebecca nodded her head at him her thoughts whirling around her mind. Joel turned to leave his hand starting to turn the doorknob. "Joel wait."

He stared over his shoulder at her. "Do you need something else."

"No, I mean yes. Thank you for comforting me. I needed it. Tomorrow morning, are we going to meet again at the lagoon?"

"You're not going to be with David?" he asked.

"No, remember, he is on duty tonight, and I won't see him until tomorrow night. We are leaving for a month long holiday. Our request has been approved for leave, and we are going to visit his family for Christmas. I won't be back until after the New Year."

"So tomorrow should be our last day to meet until next year."

"Yes." Rebecca's lips tilted into a bright smile.

"Then yes, I think we should meet in the morning. It will do us both some good."

He left the room. She stood alone for several minutes before someone else knocked on the door. Carolyn peeked her head in the room through the open door. "We are ready for you. The minister is here, David is here, all the guests are in their seats. Are you ready to get married?"

"I am more than ready."

Carolyn walked into the room and grabbed one of her hands in hers. "Then come with me Miss O'Shea. You are about to become Mrs. David Falcon."

Rebecca followed her out of the room and outside to where they set up for the wedding. Everyone sat in black chairs, the backs decorated with the same white lilies adorning her hair. The minister stood ahead, waiting for her to join them. David stood facing her on the minister's left. He wore his navy dress uniform. His eyes stared at her with adoration. Carolyn placed her hand in the crook of her arm and led her down the path to stand next to David.

"Are we ready to begin?" the minister asked.

"We are," Rebecca and David said in unison.

The whole ceremony flew by, and before she knew it, the minister pronounced them man and wife. David leaned down and pressed a light kiss on her lips. Everyone clapped with joy shining out of their eyes. No darkness came to ruin the wedding. She took that as a good sign their marriage was meant to be. David smiled down at her, lifted her hand up to his mouth, and kissed the back of her hand.

"All right everyone, if you will follow me, we have refreshments set up by the cottage." Carolyn motioned them all to where Elizabeth and Beatrice set up a table with various food items, drinks, and desserts for everyone to enjoy.

While the guests went to get something to eat Rebecca turned her attention to her husband. She only had eyes for David. They did it, they got married. Everything else would only be small things going forward. Rebecca allowed herself to feel happy and enjoy being around all of the people she loved. David pulled her into his arms and kissed her. A warm tingle spread through her as his lips caressed hers. Moments like these were meant to be cherished.

Chapter Nineteen

"YOU MIGHT THINK THIS is strange, but I want to do something different today." Joel's back faced Rebecca as he spoke. He stopped and stared over his shoulder at her. "Follow me."

Curious what he had in mind, she followed him around the bend of the lagoon and noticed an entrance to a cave. He motioned for her to continue to follow him. She got as far as the opening and stopped. Nothing was visible on the inside, nothing but pitch black.

"I don't know about this, Joel. I can't see anything."

"We will have more light when we get further inside. Come on, give me your hand. I will lead you to where we are heading."

Rebecca glanced behind her at the crystal blue water of the lagoon. The sun already rode high in the morning sky. She glanced at her watch and noted the time, half past seven o'clock. They had all day to get in one last lesson in how to control her gift. She didn't see any reason not to trust him. He hadn't let her down yet. She lifted her hand and placed it in his. With a tight grip he grasped it in his and walked inside the cave. It seemed like she followed him forever until they reached an area lit up from the sun. She glanced up and saw an opening in the cave from above. The ceiling stood at least twenty feet above her.

"This is amazing. You keep showing me places I didn't know existed on this island. What are we going to do here," she asked.

"We are going to do some meditating. The lagoon is peaceful, but this is more secluded. I know you plan on leaving this evening. I want to make sure you have all the tools necessary to block out any unwanted emotions."

"I thought we have been doing that all along."

"We have, but on a smaller scale. This is going to take all of your focus. Come over here and sit on this ledge. It has a nice flat surface, and you will be able to get a certain amount of comfort and stillness here." He pointed to an area several feet off the ground.

"I'm not sure I can climb up there by myself."

"I will give you a boost up." He strolled over to the edge and turned toward her. "Come here."

She stepped over to his side. He wound his fingers together and lowered his hands close to the ground. "Step inside my hands, and I will lift you up."

Rebecca stared at his hands and bit her lip. "I don't know..."

"Just do it, Becs. Trust me."

She lifted her foot and placed it in the center of his two hands. He lifted her up and twisted so she landed on her bottom at the edge of the flat surface. She scooted over to the center and crossed her legs, placing her hands at her knees.

"What next?" she asked.

"Close your eyes, just like we have done in the past. Picture your shield."

She did as he instructed. The shell surrounded her; she poked at it testing its strength. It appeared solid, impermeable, and sturdy. Appearances could be deceiving though as something punctured through the night before.

"Now take deep slow breaths, block out all sound. Even my voice. You are all alone, nothing can get to you."

She sat in complete silence. The world around her disappeared, her breathing even and controlled. Her mind drifted as she explored through her own thoughts. Something buzzed in her ear. A bug, no it was much louder and higher pitched. Her eyes fluttered open and stared over at Joel.

"Do you hear that?"

"It's just some planes buzzing overhead. Navy's probably doing some early morning drills."

She tilted her head in confusion. "Are you sure? Sounds like an awful lot of planes."

"The navy has a lot of planes." His mouth twitched into a smile.

Her stomach quivered, and she could feel it churning with disagreement. "I have an uneasy feeling."

Just as the words left her mouth, a loud boom rattled the cavern walls. The ground began to shake, and a few small rocks fell through the opening at the ceiling. She screamed and jumped off the ledge. Joel grabbed her and held onto her tight, preventing her from running through the dark cave.

"You don't know your way out. Let me lead."

Her mouth wobbled as tears fell from her eyes. "I'm scared. What is exploding?"

"Don't worry. I will take care of you." He pulled her into his arms. "I promise. It's what I'm here for. It's my job as a guardian."

"How long have you been a guardian, Joel. I always meant to ask you that."

"A very long time. So long, I don't know if I remember what my life was like before I took my oath of duty." He released her from his arms. "Come on. We need to see what is going on outside.

He led her out of the cave and into the open space of the lagoon. Above her, hundreds of planes flew overhead. Bombs were being dropped as they neared land. Gunfire exploded all around her.

"Someone is attacking us," she shouted.

Red circles outlined in white decorated the wings and sides of the dark green planes. They dipped and spun as they flew by. Japanese, they were attacking Pearl Harbor and the islands of Hawaii. Hundreds of them flew over and around the island. They dotted the sky, heavy, loud engine sounds drummed through her ears. One buzzed by, low just above the surface. A bomb released into the water. It skimmed the top of the water as it headed toward the harbor. Her mouth hung open as her heart thudded fast and hard against her chest.

The torpedo zipped through the cerulean waves headed straight for one of the battleships.

She ran up the hill, pulling Joel along with her, and watched battleship row in the distance. A huge explosion erupted, and a fire broke out across one of the ships. Flames ripped across the starboard side in brilliant orange and yellow, rivaling the sun in its brightness. Clouds of smoke filled the sky. Rebecca choked as she breathed in the toxic fumes. She covered her nose attempting to block the pungent burnt wood and melting paint odor drifting on the breeze. Her mouth hung open as she tried to breathe.

Another plane flew overhead and dropped a bomb from high in the sky. It whistled through the air as it cleaved through the wind. Seconds stilled into slow motion—Rebecca's breath caught in her throat. The resounding boom deafened her when the blast rocked through the ship. The bow instantly separated from the ship and lifted the vessel out of the bay. It smacked down hard against the harbor—water sprayed in every direction on its descent.

The front hull began to sink at a rapid pace. Soon, it would disappear beneath the surface, swallowed by the briny deep. The chances of any of the sailors surviving such a huge explosion were slim. Rebecca's heart sank in her chest as the horror in front of her unfolded. Her hand shook as a sob wrenched from her inner core. Tears streamed down from the corners of her eyes. All of her strength seeped out of her; knees buckling, she crumbled to the ground. It dawned on her as she studied the canvas before her. She knew exactly what ship was currently sinking into the ocean's depths.

The U.S.S. *Arizona*, the very ship David should still be aboard.

David needed her. Rebecca bolted up and marched in the direction of the ensuing chaos. Joel grabbed her hand and pulled her toward him. She halted long enough to glare into his aquamarine eyes.

"I have to find David." She pulled her hand out of Joel's. He yanked her back toward him. "Let me go. David might need me."

"If you run down to the harbor, you will die. Those planes are bombing anything that will attack back. You won't survive. If I let you go, I will fail in my duty."

"You don't understand. That's the *Arizona* sinking. David is stationed on that ship. I have to help." Tears fell harder down her face, blinding her to everything around her. "Please, let me go. He's my husband."

"You can't help him. The ship is engulfed in flames, and it's almost completely under water." Joel's voice grew quiet as he tried to reason with her. "I think you need to be prepared for the worst. Instead of rushing in where you can't help, why don't you go where you can."

"I can't! I need to get over there. I refuse to believe he's dead. He can't be. We haven't had a chance to even start our lives together. We just got married yesterday."

"Becs, I want you to be happy. You need for him to be all right, and if you need to hold on to that to get through this day, I'm not going to stop you, but you need to focus on something you can do. Let me take you to the base hospital. There is bound to be a lot of wounded men and women in need of your help. If David made it off of the Arizona, it will be the best place to find out."

Planes continued to buzz overhead. The bombs and bullets hitting their targets. More explosions and fires erupted over battleship row. She could see some planes flying inward toward the other areas of the base. They probably headed toward the airfields to destroy the planes on the island. Joel had a point. She would get herself killed if she went to battleship row. The planes didn't discriminate between anyone or anything. They kept on with their punishing assault. If she could get to the hospital, she would be able to help with the wounded. She trained as a nurse for a reason, and she couldn't let her personal feelings get in the way of that.

"Are you sure you can get me there safely?" she asked.

"Yes, I can." He nodded his head in assurance. "Do everything I say and don't stop to question it."

"All right, take me to the hospital."

Joel held onto her hand and led her away from the secluded lagoon. His eyes scanned the area every step they made. He ducked them behind corners and hid them behind rocks, cars, and buildings. Anyplace that gave them some kind of protection. They made slow progress, and every time a bullet skimmed by her, she jumped. He would pull her closer and cover her with his body. Every step they made, his first concern was to protect her and make sure she didn't sustain any injuries. It took them close to twenty minutes to make it to the base hospital. When they entered the building, chaos ensued. All the on duty nurses scrunched down, cowering in the corners, with mattresses over their heads as they took cover. Patients in the hospital sprawled next to them. Doctor Thorne ran over to her when he saw her walk in.

"Rebecca, I need you to start gathering the supplies as soon as you can safely do so. Wounded will start coming in. We are underprepared and going to be overwhelmed. I hope they leave the *Solace* alone. We need all the medical personnel available. When patients start pouring in, sort them by how critical they are."

"You want me to determine the level of their injuries? I don't know if I want that kind of responsibility."

Doctor Thorne reached over and grabbed her arms. He shook her. "I need you to do this. I can't be out there weeding through to determine if they are fatal or savable. I need to be in here patching them up and saving them. You will do more good if you don't waste my time on those that can't be saved."

"Stop it. You're scaring me."

"You should be scared. War just arrived at our shores. This is very real, and you need to wake up and start doing your job."

"What you're asking me to do is beyond my job. I'm not doing it. Find another nurse to do your dirty work."

"Fine. I will." He turned and stared over his shoulder. "You there, under the mattress, come here."

Carolyn poked her head out and studied the doctor. "Yes, Doctor Thorne." She got up and walked over to his side. "What do you need me to do?"

He gave her the same instructions he had given Rebecca earlier. Carolyn's face became pale. Her lips were almost as white as her cheeks, and her hands shook as she listened to what he wanted her to do. Rebecca turned away from them and went to gather supplies. Joel followed her every step, watching and surveying everything. She wanted to tell him to leave her alone and let her work, but she couldn't help feeling relieved he still followed her. She glanced at her watch again. An hour had passed since the last time she checked. Bombs continued to go off. The walls rattled. The day had started off so well and fell apart before she got to enjoy any of it.

She prayed David made it off the *Arizona*, but she feared he didn't. A widow before she even had a chance to be a wife. Something so tragic couldn't really be possible, could it? She shoved the thought deep in the recess of her mind not letting it take root. So much needed to be done, and she couldn't allow it to prevent her from doing her job. With her worries suppressed, she gathered all the supplies they needed and headed back upstairs. Soon, they would be flooded with wounded and enough to keep them busy for days.

Chapter Twenty

SECONDS TURNED INTO minutes, minutes into hours, and before Rebecca knew it, a whole day flew by. The wounded flooded the hospital. Injuries ranged from minor scrapes to arteries with blood spurting out, and others had limbs blown off or badly damaged. Any and every injury imaginable came through the hospital doors. Many people died. The amount of lives lost numbered thousands. Most of the injured filled the base hospital, and still others remained on board the hospital ship, U.S.S. *Solace*. Exhaustion set in as she fought the need to sleep. In the last several hours, sleep came in small increments.

She would grab a few minutes here and there when she found time. Time being a luxury many couldn't afford to lose. Lives depended on her ability to be there and capable of helping them. Still no word had come in about David. No one could tell her if he'd survived. So many were lost in the attack—the *Arizona* only one of the ships destroyed. She prayed David wasn't amongst the many aboard as it sank. Still, she half expected he'd walk through the hospital doors and hold her in his arms. Each day with no word forced her to admit he could be lost forever. She didn't want to swallow the bitter possibility. Until someone confirmed his death, she'd hold onto the hope filling her heart. Tears welled up at the corner of her eyes.

She tried to keep busy. Too much time to think would make her lose her mind. What may or may not have happened—Rebecca couldn't deal with it. Rubbing her eyes with the back of her hand, she wiped away any evidence she doubted her husband still lived. On the outside, no one would guess fear held her hostage. She lived and breathed it every second her husband remained amongst the missing.

Joel reached over and placed his hand on her shoulder. She gazed up into his aquamarine eyes. Concern flooded them, and his mouth dropped into a frown as he stared at her. "Becs, you should go home and get some rest. If you keep this up, you're going to die from exhaustion."

"I can't. I'm afraid if I leave, he will come in, and I won't be here. Don't make me leave."

"You won't do him any good if you get sick yourself. If you keep going like this, you won't even be able to help yourself. Please go home and get some rest."

"I'm not leaving."

Joel's fist slammed into the wall behind her. His eye's darkened into anger and frustration. He scrubbed his face with the palms of his hands and turned his back to her. Weariness covered every inch of his face as he leaned onto the wall and rested one hand on his hip. His back facing her as he spoke, "I don't want you to hurt. It kills me a little to see you in pain and know I can't do a thing to change it."

"It's not your job..."

He turned back around and shouted, "Yes, it is. How many times do I have to tell you why I'm here?"

"I think it's safe to say the darkness has come and gone. You can go now. I'm still here, and I'm alive. You did your job," she muttered.

"No, it's only just beginning. The darkness isn't the bombing. All the devastation brought on the catalyst. I'm not trying to prevent an attack. I'm trying to stop it from consuming you. If you let it take root inside of you, all is lost. I am here to protect you from your own shadows."

Rebecca stared up at him. For the first time, it all made sense. When she sensed the darkness, she realized it did come from deep inside herself. The pain she could feel coursing through her originated in the dark recess of her mind. She hadn't wanted to admit it to herself. She'd found it easier to keep the truth from herself than to admit where it originated.

"It's why you kept me working on my own barrier. You wanted to prevent whatever caused it to fall or at least hoped I built it strong enough to keep myself from falling over the edge."

"Yes, but you haven't gotten the news yet that is going to destroy you. Hope still courses through your soul."

A gasp of air exhaled from deep within her lungs. She studied him, and it hit her. He had news he withheld from her. Something she desperately needed to know. "No, you know what's happening with David, and you are not telling me. Don't keep it from me. I need to know."

"I'm not sure you're ready..."

"Joel, you can't protect me from everything. I need to know what happened to my husband."

"You know the *Arizona* is now beneath forty feet of water."

She glared at him, one hand over her chest the other clenched against her hip.

"Yes, quit stalling."

He rubbed his hands over his mouth. Rebecca could tell he didn't want to tell her the rest. He folded his arms across his chest and stared into her eyes. "A lot of sailors didn't make it off the ship. Many of them are still alive, but stuck on board the ship. They have no way of getting to them. Rescue is impossible. They are going to die and become entombed on the ship."

Rebecca's hand flew to her mouth as each word left his mouth. What he said couldn't be possible. All those men—they must be terrified. It took several seconds for her to realize what he didn't say. "Wait, what are you trying to say?"

"David..."

"No, don't say it," she screamed. Her heart pounded loud against her ribcage. The breaths in her chest came out shallow and forced. She put her hands over her ears to block all sound out and kept shaking her head back and forth in denial.

"It's time you faced it. You insisted. I didn't think you were ready. So now accept the reality while I'm here to help you get through it."

"You don't know for sure he is one of them."

"Becs, you know it's true. I would never ever tell you something like this if I didn't know for sure."

"You can't know..."

"I can. Say it Becs. You need to say it aloud before you can accept it."

She wouldn't admit it. David could make it out alive. So what if forty feet of water covered the *Arizona*. There had to be a way to help all of those men. Joel didn't know anything. No one deserved to die that way. She believed they would do everything possible to try and save all those poor trapped men. She still couldn't let herself believe David may be one of them.

"I can see your mind at work. There is one other thing you should know. The *Arizona* is still burning. Fuel is leaking out, fueling the fire. They fear another explosion is imminent. The *Arizona* took on a full load of fuel the day before the attack. They were preparing for a trip to the mainland. It's too dangerous to risk more lives to rescue those still trapped aboard the ship." He paused and stared at her. His eyes filled with concern as he stared into her eyes. "You know how fast the ship sank. We saw it go down. The entire ship went under in less than ten minutes. It didn't leave a lot of time for them to get off. David is lost, and he isn't ever coming back to you. I'm so sorry, Becs, but you need to accept it."

Rebecca backed away from him putting some much needed distance between them. She dropped to the floor and curled up into a ball. Her mind froze on one thought, poor David. So very young and gone before he had any chance to live. They didn't even have a wedding night, thinking they had the rest of their lives together. She quit trying to hold in the tears, finding it useless to remain brave when she just lost the man she loved. It didn't matter if he still lived in the sunken ship; he wouldn't be alive much longer. Soon, they would no longer have air, and the chances of survival didn't amount to much. Her heart mourned the loss as pain overtook her heart. It shattered into a million shards of agony. She hugged her knees to her chest and rocked back and forth.

"He's suffering," she sobbed.

"You don't know..."

"I do know. All of them are. I can feel them. Their screams, the pain, every one of them are in misery."

Fear filled his eyes as he realized what she did. He kneeled down before her and placed his hands on her knees. "You shouldn't have opened yourself up to it. Put your shield back up, *now*."

"Why should I? I can't hold him and comfort him. He doesn't have me there to hold his hand and tell him everything is going to be all right. None of them want to die. They are pounding on the ship's hull hoping against all hope someone will come to save them. No one is going to, though; soon, they will all realize it. Once they do, despair will fill their souls. Someone should be able to say for sure what happened to them all. They need a voice. It's the very least I can do."

"If you don't put up a barrier, you will become their pain. It isn't enough to make a note of it; their open wounds will become yours. It will begin to fester until you no longer exist. You *will* get lost in a sea of anguish. The Becs we all know and love will cease to be. Please, block it all out again. I'm begging you, do it now before it's too late."

"Don't you understand," she shouted, her rage filling every facet of her voice. "I'm already there. My emotions are mingling with theirs. I don't just feel their pain, I am it. My husband lies beneath forty feet of water, a place that will ultimately be his final resting place. All I can do is *feel*. The loss, the despair, and every bit of pain coursing through them, someone should know their pain. What's more, I have every right to. It's my choice to make. I want to know what is happening to them, and you need to stop asking me to let it go. I can't do that. I won't. Don't tell me to block it all out because what kind of person would I be if I did?"

"Alive, Becs, you would be alive. If you persist in doing this, you won't be. I keep trying to tell you over and over. You're an empath, a very strong one. If you take on too many emotions, they will destroy you. Please, I'm begging you one last time, put up a shield and protect yourself."

"No."

Rebecca closed her eyes and leaned her head against the wall. She reached out into the space filled with so much pain, one far beyond the hospital walls, deep down beneath the water of Pearl Harbor. So many voices screamed in her head. She searched for one, the voice she needed to hear one last time, David, her husband. After a few minutes, she focused long enough and found him. His emotions filled her to the brim. Fear filled him, mixed with so much regret. Like many of the men around him, he didn't want to die; he had so much to live for.

He struggled to breathe and weakness overtook his body. She could tell he didn't have much time left. As much as she wanted to be with him until the end, she knew Joel was right. If she held on, it would destroy her. She loved David, but losing him and feeling it at the same time would be her undoing. Tears fell down her face, drenching her cheeks. She kept wiping them away with her hands, trying to stop them from leaving a trail down her neck and soaking through her blouse.

An overwhelming need spread over her—what about her friends? Did they make it through the attack? She spread her gift in a wide net and located them. She ticked off each one and breathed a sigh of relief. Until she couldn't find two of them in her search...

Rebecca needed to let go. Something she found so very hard to do. With a heavy heart, she pulled her shield back into place. Once she believed it to be complete, she opened her eyes and stared back at Joel.

"What else are you not telling me?"

His eyes glanced away from her. "I don't know what you mean."

She stomped her food. "Don't play games with me"

Joel pushed his fingers deep inside of his pockets. His eyes studied the tiled floor at his feet. "You don't need me to tell you anything."

No, it couldn't be true. Not only David—but Maxine and... She gulped down a lump in her throat. Virginia, her dear friend, the light inside of her blinked out too.

Rebecca's hand flew up and glided across Joel's face. A deep red mark spread across his cheek. "You evil bastard."

"It's not like that, Becs..."

"It's exactly like that Joel." She glowered at him. "You and your friends could have stopped this. So much life lost—for nothing."

His gaze landed across her face, anguish pouring out of his eyes. Rebecca's insides quivered as pain stabbed her entire body. Her friends, her husband, all the people in agony around her amplified it by thousands. She couldn't—wouldn't—accept his grief too. He could live with his own choices.

"Please," he begged.

Rebecca turned away from him, refusing to give him any kind of reprieve. Her insides were raw and ripped apart from the emotional overload.

"I want you to leave."

He shook his head. "I can't."

"I don't care what your job is. I can't be around you."

"Listen..."

She interrupted him before he could lecture her further. "No, you need to listen to me. I did what you asked. I put the shield back up, but being around you hurts too much. If I'm going to keep it intact, I need you gone. Otherwise, I will fall apart again. It's too much for me to handle. So leave."

He stared at her for several seconds and inclined his head in agreement. "I will leave, but you need to understand one thing before I go." She started to stop him, but he held his hand up indicating he wanted her to be silent a few moments more. "Don't interrupt me, let me get it all out, and then I will walk away. I'm a guardian. I don't think you understand what it means. It means I have charges assigned to me, and my job is to protect them, even against themselves. Just because you don't see me, doesn't mean I'm gone. I will always be here, and if you ever want to see me, say my name. My real name, you know what it is. Just be really sure you want me there before you do, because I'm not leaving again, no matter how nice you ask or how much you believe you want me gone."

After he finished speaking, he walked away from her fading with each step he took. She didn't know what it meant to be a guardian until she saw him vanish in front of her eyes. Joel, or Jaoel, as his world knew him, wasn't just a guardian. No, that would be much simpler than the word implied. Her very own guardian angel honored her wishes and disappeared from her life. What had she done?

Chapter Twenty-One

THE HOSPITAL FINALLY calmed down into normal activity a week after the Japanese bombed Pearl Harbor. Rebecca stayed at the hospital the entire week, finding little time to sleep. She would rest only when someone made her and only for short periods of time. So much needed to be done, and they didn't have enough people to spread out the workload. It helped her to remain busy, to not think about what this tragedy cost her.

Joel kept his word and didn't come around, at least not that she could tell. He could be hovering around invisible for all she knew. Part of her hoped he did because a tiny part of her missed him. She still didn't want to see him because she associated what she lost to him. It might be unreasonable, but she couldn't help the feelings coursing through her. Until she got them under control, she couldn't be around him. She needed to deal with her loss the only way she knew how; and for the moment, she did so by throwing herself into her work.

"Nurse, nurse."

Rebecca turned to see one of the patients attempting to get her attention. She wiped her hands on her uniform and pushed a stray lock of hair behind her ear as she walked over to his side. "What can I do for you?"

"I'm thirsty. Can I have some water please?" he asked.

She nodded her head at him. "Yes, of course. Give me a minute, and I will bring you some."

Rebecca walked away to get a pitcher of water and a cup for him to drink it in. She filled the pitcher up with water from a nearby sink and brought the items over to his bedside. The man pulled himself up into an upright position as he watched her. She filled the glass up and assisted him as he took a sip of water.

"What's your name?" she asked.

"Keith," he replied.

She studied him, his stone grey eyes staring back in equal perusal. He had a deep gash with hundreds of stitches across his forehead leading to the top of his head. His pale blond hair almost white, shaved close to his scalp, gave the impression he had no hair. He seemed so familiar to her, but she couldn't figure out why.

"Have we met before?"

He nodded his head. "Yes, ma'am, we did, on Thanksgiving."

Sadness filled her at his words. She understood why he stared at her and how she knew him. Rebecca recalled the day she met him. Keith Ernest, a friend of David's. She cleared her throat to try to remove the lump beginning to settle there. "I remember now. David introduced us."

"Yes, he did, along with Doug Logan."

"It's a day I won't forget anytime soon. One of the happier times over the past month." She played with her hands, having difficulty staring into his eyes. "How is Doug? I mean, I guess there is no easy way to say this. Did he survive? Is he injured?"

"He did, survive that is." He grinned, releasing a soft chuckle. "I guess you could say he got lucky. He wasn't on board the ship when the attack started. He, uh, stayed overnight with a friend. Although he did get injured trying to get to safety. Got too close to a bomb blast and sent him flying into a wall. Some cuts and bruises along with a minor head wound. Nothing like I have going here. I have a broken arm, torn ligaments in my leg, and a three-inch gash on my head. They had to shave off some of my hair to patch me up."

"Some would say you are pretty lucky yourself."

Rebecca couldn't help wishing David had found some of that luck. At least if he were injured, he would still be with her. You can't heal from death. Dead is dead and nothing could bring you back from it. Melancholy and exhausted, she patted him on the shoulder before starting to walk away.

"What about David?"

She stopped in her tracks and glanced over her shoulder. Concern etched across his handsome bruised face. He truly didn't know. Rebecca didn't want to be the one to tell him about David. She didn't even want to think about him. If she did, she might lose control, and she didn't want anything to break her shell.

"He didn't..."

The words refused to leave her mouth. She thought them all the time: *David's dead.* He's gone and never coming back, trapped in a watery grave. Anytime she tried to say the words aloud, they refused to leave her mouth. To do so was her final admission, and she would truly have to let him go. Something she didn't believe she would ever be able to do. She lowered her head and whimpered, covering her mouth with her open palm. She didn't cry for the loss of her husband, but for the loss of her hard won control. If she let go, she would shatter.

"You don't have to say it. I understand. A lot of people died; so many lost lives. I don't even know how many of my friends are gone. If Doug hadn't happened upon me one day, I wouldn't know he lived. David though, he was on the *Arizona*. Doug and I were on the *Oklahoma*. I saw the *Arizona* go down. It happened so fast, but I couldn't think about what it meant to him. We were all trying to survive and bombs were going off everywhere. I'm sorry; I know how much you meant to him." His voice cracked as he spoke forcing him to stop and take a deep breath, regain his composure. "He loved you and couldn't wait to get married. I'm so sorry. I know I said that already, but I can't say it enough."

"I know, and I'm sorry too. As much as I'd like to talk about it—I can't."

"It's all right. If you ever feel like you can, or if you want to just talk, I'm here. We all have a lot to work through."

"Thanks for the offer, but I'm hoping to get a transfer soon. I may not be here much longer." A wobbly smile formed on her face.

"You want to leave Hawaii? Why? Where would you go?" he asked.

"I asked to be stationed on the U.S.S. *Solace*. It's scheduled to follow the Pacific fleet on all of their missions. I want to be able to be more help to those in need. I don't have—well nothing is keeping me here anymore. This seemed like the best opportunity for me to use all of my skills."

"I see. When did you decide this?"

Rebecca bit her lip and fidgeted. She didn't like explaining her choices, but she considered it to be good practice. She knew some of her roommates would also question her decision. The ones still alive anyway. Another thing she didn't like to think about. So many deaths... "I put in the request this morning. I overheard the doctors talking and how much good the hospital ship did after the attack. If they hadn't been there, so many more lives would have been lost. It made me think I could use a change of scenery, and it seemed like a good opportunity."

"If it's what you want, I hope they let you go."

She smiled, hoping it reassured him. Rebecca didn't know him that well, but as a friend of David's, she didn't want to cause him worry. She couldn't be concerned about his friends' outright concern when she had a hard enough time getting around without him. Being on the island and in all of the places she used to see him had become a bit stifling. She needed to get away from all the reminders. "It is. I need to go now. I've been working nonstop for a week, and it's time I went home and took care of myself. Get better soon."

"I will do my best." He flashed her a smile. "Please let me know if you get your transfer."

Rebecca nodded her head in agreement. "Certainly, as soon as I know."

She smiled at him and then turned to leave. As soon as he could no longer see her face, she let the smile fade. Rebecca didn't have much to grin about. A smile became a reflex—a way to pretend the world hadn't been ripped apart before her eyes. A vacant carcass continued to beat in place of her heart. Emptiness permeated her soul—a body, but no substance.

She couldn't even claim to be numb.

No, when she put up her shield again at Joel's insistence, she also took great care in removing all remnants of any emotions from within. It made things much easier if she didn't have to fight off every possible sensation from invading her. So she didn't simply put up a barrier. She became it.

She crossed the hallway and left the hospital. A place filled with souls in need of care, something she could easily aide them in. If she could open herself up to it and allow herself to feel again. They ached in more than physical ways. Before she blocked everything, she sensed ways she could ease their suffering, but she couldn't do it. Rebecca would do whatever she could to heal them physically, but not anything involving emotions. She may be a strong empath, capable of helping where other people couldn't; however, the cost of her assistance was a price way too high to pay. So she ignored her instincts and removed herself from the temptation.

The walk to her cottage from the hospital took longer than normal. Her exhaustion caught up to her with each step she took. She couldn't wait to get there and sleep for several days. She would overlook the empty bed in her room, the one where her dear friend should be. Another loss she couldn't, wouldn't cope with. She reached the front door and pushed it open. Two of her roommates sat on the wicker furniture, expressions of sadness on their pale faces.

"Oh, Becca, I'm so glad you finally came back. We were beginning to worry about you." Carolyn leaped off the chair she occupied and crossed the room to wrap her arms around her. "How are you doing? Do you need anything?"

Beatrice's coffee-brown eyes were rimmed with red. A result of crying and the misery they all experienced the past week. "I can see if Lizzie is up to making something to eat if you're hungry."

Rebecca shook her head and pulled herself free from Carolyn's grasp. "No, I don't really have much of an appetite. I'm going to take a shower and get some sleep. I'm sorry if I worried you guys, but I needed to keep busy. I—keeping busy made it easier for me. It gave me less time to think."

"All right, but if you need anything—" Carolyn began to say.

"I don't." Rebecca cut her off before Carolyn's could gain control.

"We are only trying to help." Bea's voice quiet, almost in a whisper.

Rebecca smiled her fake reassuring smile. The one which never reached her eyes. "I know, but right now all I need is some space. I'm going to go retrieve my things for a shower and then get some much needed rest. We can talk more tomorrow. I'm sure there are arrangements we need to make..."

"For Maxine and Virginia's things," Carolyn supplied.

Rebecca inclined her head in agreement, not wanting to speak their names aloud. "Yes. For now, please just let me be. It's been a trying week for us all. I need some space. I hope you understand."

"We do," Bea replied.

"Good. If you'll excuse me, I'm going to go take my shower now."

Rebecca walked away from them and went into her room. She didn't allow her eyes to wander across the room—because she would notice the emptiness. Anything that might crack the shell around her, she blocked out. She couldn't allow something to damage her hard won control. After grabbing her things, she left the room as quick as possible. In the bathroom, her shower was just as rapid, scrubbing away all the dirt and grime. Quick sponge baths only went so far. Clean once again, she dressed in her nightclothes and sought her bed. Her mind emptied of all thoughts, she soon fell asleep, dreams eluding her.

Chapter Twenty-Two

"BECCA."

She could feel someone shaking her. Carolyn from the sound of the voice calling out to her. Her eyes fused shut, refusing to open and face the day she ignored them.

"Wake up, now. You have been in this bed for two whole days."

Giving up on the pretense of sleep, she rolled over and opened her eyes. Carolyn stared down at her with concern in her eyes. She had one arm leaning on her hips and the other one swinging loose at her side. From the looks of it, she had the beginnings of a lecture forming on her mouth. Rebecca had no intention of listening to it.

"Don't you think I deserve a few days rest? I've been through hell."

"I know," her tone softened. "But it isn't healthy to stay in bed. We all need to talk, and we can't get things done without your input."

Rebecca sighed and pulled herself into a sitting position, her legs swinging over the side of the bed. "Fine, you win. I'm up. Can I at least have a shower before I'm bombarded with things I don't want to deal with?" Sarcasm infused the question as she glared up at Carolyn.

Carolyn ignored the scorn and answered her. "Of course you can, but don't take too long. Lizzie made lunch, and we are going to talk while we eat."

Oh joy, she would get to push food around her plate and pretend to eat. On top of that, she got to stomach some well-meaning concern and force down the pity shining off each of their faces. So much to look forward to. Maybe she would get good news soon that her transfer to the *Solace* had been approved.

"Fine, I will forego a shower and just pull on some clothes. If I get under the hot spray right now, I will be reluctant to leave. I suspect lunch will be ready soon."

Carolyn shrugged and began to walk out of the room. She stopped at the door and turned her head to stare at Rebecca. "You're right of course, but we will wait for you to join us before we start. I'll see you soon."

She watched as Carolyn left the room, her eyes glaring at her, wanting to hurt her somehow. Some emotions had begun to seep in while she slept. None of them any good. With her unaware and unable to keep her shell fortified, they slipped through the cracks. So inside, she brimmed with anger and frustration. The need to make someone feel her pain consumed her. No time like the present. She had some willing victims waiting for her. An evil smile formed on her face and malevolence filled her soul as she dressed. Satisfied with her appearance, she left her room and joined her roommates.

"I'm glad you decided to join us." Bea pushed her glasses up her nose and glanced up at her with a hopeful expression.

"I'd rather not, but then I didn't exactly get a choice."

Rebecca saw the stunned expression on each of their faces and sauntered over to an empty chair then took a seat. She crossed her legs and studied her nails with nonchalance.

"So where's the food? I only came out because Caro said I'd get lunch."

"Um, yeah, I will go get it." Lizzie jumped up out of her seat, and with quick strides, left the room.

"I'm going to go help her," Bea mumbled.

Rebecca watched her retreating back and leaned further into her seat. "So, Caro it's just you and me. What shall we talk about?"

"Why are you acting like this?"

"I don't know what you mean." A wicked smile took form on her face.

"You're grieving, I know, but..."

Anger burst out of her as she glowered over at Carolyn. "Don't presume to know what I'm going through. You have no idea. I don't appreciate being ordered around. I can't wait to leave this place."

"You plan on leaving? Where would you go?" Lizzie asked as she entered the room. Her arms filled with a tray of sandwiches.

Bea followed close behind her with another tray. This one with drinks and a bowl of fruit. "Who's leaving?"

"I am as soon as my transfer request is approved," Rebecca replied.

"I understand. It has to be hard being around everything reminding you of what you lost." Tears formed in the corner of Beatrice's eyes. "When will you know?"

"I asked a couple of days ago." Rebecca shrugged. She wanted this lunch and intervention over with. Why couldn't they leave her alone?

"Did you request someplace in particular?" Carolyn asked.

"I did."

Carolyn raised an eyebrow questions shooting from her eyes. "Are you going to share it with us?"

Rebecca didn't answer, just stared at them for several seconds. She could almost feel the time ticking by with the beat of her heart, the silence stilted and full of tension.

Carolyn decided to fill the quiet void with words. "Well, I guess it would be a good time to tell you all I requested a transfer as well. Although I didn't ask for some place specific. I want off this island."

It was Rebecca's turn to raise her eyebrows. "Oh really? Maybe we will be sent to the same place."

"Are you going to tell us where you want to go?" Lizzie asked, once again trying to dig information out of her.

Rebecca knew on a visceral level her actions were way past the difficult stage. They had to be getting frustrated with her. She couldn't help herself though, something else seemed to take over. What harm would it be to tell them where she requested to go? As far as she could see, none, but she wanted to hold back the information. She forced the details out so they could drop their insistent questions. "The U.S.S. *Solace*, they are going to be traveling with the Pacific fleet."

"But you would be in the brink of battle. Haven't you seen enough?" Bea inquired.

"I feel it is the best place for me. I can help those who need immediate attention."

Carolyn stared at Rebecca, her face devoid of emotion. "I think it's very brave of you, but are you sure you will be able to handle it?" Each word enunciated with careful precision.

No, she didn't know if she could handle it. She did know one thing for certain: she couldn't remain on the island. Rebecca didn't want to explain any of it to them. So she nodded her head in the affirmative. "Of course I can handle it. I worked myself into exhaustion for a week after the bombing. I can handle anything. Besides, work gives me an outlet. It's something I understand and can do instinctively. It's not like I'm rushing into battle. We just go in the aftermath and help any wounded we find."

Carolyn shook her head and explained, "I don't think it will be as simple as you are describing. It may end up being more traumatic than you think."

No way would she concede Carolyn had a point. She would not sit and argue with them about her decision. She made it, and she intended to stick to it. What she needed was a change of subject. "Doesn't matter, I'm doing it. So what did you want to discuss that required dragging me out of bed. I might add, rest I very much needed too."

"We need to pack up Ginny and Maxi's belongings. They are going to come by and pick them up to ship to their families." Lizzie twisted her hands in her lap.

"Is there anything of theirs you want to keep as a token of remembrance?" Bea asked.

Good Lord no, she didn't want anything to remind her of the losses they all suffered. It's why she wanted to escape this place as soon as possible. She didn't even want to touch any of the stuff to pack it up. "No, I'm not sure I will be able to take much on the *Solace*. I'd rather not commit to anything. Do whatever you want with it all. I say just send everything to their loved ones. Not our place to pick through it all."

Bea gasped. "We didn't mean it like that..."

Rebecca held her hand up stopping her from further explanations. "I don't need you to break it down for me. I don't want anything. If I'm being honest, the idea of a reminder makes me cringe. I want to forget this ever happened, although I'm positive I can never forget. Why add to that burden."

Lizzie and Bea began to sob, tears streamed down their face. They each attempted to wipe them off, but failed to clear them away. Their pain fed whatever brewed inside her. A beast hungry for more agony, perhaps it was one of the reasons she wanted to go on the *Solace*. It had its fill of the tragedy on Pearl Harbor. Now it sought other ways to gather sustenance. She had enough of their pitiful expressions and words wrapped in concern. Rebecca had better things to do with her time. She stared over at her untouched sandwich and picked it up off the plate as she stood up.

"Are you sure..." Beatrice began to ask.

"We will pack everything up. If you change your mind," Carolyn finished for her.

"I won't," Rebecca interrupted her.

"We understand, and I promise we will not push you anymore," Lizzie whispered. "We do have one question though."

"What's that?" Rebecca asked.

"Are you going to have a memorial for David?" Carolyn inquired.

Rebecca jumped up and paced the room. Why couldn't they stop talking about him? She couldn't deal with this. She needed to get out of the cottage and put some distance between them.

"No, I can't do this. I need to get out of here."

"Becca, wait." Carolyn called.

Rebecca turned to face her. "I'm not doing this. If you want to do something—I won't stop you, but don't include me."

"All right, I assume you feel the same about Ginny and Maxi?" Carolyn whispered.

"Yes."

They each nodded, the realization of her stance on it all finally dawning on them. Good, they were finally beginning to understand. She wanted nothing from them and only wanted to escape this hell on Earth. Rebecca had plans, and not one of them included being forced down a path of constant reminders.

"If we're done here, I'm going to go for a walk."

She didn't wait for them to reply as she strolled out the front door—no reason to stay and a beautiful afternoon to enjoy. Perhaps she would go visit the secluded lagoon. She brushed that thought aside and took a bite of her sandwich. No, she would go to her commanding officer and check up on her request. Perhaps nudge him into approving it. She continued her walk, munching the sandwich on the way. Once she finished, she brushed the crumbs off of her hands and smiled. She was a little hungrier than she thought. A semblance of a happy smile filled her face, but anyone who knew her would recognize how false it truly was. Rebecca didn't do happy anymore and had no plans of finding it ever again. Happy ever after ideals were designed for fools.

Chapter Twenty-Three

"WELCOME ABOARD," A nurse greeted Rebecca as she stepped aboard the U.S.S. *Solace*. "My name is Jacqueline Martin. I'm the head nurse in ward five. You are going to be working with me and Geraldine Varbel. As soon as our other new nurse arrives, I can show you around."

Her request came through, but not as soon as she wanted it too. She didn't hear for weeks if they would allow for her transfer. She suffered through them as best as she could, but the holidays had been the worst. Christmas became a long suffering affair where they didn't talk to each other. Gift exchanges didn't happen, and for once, Bea didn't get thrown into the details of decorating and making crafts as she was known to do. Lizzie cooked a meal, but nothing elaborate or special.

An ordinary day in their very unordinary lives, something mundane as they went about functioning, merely existing after the world as they knew it fell apart. Life at the cottage slowed down, and any happiness drained out of its walls. Now a new year boomed forward, giving hope things would begin to get better. The notice giving permission for her transfer to the U.S.S. *Solace* came in a week after New Year's Day.

The missive explained she needed to report to the ship for duty on January twenty-second, giving her two weeks to pack up and leave all her memories behind. During the last two weeks she didn't speak to any of the women living with her at the cottage. She cut herself off from them, not wanting to have any ties remaining anywhere near Hawaii. At some point, the *Solace* would leave and follow the Pacific fleet into battle. Rebecca didn't need any reminders of the place where she lost so much.

Rebecca allowed her lips to turn up into a smile. "I'm not the only nurse joining the ship?"

"No, you and one other nurse applied for a transfer. We are going to need all the help we can get. This tour is going to be long and strenuous on us all."

"Sorry to keep you waiting. I got stuck on duty at the base hospital overnight."

Rebecca turned to see Carolyn standing behind her. Any remnants of a smile on her face faded at the sight of her. She wanted to get away from them all, and here in front of her was a walking talking reminder of everything she wanted to forget. She knew Carolyn asked for a transfer, but hoped she wouldn't get assigned at the same place she did.

"I expect you're tired, then. The tour shouldn't take long. I'll show you where you'll be working, taking meals, and finally, I'll take you to your quarters to get settled in. You're not expected to start working until tomorrow. The schedule is up in the ward. You will get a chance to study it when we walk through."

Carolyn nodded her head. "Sounds good. I would like a little time to get settled in."

Rebecca ignored her and stared over at Jacqueline. "I'm ready to start whenever you are."

"Good. If you both will follow me, we will head over to the ward first. Leave your belongings here, and we will circle back and collect them before we go to your room." Jacqueline motioned with her hands which direction they were heading. "The ship actually has several wards. The *Solace* is equipped to handle a fair number of patients at one time, over four hundred enlisted and fifty-five officers. For the most part, you will work in the ward dealing with the enlisted as it is where we need the most help, but sometimes you might be pulled into the officer's ward to provide relief."

Jacqueline set a brisk pace as she led them down to one of the lower decks of the ship. She rattled off information as fast as she walked. Rebecca decided it didn't matter anyway. Learning on the job would be far easier than trying to remember everything the nurse said. Chances were she would forget at least half of it anyway. Carolyn, on the other hand, had a notebook out and took notes. Her mouth tilted into a smirk. Some things didn't change much. She still relied on her many lists to get by and gain control over a situation.

They walked into a room housing several beds, almost every one of them full. Men with various different injuries occupied each one. All of them victims of the bombing of Pearl Harbor. Each one lucky to be alive even though they suffered serious injuries.

Still jotting down notes, Carolyn stopped, lifted her head, and raised her hand. "Quick question, how many patients can be held in each ward?"

Jacqueline stopped and gave Carolyn her full attention. "Most can handle at least fifty patients maybe a little more.

It's set up so we can take on as many injured as possible. There may be times we are over capacity, but of course, we pray that is never the case. If it ever becomes an issue, we will have to make a stop to unload extra patients at a base hospital or transfer them to another ship."

"But you don't expect it to be an issue, right?" Rebecca asked.

"We can't even begin to guess what we will encounter once we begin following the Pacific fleet, but no we don't think it should come to that," Jacqueline explained.

"Do you have any idea how long we will be docked here in the harbor?" Rebecca wanted to ship out to sea and as far away from Hawaii as possible. She needed some distance between her, the island, and the memories it forced upon her. So the sooner they departed, the happier she would be. She didn't believe happiness would ever find her again, but at least being away from the constant agonizing flashbacks would be a good start in finding some semblance of peace.

"We have not received our orders yet. I suspect it will be after a lot of our current passengers depart. We don't have any place to send them yet, and none of them are ready to leave. Maybe in month or so, we will have some place specific to go. Until then, we will remain in the harbor taking care of the victims from the bombing." Jacqueline walked them through the ward pointing out certain areas where supplies were located. "All right, I will show you where the galley and mess hall is located."

Rebecca and Carolyn followed her through some narrow passageways and down a few ladders until they reached a staircase to climb up. They walked up on a lower deck and around another hallway until they located a large room with a bunch of tables. On each side of the tables, a long bench seat sat in front of it.

"We eat meals on a strict schedule. If you want a meal, you are expected to report at those times. Breakfast is precisely at seven hundred hours, lunch is at twelve hundred hours, and dinner is at eighteen hundred hours. The only exception to it is if we have a bunch of emergency wounded to care for. In those instances, you can come to the galley and request a special tray made up for you. Do either of you have any questions?" Jacqueline led them through the mess hall so they could get an idea of how everything worked. "Over here is where the meal is served. Make sure you grab a tray and your utensils and then go through the line for food. Once you have your meal, find a table to sit at."

"It all appears pretty straight forward," Carolyn replied.

"I don't have anything to ask. Guess that means we only have to find our quarters." A separation between her and Carolyn needed to happen soon. Rebecca didn't want her to think they were still on good terms. Not that they were on bad terms, she just didn't want to resume their former friendship. The whole point in asking for a transfer was to get away from the things that reminded her of what she'd lost. She wanted to do her part in aiding those injured in the war, just not on the island of Hawaii anymore. Carolyn was a part of the memories she was trying to get away from.

Having her close on hand didn't bode well for her peace of mind.

"Of course. If you will follow me, I will show you where you will be bunking. First, of course, we will stop and pick up your suitcases. Now, we only had one room available, but lucky for us, it works out well. It's on the small side, and you will not have a lot of room, so I am glad neither one of you brought along too many personal items."

Rebecca didn't want to bring any personal items. She donated most of them to a local charity. Not out of the goodness of her heart, she couldn't claim to have any of it left to boast about. No, she did it for far less altruistic reasons. They carried too much baggage with them. Carolyn probably realized she couldn't bring so much along with her on the ship. It explained her one lonely suitcase. As they walked up to the deck and collected their belongings, Jacqueline's words sunk in.

"Pardon me, Nurse Martin, did you say you only had one room available? Does that mean we are going to be sharing?" Rebecca asked. Please let her say no, she didn't want to share any quarters with Carolyn again. Especially in such a cramped space.

"Yes, you will, and please call me Jackie. I don't believe in formalities."

Rebecca smiled sweetly at her. "Of course, and you can call me Rebecca."

She didn't want to be on friendly terms with anyone, but for the moment, she was willing to humor the head nurse.

"I prefer to be called Caro, Carolyn if you want something a little more formal."

"Caro works fine. I like nicknames. When you get around to meeting Geraldine, she will probably request you call her Gera. When things get crazy around here, first names work best."

They walked down some more narrow passageways until they reached a tiny room. It displayed bunk beds on one side of the wall. She couldn't help but note it was a good thing they were both slender or the beds wouldn't be able to hold them. Two small sets of drawers on the other were built into the other wall and flanked by a tiny closet on each side.

After perusing over the room, she realized bringing very little belongings on board had been a good idea. They wouldn't have been able to store much more than what they already had. Describing the room as cramped gave it more justice than it actually had. There would be no escaping each other in such tight quarters. Rebecca couldn't help a grimace from forming on her face. Oh joy, her and Carolyn could continue to bond over their shared tragedy.

"All right, I will leave you two to settle in." She glanced at her watch to note the time. "Lunch is in a couple hours. If you're hungry, make sure to get there on time. I will see you both later."

"Do you have a preference on which bunk you would like," Carolyn asked.

Rebecca didn't want to have a conversation with her, but she knew shrugging would get her nowhere. She wanted the bottom bunk. It would be easier to escape from if needed.

"I'd prefer the bottom bunk, if you don't mind."

"Not at all. I don't have a preference. I can take the top. I'm going to unpack now and rest for a while."

Carolyn grabbed her suitcase and began hanging her uniforms and a couple casual dresses in the closet. Rebecca decided she might as well unpack as well. Soon, they both had everything unpacked. Carolyn didn't say a word to her the entire time. Maybe she had gotten the message over the past month. Rebecca didn't have any energy for small talk anymore. Without saying a word, Carolyn crawled up on her bunk and fell asleep. Rebecca took the time to lay on her bunk, but sleep eluded her. Soon, they would be thrown into the workload aboard the ship, and maybe it would be enough to keep her mind from thinking about everything that bothered her. She could only hope for the numbness working filled her with.

Chapter Twenty-Four

"REBECCA CAN YOU COME over here?"

She turned to see Doctor Thorne motioning for her to join him at the side of one of the patients still aboard the *Solace*. What did he want now? The doctor's presence a surprise she hadn't banked on and not a pleasant one either. Shock had been her first reaction when she saw him aboard the ship, followed by a quick what are you doing here. Apparently, they had been short staffed on more than nurses. The ship desperately needed more doctors on the *Solace* as well and transferred him aboard along with her and Carolyn. For two weeks, she had both of them as constant reminders. Some days, she believed escaping the bad memories plaguing her were futile. They were a part of her now, and because of those experiences, she didn't recognize the person she'd become. No reason to fight it anymore. She accepted her destiny with open arms. Although, just because she accepted her fate, didn't mean she needed to be nice about it.

"What can I do for you?" Rebecca folded her arms over her chest and glowed at the doctor with a mutinous glare.

"I need you to help me cut off his cast." The doctor motioned to the patient's broken leg, ignoring her bad attitude. "He will have a bit of atrophy. I understand you have some experience with physical therapy?"

Rebecca rolled her eyes. He knew exactly how much training she received. The good doctor had reviewed her credentials with her when she started working at the base hospital. "I have some training, yes."

He waved his hand at her and gave the patient his full attention. He didn't dismiss her exactly, just put her in her place. A lowly nurse with a little bit of special skills, and of course, Doctor Thorne knew everything. "Good. For the next several days, I want you to start him working on building muscle tone in his leg. I think he will be ready to be discharged soon."

They began the process of removing the cast from his leg. After several minutes and some strenuous cutting, they were able to separate the plaster. Doctor Thorne pulled it apart and slid the patient's leg out. He turned his attention back to Rebecca and gave her further instructions, "All right, wash his leg and make all necessary notes in his chart. I have other patients to attend to. After you devise a strategy for physical therapy, show it to me so I can approve it."

Rebecca inclined her head agreeing with his orders. "I will work up a plan, and if you approve it, I will begin it this afternoon." She turned her attention toward the man lying in the bed. His chestnut hair shaved close to his scalp and his dark blue eyes narrowed in on her. "I'm Nurse O'Shea, what's your name?"

David died one day after her wedding. Rebecca was never given the chance to even feel married and didn't believe she deserved to use his last name. So she never updated her paperwork with the Navy and kept her maiden name.

"Ray Spragg, ma'am" A voice with a soft southern lilt accented each word.

"We're going to be working closely the next couple of weeks to try to strengthen this leg of yours. I hope you're ready to work hard."

"Yes ma'am"

"No more ma'ams. From this point on, call me Rebecca."

Ray shook his head back and forth. "No, I don't know if I can do that, ma'am. My mama didn't raise me to use a woman's first name. It's too personal and doesn't show respect."

"All right, if you can't call me by my first name, then I at least insist on Nurse O'Shea. I'm not a ma'am."

Rebecca examined his mangled leg. Doctor Thorne was right. The muscles in his leg had severe atrophy. With some serious physical therapy, they could build the muscle back, and he should regain full range of motion in his leg. She needed to give a full assessment of what he could do before she worked up her report. In order to do that, she would have to get him to do a series of exercises. Afterwards, she could draw up the report and show it to Doctor Thorne.

She didn't mind the extra work. In fact, she looked forward to it. What she didn't want to do was have any kind of conversation with the doctor. He grated on her nerves and angered her. He had always talked down to the nursing staff, and no one liked him. Rebecca used to push it aside and do her job, something she believed might prove to be impossible now. She didn't have the time or the energy to placate his sense of superiority.

"Today, we are going to do a few simple exercises in the bed. They might be a little bit painful at first. You haven't used your leg in several weeks, and it has caused you to lose muscle mass. I need to make a solid assessment of how much dexterity you have lost and what we will need to do to improve your strength. Once I know where to begin, we will work at a slow pace to begin to strengthen all the muscles in your leg. I hope by the end of two weeks we can get you walking with a cane." She ran her hand over his leg and tested the agility of his muscles. "Are you ready to begin working? By work, I mean a little bit of exercise. The real work won't begin until tomorrow. You might hate me by the end of this."

"Yes ma..." He stopped and corrected himself. "Nurse O'Shea, I want to improve my leg. I promise I will do whatever you ask of me and won't hate you for it. I know you are trying to help me."

She walked around to the foot of the bed, lifted his foot, and kneeled on the bed. Rebecca bent his leg and placed his foot at the base of her hipbone. "All right, I'm going to lean forward, and I want you to push against me as much as you can."

As she leaned forward, he pushed up with is leg muscles. She didn't move forward much as he struggled to push her weight away from him. The atrophy in his legs appeared to be much worse than the doctor anticipated. His belief he would be able to leave in two weeks might be a tad optimistic.

"I'm sorry, I don't have a lot of strength," he apologized.

He appeared contrite and embarrassed at his inability to move her with his leg. At least her training in physical therapy finally had some use. This kind of activity would give her something to occupy her mind with. With her body and mind still numb from the removal of emotions, faking empathy was starting to get more difficult. Staying busy with work made it easier for her to limit social interactions.

"No, you are doing well. I didn't expect you to have a lot of strength. If you did, you wouldn't need any physical therapy. I'm looking forward to helping you improve your strength it's nice to have someone willing to put the work in to get better. Not everyone is eager to start physical therapy."

She watched as Ray stared down at his leg, the mangled mess of skin sewn back together after living through the bombing. From what she read in his chart, they hadn't been able to put a cast on it at first. All the stitches and broken skin needed to heal enough first. So for the first week, they had a splint on his leg and wouldn't let him move. He glanced back up at her and asked, "I suppose you have a point. You think doing these exercises will help me to regain the strength in my leg?"

"I do. It's my job to make sure you can get back as much mobility as possible. If we can't finish helping you here, maybe some work with a physical therapist once you go home will help to continue on the path of recovery."

He gaped up at her with a startled look in his blue eyes. "You think they are going to send me home?"

She smiled at him and explained, "I do. The injuries to your leg are extensive. While I believe we can help you to gain mobility again, I don't think it will be without a limp. Which would be a hinder as a soldier, sailor, or anyone who needs to be able to move quickly."

"I suppose it could be worse." His lips tilted down into a small frown.

She gawked down at him, surprise filling her eyes. "You don't want to go home?"

"No, I mean going home isn't the issue. Under different circumstances, I suppose going home would be my fondest dream. It's just I hoped I could help our country fight. We just entered this war, and it's far from over. Really, it is just now beginning, and they are going to need every bit of assistance they can get if they want to win it."

His word sent her into flashbacks. Bright lights flashed through her mind and loud booms echoed inside her eardrums. Breaths came out rapid from her lungs as she struggled to regain control. As her heartbeats pounded in her chest with a resounding echo mirroring the sound of bombs exploding, she focused on calming her nerves like Joel taught her to. She blocked out everything and found her center and numbed herself again.

"Nurse O'Shea, are you all right?" Ray's voice filled with worry as he stared at her.

"I'm fine," she reassured him

"You appear like something is bothering you. We're you in the bombing?"

"I'd rather not talk about it." Rebecca brushed off his concern. "Why don't you tell me about you. Where is home?"

"I understand if you don't want to talk about it. That day, it was hard on us all. We lost so much and so many people we knew. Not one person on the island escaped unharmed. Even if they managed to get out with no physical injuries, they still carry scars on the inside. I'm taking from your reaction you lost someone important. Just know if you want to talk, I'm willing to listen."

Rebecca let his words register inside of her. She was so tired of people offering to listen to her. Why did they think she needed to spill out every detail of her pain? Some things were too unbearable to speak about. She would not sit down and cry again. No one needed to know how much she ached inside.

"I said I didn't want to talk about it," she snapped at him.

"I apologize."

She didn't acknowledge him. Rebecca blocked out all sound. The session with Mister Spragg was about to halt rather abruptly. If days like this kept creeping up on her, the careful control she had achieved would shatter. She put his leg down and smoothed his blanket back over it.

"I think that's enough for today." Rebecca got up and walked away.

"Texas, Galveston to be exact."

She stopped, stared over at him and replied, "Excuse me?"

"It's where I'm from. You asked me where home is."

"I see. Do you miss it?"

"Sometimes. I miss my mom. She's a fantastic cook and always looking out for me. I thought joining the navy and seeing the world seemed like a good idea. When I told her about my plans, it terrified her. Her brother died in the first big war. She didn't want me to join, but gave in when I explained why it meant so much to me. I know she'll be relieved I'm coming home."

"It will give you something to look forward to. Your mom will be so happy to have you back where you are safe. I think you should appreciate this injury for what it is."

"And what do you believe it to be?" he asked.

"A gift."

"I never considered it quite like that. In a way, I suppose you're right."

"Of course I am," she replied.

"Thank you."

Startled, she turned to him and asked, "Your welcome, but for what?"

"For making me see there are blessings in my life even through all the bad things. Sometimes you need someone to point them out to you for you to realize good does still come when you need it. My mama will be glad to have me home. I'm going to work extra hard to make it back to her, soon and I will appreciate it even more if I can walk into her arms."

"So what you're saying is you are looking forward to the torture I am going to put you through over the next couple of weeks?" Rebecca smiled down at him.

He nodded his head and replied, "Yes, I am. Maybe we can talk more about home as we work. Give me incentive to keep going when it gets painful."

"We can do that. I will see you tomorrow."

Rebecca turned and walked away. She set a rapid pace to gain some distance between her and Ray Spragg. He meant well, but in a lot of ways he reminded her of David. If everything had gone as planned, they would have went on leave. While away from Hawaii, she was supposed to meet his family. She had looked forward to it, and yet when the time came to leave, she hadn't spared them a second thought. Now she had to work every day with a man who would constantly remind her of her husband. Ray seemed kind hearted and respectful, but he might tear open her wounds and make her face the one thing she wanted to avoid.

Chapter Twenty-Five

WHEN REBECCA REQUESTED to be transferred onto the *Solace*, she believed it to be a good idea. After a month on board the ship, her views were starting to change. They were still harbored in the one place she didn't want to be. When were they going to do something? They needed to start moving and soon. At least she had the physical therapy work to keep her occupied. The wounded were almost all gone from the wards. Only a few remained, and at the rate they progressed, even they would be sent home. The first physical therapy patient she had been assigned still remained on board. He'd made remarkable progress, and she believed Ray Spragg would be sent home soon.

"Where you heading off to?" Carolyn blocked the doorway preventing her from leaving their shared room.

"I don't have time to deal with whatever histrionics you are getting ready to unleash. I have a patient waiting for me." Rebecca tried to push her way past Carolyn and escape, but her roommate had other plans. She pushed back, and Rachel fell down, her bottom hitting the ground with a hard *thud*. "Good grief, is this necessary?"

"Yes. It's time you and I had a long talk. I'm sure your patient can wait. No one is in danger of dying as most of the injured left on board this ship are well on their way to a full recovery. So you are going to sit down and listen to what I have to say."

Great, just what she didn't want to do. Have a heart to heart talk with Carolyn. She had to find a way out of this predicament. Some kind of diversion to distract her so she could make a quick escape, but what could she do? Nothing popped into her head so she scooted over and used the bed to help her get to her feet. She stood up and brushed her uniform skirt down to smooth it back into place.

"Go ahead say your piece, so I can leave. I don't have a lot of time to humor you."

"What happened to you? Why are you acting like a first rate witch? You used to be so nice and generous, and now no one can stand to be around you."

"Now, that isn't fair. Some people can still tolerate me, and you know exactly what happened to me."

Carolyn crossed her arms across her chest and tapped her foot. "Your husband died. A lot of people died that day. They didn't set out to target you specifically, and yet you act like you are the only one devastated by it. What truly confuses me is you don't even seem to be mourning anyone. You're just mean and hateful."

How dare she? She didn't have a clue what was going through her head. She had every right to her feelings—or lack of them in her case. It's why she numbed herself from experiencing them. Carolyn could throw as many hissy fits as she wanted to. Rebecca had no intention of allowing herself to feel the grief of losing not only David, but also her dear friends, Virginia and Maxine.

"Oh? Like you are now? Why can't you leave me be? If I wanted to discuss any of this, I would have already. I am not going to explain myself to you or anyone else. Now if you're done with your temper tantrum, I have work to do."

"No I'm not done." Carolyn glared at her and pinched her eyebrows together. "If we are going to share this room for who knows how long, we need to settle a few things between us. Starting with your refusal to acknowledge those we both lost."

"I don't have time for this." Rebecca tried to push her way past Carolyn again. Carolyn thwarted the attempt and slapped her.

Rebecca stopped, shock filling her as she rubbed her cheek. Her immediate response was to raise her other hand and smack Carolyn back—her hand seemed to make contact with Carolyn's cheek of its own volition. "Don't ever lay your hands on me again. I'm willing to let this go, but if you keep pushing me, you will regret it."

Carolyn shrugged. "I thought it might help."

"Help what? Making me angry? Congratulations, you succeeded. Now all I want to do is pummel you. Thanks for that. This is how I wanted to start my day. Why don't you do me a favor and leave me alone from now on."

"In my head, this went so much better than this." Carolyn's eyes filled with sadness. "I want to understand. It's like you don't feel a thing for anything or anyone."

Carolyn stopped and stared into Rebecca's eyes. She studied them as if trying to find the elusive answers to all of her questions. She took a step forward, narrowing the distance between them, so close they shared the same breathing space.

"What are you doing? Quit invading my personal space."

"I think I get what you did. It all makes so much sense now. If only I'd have seen it sooner, I may have been able to stop it."

Rebecca rolled her eyes. "What are you going on about now? There isn't anything to understand."

"I remember what happened to you the day before Thanksgiving."

"What about it?"

"You were drained and could barely walk. Virginia and I had to help you into the house. You refused to go to the doctor. I agreed it was a bad idea after you explained what happened."

"I remember. Why are we going over our shared history?" Rebecca took a step back to put some distance between them. She had a feeling she knew where Carolyn was heading with this line of talk.

"You could sense emotions. It occurs to me if you can sense them, you must need a way to block them all out. You wanted to talk to that army mechanic because you believed he could help you. Tell me, Becca did he? How close did you get with him?"

Rebecca gasped in shock. "What are you insinuating?"

"Well, I must be a tad closer to the truth than you would like by your reaction. So spill it, or should I continue on with my own conjecture?"

"I don't know what you are talking about. I really am done this time."

Rebecca shoved Carolyn out of the way. She managed to succeed this time, but Carolyn's next guess stopped her dead in her tracks.

"You shut off your emotions, didn't you?"

Her whole body stood frozen. How to answer Carolyn? Denial immediate on her tongue, she turned around and glowered at her. "I'm not going to say this again, Caro. Leave me alone."

"So he did teach you, didn't he? You were gone every morning for weeks. Said you were going for a walk each day. We didn't question it, why would we? You didn't act out of the ordinary, and a walk was harmless. I can see it all clearly now. Why did you hide it from us? Ginny and I were on your side every step of the way. We supported you, and we would have kept your secret." Carolyn paused and tapped her chin in thought. "Did something happen between you and Joel? I admit I found him to be quite attractive, not as much as his friend Kenneth. Still, he held a bit of appeal. Is he the reason you shut off your feelings? Did you betray David somehow?"

Rebecca stormed forward and pushed Carolyn to the ground. "I have never, nor would I ever, betray David."

"Well at least you are finally reacting to something. I think Joel might be your trigger. You do protest a little too much, my dear.

"You don't know what you're talking about."

Carolyn scooted backwards and rolled over on her side to help herself to her feet. She stood before Rebecca and stared her directly in the eye. "Where is Joel? I haven't seen him around much. In fact, I believe the last time I saw him was your wedding day."

"I don't know where he is." She didn't because Rebecca had sent him away. "Why would I?"

"Oh, I get it. You were acting like this with him too, and he couldn't stand to be around you. You are getting real good at pushing the people in your life away. Well I have news for you, Rebecca O'Shea. We are not that easy to get rid of."

Rebecca sneered at her. "I already noticed that. Thanks for pointing out the obvious."

Carolyn smiled at her. A smile that spoke of triumph. Rebecca didn't like it one bit. By the expression on her face, she was in the throes of planning something. Carolyn always did create the best plans, and it didn't bode well for Rebecca to be the subject of one.

"I think I might try to track down Joel. He might be the key to getting through to you. If he is like you, he could spark some emotion in you."

"Don't bother. He isn't coming back."

He better not be...

"Oh, I thought you didn't know where he was?"

Panic settled in Rebecca's stomach. She had said too much and needed to steer Carolyn in a different direction. "I don't. I know he won't be around."

"And why is that? You did send him away, didn't you?"

"Of course not. I don't have that kind of control over him."

If only she knew... Carolyn was too intuitive for her own good.

"I think you do, and I will find him."

"You can try, but you won't succeed." Rebecca flashed Carolyn a smug smile. Joel was not going to be so easy for her to locate.

"You sound so sure of yourself."

Rebecca shrugged. "Because I am."

Uncertainty filled Carolyn's eyes as she tilted her head, studying Rebecca. "I believe you are trying to talk me out of searching."

"Look all you want. I don't care. Even if you do find him, it won't matter."

"Then why are you so scared?" Carolyn asked.

"I'm not. You're projecting your own feelings on me."

She couldn't let Carolyn see how much the conversation bothered her.

"You don't think Joel can help fix you? Why?"

Rebecca let herself smile—one of the fake ones. "Because he isn't like me. He can't force me to feel anything. No one can. I am the only one who can do that. So do whatever you want. I'm going to continue on exactly as I have been. Oh, and Caro, there isn't a damn thing wrong with me. Quit trying to fix me."

With those words, she sauntered out of the room. Her hips swayed with each step she took. Carolyn could search for Joel all she wanted. The only way he was going to come back is if she asked him too. He said he wouldn't unless she called out to him using his real name. *Something she never intended to do.*

In the meantime, she would go up to the hospital ward and give Ray Spragg some good news. She intended to ask Doctor Thorne to discharge him. He was ready to go home. Whatever physical therapy he needed, he could do from the comforts of his own house. The only satisfaction she got any more involved working with the patients. It gave her a small thrill to see them improve with small measures. She could plot and plan their treatments until she saw results. She didn't need to feel anything in order to have a fulfilling life.

All she needed to do was continue to work and help make people better. She became a nurse and physical therapist to help people heal. With the treatment of Ray Spragg, she had her first successful case as a physical therapist. So with a proud smile displayed across her face she pushed her way into the ward.

She walked over to his bedside and told him soon he would be home in Galveston, Texas. His mom could breathe a sigh of relief. For Rebecca, she would know she prevented one person from going to war and their potential death.

She closed herself off from feelings, but she couldn't stop her mind from thinking. David and Virginia and Maxi always crossed her mind. Not a moment went by without one of them lingering through her thoughts. Some days, it seemed like they were still reaching out to her, trying to catch her notice. Rebecca knew one thing for certain; she would never get over their senseless deaths.

Chapter Twenty-Six

A QUIET THRILL RUMBLED through Jaoel's body. He couldn't express it, but he had a deep desire to shout with joy. Carolyn laid down some seeds he could use to his advantage. He smiled as he followed Rebecca while she walked through the hospital ship. Staying in the dark shadows and only observing had taken a heavy toll on his ability to help Rebecca.

He watched, keeping his distance as promised and not liking anything he saw. He needed to be around to push her in the right direction. The little argument she had with Carolyn was a step in the right direction. She might be able to fool her friend, but Jaoel knew exactly what she attempted to hide. Rebecca sent him away because she knew he would be the only one to stop her from keeping a barrier up. It needed to come crashing down, and he happened to be the person to start tearing it to pieces.

It just needed a few cracks, and it would shatter into a million shards of nothing.

A shield should only be created to protect her from experiencing too many emotions at once. She took it to a level it had never been designed for. The first step in his plan revolved around getting on board the ship. Jaoel the army mechanic was about to be reassigned as a medic on the U.S.S *Solace*. He needed to get a hold of Michael and get his assistance in weaving the proper magic. Everyone needed to believe he had the credentials to make the transfer seem reasonable. He didn't need to heal people, but rather be the person to do the grunt work on board the ship. Jaoel sent out a silent call to his leader. It didn't take him long to answer.

"What do you need?" Michael asked.

"I honored her request by keeping my distance." Jaoel stopped and gestured toward Rebecca as she talked to her patient. "It's time to make myself a physical presence in her life again. My absence hasn't helped her. She is spiraling, and if something doesn't stop it soon, she will be consumed by the darkness."

"She isn't lost yet?"

Jaoel shook his head. "No, far from it. She might have closed herself off from most emotions, but she is still capable of feeling them. Rebecca thinks she blocked them all out. What she doesn't realize is she only blocked the happy ones out. She doesn't feel joy or love, only anger and mistrust. The kind of emotions the darkness feeds on."

"What do you propose to do?" Michael asked.

"Joel Remak is going to get reassigned to this ship. I need your help accomplishing it."

"In what way?"

"He's an army mechanic, or well I am in the eyes of everyone on this base. I'd change the name a bit, but it's kind of too late for that. Help me with a glamour of sorts. I need it set so they don't question my transfer too much. I'm going to add a little addendum to my military file to say I have some medical training. This ship is willing to take on any volunteers with medical skills. They are preparing to follow the Pacific fleet into battle."

Michael stared across the short distance and studied Rebecca. After a few seconds, he turned his head and stared at Jaoel. "Consider it done. Keep me apprised of everything. I hope you're right, and she isn't lost."

"Thank you. I'm going to start working on board the ship immediately. After you leave, I'm going on board with my transfer paperwork in hand. I took the liberty of starting the process before I called you."

Michael inclined his head. "No one will question it. Now I must leave."

In the blink of an eye, Michael disappeared from sight. He could move about without much effort. Jaoel could disappear from sight, but he found traveling by anything other than normal means too taxing. So he had to take the longer route, meaning he left the ship and re-boarded it in his physical form.

As he stepped on deck, he knew he made the right decision. Carolyn exited a nearby room and walked along a path on the deck, her back to him. As if she sensed his presence, she stopped and glanced over her shoulder. Her lips tilted into a smile, one filled with pleasure and excitement. Good, she would come to him, and he wouldn't need to arrange a coincidental meeting. He turned away from Carolyn and walked toward another nurse on the deck with a clipboard in her hand.

"Hello, I've been reassigned to your ship." Jaoel handed her his paperwork.

"It says here you have limited medical training and are going to be assigned as an emergency medic. You know what that means right?" Her green eyes searched his for answers.

Jaoel nodded his head and replied, "Yes, I get the grunt work on ship and the joy of being sent out into the war zone to retrieve any injured to bring back on the ship."

"You're correct. We are pretty close to having all of the patients discharged or moved to a new location. We received orders to join the Pacific fleet. It's only a matter of time before we leave port and head out to join them. I'm not sure what our destination will end up being."

"I'm all right with that. I want to help where I can. I'm not needed here on base anymore. This ship is where I need to be. Point me in the direction of where I'll be bunking so I can settle in."

Her green eyes studied him as if trying to figure him out. He didn't know if she got the answers she sought or gave up. "I'm one of the head nurses, Jacqueline Martin. I meet all the new recruits and give them a tour. You'll be bunking in a large area with a lot of the men. I don't have any private quarters left on the ship."

"Not a problem I just need a place to lay my head down and rest." He did his best to reassure her, not really understanding why she seemed to want to talk him out of joining the crew. "I'm ready to do my duty and serve."

"Joel, are you going to be on the *Solace* now?"

He turned his head and saw Carolyn standing on his right. Her face filled with jubilance as she practically bounced in place. He had to force down a grin at her eagerness to talk to him. "I am. I explained everything to Nurse Martin. She is getting ready to show me where my bunk is and give me a tour of the ship."

"Oh I can do that for you, Jackie. I'm not on duty, and I know how busy you are," Carolyn offered.

Jacqueline bit her bottom lip between her teeth. "I don't know..."

"We're old friends, and I know the ship well after being on it for a month. Tell me which quarters he will be staying in. Don't you have another nurse to wait for?"

"I do. If neither one of you mind, it would save me some time."

"I'm all right with doing what Carolyn suggests. We are old friends, although I haven't seen her in over a month. I didn't realize she would be here."

Jaoel didn't want the head nurse to think they had some romantic involvement. He wanted to talk with Carolyn without other ears around. So her plan of showing him around fell right in line with his own needs.

"Go ahead and show him around, Carolyn. He is going to be in the main men's quarters. Make sure to show him where ward five is. It will end up being his main area to work in when he isn't needed for his other duties. Explain the galley's strict time schedule before showing him to his quarters."

Carolyn nodded her head and folded her hands behind her back. "I'll show him everything. If you'll excuse us, we can begin the tour."

Jaoel inclined his head at the head nurse. "I suppose I will see you another time. It was nice meeting you."

"Come along, Joel. We have a lot to get through." Carolyn tugged at his arm to pull him in the opposite direction. Once they gained some distance between them and the head nurse, she whispered, "I also wanted to talk to you about Rebecca."

He raised his eyebrows. "Oh really? What about her. I haven't seen her in quite a while. Not since the week of the bombing anyway."

"Oh you saw her after her wedding?"

Jaoel fought a smile. Carolyn was one astute woman. "Yes, the day after the bombing while she worked in the hospital. We had a brief discussion—something clearly bothered her. She told me to leave and never to come by again." They continued to talk as they strolled through the ship's corridors.

"She must have found out about David and took it out on you."

Yes, Jaoel stood by his first assessment. Carolyn had to be the most astute person around. She picked up on subtle cues and played them to her advantage. "What happened to David?" Jaoel decided on playing on the side of cluelessness to see how much information she would be willing give him.

"He died," she whispered. "I don't think Becca is taking it well."

"Would you?"

"Probably not. Still, she is different. She is cutting off everyone who cares about her. Someone needs to shake her out of this mood."

"You're discussing this with me because?" His eyebrows scrunched together as he played the part of a confused person.

"I know you two got close after Thanksgiving. She said she thought you were like her."

Not exactly like her...but he was close.

"You're going to have to give me more to go on than that. In what way am I like her?"

"She can sense emotions."

"I didn't know she told you about her gift," he muttered.

"I found out by accident. She did approach you for help, didn't she?"

He fought the urge to smile. This was going better than expected.

"Yes, she did."

"So?"

"So what?" he asked.

"Did you help her?" Carolyn stopped and turned to face him, her hand on her hips glaring at him. "Quit stalling and tell me."

How to play this? Should he admit to helping or not? He decided to give her a little bit of information. "I did help her."

"You were the person she met each morning on her walks."

"Apparently she told you everything." Jaoel nodded, exasperation flooding his features. "Why are you harassing me?"

"Because she closed herself off, and I think you can help her find her way back to the person she used to be."

"I hate to tell you this, but Becca will never be the same again."

"She has to be. This person she has become—I don't like her very much." Carolyn pouted as she studied Jaoel.

"Does that look usually work for you?" He flashed her an amused smile.

"Most of the time, yes it does. Are you going to help me?"

Jaoel sighed and pretended to be put out by the idea. "I don't know if I can. I'm willing to try, but we have to go about it slowly. Let me assess the situation, and then we can talk."

"So we can form a plan?" Carolyn's eyes lit up with eagerness. She did like to plan. Jaoel remembered Rebecca saying how much she enjoyed making lists and organizing things.

"If need be, yes. Give me a week, and I'll come find you to discuss what should be done."

"We have to wait a whole week? Why can't we start right away?"

"Because I need time. We don't want to cause more harm than good, do we?"

"No, I guess you're right." Carolyn bit her lip.

"Good, now show me everything I need to know about this ship." He stopped and held his hand out to stop her from advancing down the hall. "One other thing, don't tell Rebecca I'm on board yet. I think the element of surprise would work best for us."

Carolyn tilted her head and studied him. After a few seconds, she nodded her head. "Yes, I can see how it might be best. I won't say anything, but you better let me know what you figure out. I don't like keeping secrets or people who shut me out."

Jaoel nodded and resumed walking, Carolyn just ahead of him as they passed through the corridor. He followed behind her and listened to her speak. She showed him the ward and the mess hall, making sure to outline the meal times. Afterward, she showed him to the men's quarters. She left him to get settled and left to go to her own room. Jaoel watched her leave and couldn't help but be pleased at how well everything went. Soon, he would be back in Rebecca's life.

What he didn't explain to Carolyn was he needed Rebecca to say his name so he could appear again in her life. He shouldn't have made it a condition of his return, but he had wanted her to need him. A silly feeling in retrospect, and now he was stuck waiting for her to say his real name. He might have to visit her in her dreams and trick her into saying it. If she didn't say it by the end of the week, he would do just that. For now, he was content with waiting. He smiled and settled into an empty bunk. Soon, Rebecca would be on a path to healing, and he couldn't wait to begin the process.

Chapter Twenty-Seven

"ORDERS HAVE COME IN for us to join the Pacific fleet." Jacqueline walked through the ward as she imparted the news. "We are scheduled to depart at six hundred hours tomorrow morning. Make sure you are here and on board by twenty-two hundred hours tonight. We need to make sure everyone is on board well in advance of our departure. Do any of you have questions?"

The months had flown by. December almost a distant memory as March rolled in. Rebecca couldn't believe how everything kept moving forward. Now the long wait to leave Hawaii had arrived. She had a couple questions. Where were they headed, and how long would they be at sea?

Carolyn raised her hand and waved it in the head nurse's direction. "Pardon me, Jackie, Do you know where we are heading?"

Of course Carolyn would jump right in and ask what everyone wanted to know. Rebecca would have gotten around to asking once she got over the excitement of finding out they were finally leaving. She glared at Carolyn's back, wishing for the millionth time she had not been assigned to the *Solace*.

"The destination is the South Pacific. Other than that, I don't know. I guess we will find out when we get there." Jacqueline stared at the papers in her hands and then over at everyone. "Now you all know what you need to do. Go say your goodbyes if you need to and get back on this ship. See you all in the morning for rounds."

The head nurse walked away and left them all to discuss the new development. Chatter filled the ward. The nurses excited and scared to be finally going somewhere and be a part of the cause.

"So, do you have anyone you want to say good bye to?"

Rebecca turned to see Carolyn standing directly behind her. "Of course not. Who would I need to say good bye to."

"Bea or Lizzie for one."

"Seems I already did that before I came on the ship."

Carolyn raised her eyebrows in disbelief. "You actually went and told them good bye before you left? I somehow doubt you did. If I were to guess, I'd say you did your best to sneak out when no one was around. You avoid anything messy—mix in a little emotion, and you go running faster than I could say boo."

"I don't know what you're talking about." Rebecca pushed by Carolyn and began to leave the ward.

"What about Joel. You going to go see him?"

Rebecca spun around and faced her. "What is it with you and Joel? You don't even know him that well, and you keep bringing him up."

"Oh, you mean like you keep getting defensive whenever I bring up his name." Carolyn raised an eyebrow. "I don't care what you say, he means something to you. Now before you start getting mad, what I mean is you care about him, more than you would like. I am not saying you loved David any less because of it."

"You don't know how I feel or what is going through my mind. David is not a subject I feel like visiting now or ever, and as far as your other obsession...I'm done talking to you about Jaoel too, I don't need you to approve of anything, Carolyn. I'm fine with how everything is right now."

"What did you say? Who or what is *Yah-el*?" A puzzled expression spread across Carolyn's face.

Rebecca's mouth hung open as shock reverberated through her whole body. What did she say? No, Carolyn only repeated what she said. Maybe her roommate had a point. She couldn't stop thinking of him and couldn't help wishing she hadn't sent him away. So her slip in saying his real name was perhaps her way of getting something she would never openly admit. Which is why she decided to act like she had no idea who or what Jaoel was.

"How am I supposed to know?"

"Don't play stupid with me. You said the name, so you must know what it is." Carolyn leaned her arm onto her hips and glared at her.

"It doesn't matter. The point is, I'm done with this conversation."

"Before you run away again, there's something you should know."

Rebecca decided to humor her and stared at her with her eyebrows raised. "All right, I will play along. What do I need to know?"

"Hey Caro, do you want to join me for dinner?"

Rebecca froze at the sound of a voice she wasn't prepared to hear. The one person she just had on her mind and wished to be on the ship. He stood behind her, and instead of talking to her, he invited Carolyn to dinner. Anger flooded her as she spun on her heals to stare into his ancient aquamarine eyes.

"What are you doing here?"

His eyes pored right through her, as if she hadn't spoken and turned his attention back to Carolyn. "So yes or no?"

"I could eat. Let me go freshen up, and I will meet you on deck." Carolyn smiled at him and then turned her attention to Rebecca. "I thought you might want to know Joel's on board."

Rebecca rolled her eyes. "Thank you, Nurse Obvious."

Carolyn ignored her, giving all her attention to Joel. "I'll be done before you know it. I am looking forward to having that conversation you promised."

"Good. I thought we could enjoy our last night on land for a while. There is a nice diner I have been meaning to try, unless you would rather stay and eat on the ship."

"I think it is a lovely idea. We'll be eating the ship food for some time now. Might as well eat something different before we are stuck in purgatory." Carolyn stared over at Rebecca with triumph in her eyes. "Talk to you later, Becca."

Carolyn appeared way too happy about this new development. She needed to find out what was going on and fast. No way would she put up with this nonsense. Jaoel, Joel, or whatever, should not be on the ship. He said he would stay away.

"You didn't answer me. What are you doing here?"

"I work here."

Rebecca rolled her eyes.

"Yeah, I see that, but you said you would stay away."

"And I have," he replied with a simple shrug.

"No you're here, so clearly you are not staying away." Rebecca threw her hands up in frustration.

"I never once said I would go away. In fact, I believe I told you my job was to be here for you if you needed me. I even said if you wanted me to come back to say my real name, and I would be here."

"I'm failing to see your point. You are standing in front of me clearly visible. I don't want you to be here, so leave again," Rebecca demanded.

Joel stared down on her with his mesmerizing eyes. She could feel herself being drawn back into his sphere again and needed to mentally put some distance between them. She shook her head to clear it away. He stood there and laughed.

"Sorry, I can't do what you want, Becs."

She stomped her foot and shouted, "Why not?"

"You said my name."

She groaned out loud at his words. "Again, why does it matter?"

"You wouldn't have said it if you didn't want me here."

"Now that's ridiculous. I didn't actually mean to say your name. Carolyn had me so frustrated." Rebecca waved her hands in the direction her roommate had left. "Which brings me back to my point. From what I just saw, you and Carolyn have gotten pretty comfortable around each other. That tells me you have been around for some time. My saying your name doesn't mean anything."

"Apparently, I need to repeat myself often around you. I told you I wasn't going anywhere. I've always been here. You haven't seen me because you didn't want to. As soon as you said my name, you opened that particular door. Now you need to deal with it. I'm not giving in to your desire to make me disappear again. You need me here whether you know it or not."

"Well, I don't like it." Rebecca folded her arms across her chest and pushed her lip out into another pout. Apparently she found her new habit when dealing with Joel. Sulk a little in the hopes he would give in to her demands. So far it didn't work, but she didn't believe in giving in on the first try. He would come around to her way of thinking. It might take a little longer than normal. If he was truly on her side, he wouldn't stick around Carolyn for very long. He would need to see what Rebecca had going on in her life.

"Too bad."

"Are you going to have dinner with Carolyn?"

"I am. She actually likes to be around me. We can talk again later. I have to go meet her on deck." Joel moved around, impatient to leave the room. He hopped from one foot to the next as he took a couple steps back, gaining some distance between them.

"Can I come along?"

Rebecca had no idea where the question had come from. It spurted out of her mouth before she realized what she said. A small part of her didn't want Joel to hang out with Carolyn. She didn't know what to make of it, but if she didn't know better she would swear she was—*jealous*. Good grief, no it couldn't be possible. Could it? She swallowed the emotion and didn't like it one bit.

His eyes grew weary, and he glanced everywhere, but at her. Appearing uncomfortable with her desire to go along with him. "I'm not sure it's a good idea. From what I could see, you and Carolyn aren't exactly getting along these days."

"Aren't you supposed to be on my side?"

Rebecca pouted when he said he didn't want her to go. She didn't recognize herself and had no clue why she continued to act this way around him. Yes, she missed him. More than words could express, but she didn't want to beg him to spend time with her. She needed to admit to herself she screwed up. Joel had every right to put some distance between them.

"I'm always on your side. Which is why I think you should leave this be for now."

"You're truly working on this ship?" she asked.

"I am," he replied.

"But I thought you were an airplane mechanic."

"I am whatever the world needs me to be. I used to be an airplane mechanic, but now I'm an emergency medic."

"I don't understand. How is that even possible?" Rebecca tilted her head with questions in her eyes, irritated by his simple reply.

"Michael."

His boss could make him into anything he wanted? Something wasn't adding up, and Rebecca wanted a better explanation. She believed Joel was actually a guardian angel, but she needed him to confirm it. He seemed so human, mortal even. How could he actually be an angel? These were all questions she desperately wanted answers to.

"I fail to see how Michael can make the military that flexible with your job description."

Joel sighed and rubbed his hands over his face. "I'd love to sit here and explain it to you, but I have someplace I need to be. Why don't you meet me on deck at midnight? We can talk about it all in depth."

Rebecca didn't want to give in. What she honestly desired was for him to go tell Carolyn he couldn't make it and cancel the dinner. Joel must be up to something inviting her friend out. Something else she would need to get him to talk about. Maybe meeting later would be better for her as well. She needed to dig a little deeper and have a lengthy conversation with Jackie. No one got on board the ship without going through the head nurse. She handled all new arrivals.

"All right, fine. I will meet you later."

"Good. I need to go now. We have a lot to discuss."

"Indeed we do."

Joel turned to go before she called out to him. He stopped and stared back at her. "What?"

"You better be ready to explain everything. I'm tired of you talking around me. This guardian thing you have going for you is clearly not normal. I want to know what you are exactly, and why you have to protect me in particular. So don't come tonight if you are not prepared to give me all the answers I want."

"Duly noted," he replied. "I don't have anything to hide."

"You better not because even if you don't show up I plan on hunting you down and making you talk."

A smile fluttered across his face before he twisted his head back around and left the room. She might not have all the answers, but she would soon. Joel's days of evading her questions had ended. If he didn't want to tell her the truth, he should never have revealed himself to her again.

Chapter Twenty-Eight

SOUNDS SURROUNDED THEM as everyone in the diner carried on their own conversations, filling it almost to capacity. The restaurant was decorated in red and white. Nothing within could be called spectacular, but every piece inside entirely functional for what it had been designed for. Jaoel led Carolyn to a corner booth so they would have privacy to talk about their mutual concern. Once they were seated on opposite sides from each other, a waitress came over to take their order.

"What can I get you," she asked, a pulling a pen from behind her ear, a notepad in her other hand.

"I'll have a cup of coffee." Joel smiled. "What do you want Carolyn?"

"Give me the same."

"No food?" The waitress glanced back and forth between them.

Joel shook his head and replied, "Not right now. Maybe later."

"Suit yourselves; I'll be right back with your coffee." She replaced her pen to its previous location and put her notepad in the pocket of her apron as she walked away.

"So Rebecca didn't seem to like the idea of you and me going out to dinner." Carolyn jumped right into what they needed to talk about taking a particular glee over her friend's discomfort.

"You're probably reading way more into it than you should. She doesn't like surprises, and this one took her for a loop."

Jaoel understood how much Rebecca had been driving Carolyn crazy over the last couple of months, but there were greater things at stake. He couldn't let her get caught up in the desire to give a little of her own animosity back in return.

Carolyn set her elbows on the table and weaved her fingers together. A smug expression filled her face as she replied, "No, I'm willing to bet everything I have it's a pretty accurate accounting."

"It doesn't matter."

"Doesn't it though?"

"No, it really doesn't. This dinner is to talk about how we can get Rebecca back on track. Idle musings about what you believe she may or may not feel isn't going to solve anything."

Carolyn leaned back into her seat and waved her pointer finger in a circle. "Now that is exactly where you are so very, very wrong, Mr. Remak."

"How so?"

"Rebecca's feelings for you are how we are going to get her back. She loved David, I don't doubt that for a minute. His loss is the reason she has cut herself off from everybody. She is almost numb and going about her life without actually experiencing anything. She has all these negative emotions still lying around. She is constantly angry. It doesn't take much for her to spout out a scathing reply."

Jaoel raised his eyebrow and asked, "So how are her feelings, as you put it, for me, any different?"

"She's jealous, and I think we should use it to our advantage."

"Pretend I'm dumb and explain it to me."

"As if you could ever be confused with someone lacking intelligence, please." Carolyn's loud boisterous laugh filled their small space in the diner. "But I'm willing to participate in whatever game you're playing."

"It's not a game." Joel frowned. "I'm not following your thought process."

"She suppressed how she feels about you. Why do you think she sent you away?"

"Because she was grieving the loss of David."

Carolyn nodded her head. "And if you were around more often, she would be forced to admit she loved you far more than she ever loved David."

No, she couldn't be right. Carolyn didn't know what she was talking about. Rebecca didn't have those kinds of feelings for him. She sent him away because he happened to be the one who broke the bad news to her about her husband. Having him around all the time would be a constant reminder of what she lost.

"No, she doesn't love me."

"Of course she does. Tell me what happened the last time she saw you."

The waitress brought over their coffee and set it on the table, giving him a brief reprieve from Carolyn's question. After the waitress left, he turned his attention back to her. Where should he start? The beginning? No, he would give her a brief amount of details.

"The base hospital overflowed with injured, and she kept busy helping anyone and everyone she could."

"What day did you see her?"

"The second day, after the bombing."

"Did she know about David yet? I assumed she knew when we spoke before, but I've had time to think about it. You're the one that broke the news to her didn't you?"

How could she possibly have figured that out? Jaoel knew Carolyn had intelligence to spare, but he clearly underestimated it. She saw more than he wanted her too. Before she could start on how much he loved Rebecca, he should maneuver the conversation in a different direction.

"How would I know what happened to her husband?"

"I'm not sure how your gift or hers works, but I think you both would know things in advance to any of us mere mortals."

Joel shook his head. "I don't share Rebecca's gift."

"Now I'm the one confused. If you don't have a similar gift, how were you able to help her."

"Because I see auras. I can see her gift and what she is capable of. It gave me the ability to guide her and help her to control it."

He didn't need to give her all of the details. For instance, Carolyn didn't need to know about his guardian status and why he found himself a part of Rebecca's life. He recognized in order to get her help, she would require a certain amount of information. So he made the decision to share a little with her. It gave him a twofold advantage: he would gain her assistance and get off the topic of love.

"I see. You must have been an amazing find for her. She trusted you inexplicably, didn't she? Yes, I can see it all so clear now. You were a forbidden desire for her." Carolyn tilted her head a faraway look came over her face. "I stand by my assessment. You can break through and make her see her mistake."

"I'm not disagreeing with you, well not entirely. I think I can help, but I will need yours as well."

"What can I do?" Carolyn leaned her arms on the table giving her full attention to Jaoel.

"Follow your instincts for the most part."

"It can't be as simple as that," she said, disbelief evident in her voice.

"I need you to keep pushing her. Anger isn't a pleasant emotion, but it shows she already has cracks in her shield. Rebecca isn't quite as protected as she thinks she is."

"So you're going to swoop in and get her to accept all of her emotions again."

"I suppose that is the simplest way you can put it, yes."

Carolyn tilted her head and studied him. "You're in love with her too."

Jaoel had hoped they were off this particular topic. Carolyn wouldn't leave well enough alone. He didn't want to travel down this particular road, but he still needed her help. He wanted to get this squared away before he got back on the ship. Rebecca waited there for him.

"I don't know where you get these ideas."

"I'm good at reading people. When you see Becca again, test my theory. See if I'm right."

Jaoel raised his hands and asked, "How do you propose I do that?"

Jaoel didn't want to admit he hoped she was right. He wanted Rebecca to be in love with him, but he didn't want to openly admit it. His feelings for her were something he kept buried deep inside of him. If he admitted them, he might feel obligated to act on them. He was her guardian, and her life had to be his first priority.

"Kiss her."

Shock filled him at her words. He couldn't have heard her right. No, he couldn't kiss Rebecca. Something like that went way beyond the scope of his duties.

"No, I can't do that."

Her lips formed a smirk as she asked, "Why not? Are you afraid?"

"It's not possible. Leave it Carolyn."

"I can't do that. I think you would make a lot of progress if you followed my advice. Next time she starts shouting at you, pull her into your arms and shut her up with your lips. I bet you get a lot of answers you weren't counting on."

Exactly, something he was very much afraid of. He might find out something he didn't want to know. What if she didn't feel the same way? What if she did? So many questions with answers he didn't know he if he wanted or not. Maybe he should follow her advice and see what happened. No, he couldn't take the risk.

"I think we need to let go of your theory. I'm not going to be kissing Rebecca any time soon."

"So you plan on doing it in the far reaching future?"

"Quit hearing what you want to hear. I didn't say that. I have no plans to kiss Rebecca now or in the future." Frustration filled his voice as he emphasized each word.

Carolyn picked up her coffee and took a sip, studying him for a few moments. "All right, I can live with that response. Sometimes the best kisses are the ones you don't plan for anyway."

"Now that I have you back on topic, are you going to help me or not?'

"By continuing to make Rebecca angry all the time? I do that just by breathing, so yeah, you can count on me. I hope it doesn't take too long, because if it does, I might hurt her."

"Leave her to me. In a few short weeks, she should be as close to normal as possible. She might never be the same, but she won't be so belligerent with everyone."

"I suppose it's all I can ask for. I want my friend back, and you're my best bet at getting it. So work fast." Carolyn's coffee cup still rested in her hands. She played with the cup rolling it back and forth as she pondered something. "Are you sure whatever you have planned is going to work?"

He nodded and replied, "I am."

"How?" she asked.

"I've had experience with it before."

"I still say my suggestion would work a whole lot better. It would probably be a lot quicker too." Carolyn set her coffee cup down and sighed.

"I don't..."

She held her hand up and interrupted him, "Don't worry. I know when to let things go. At least for now. I think we should head back. We've been gone for a couple of hours now. I'm sure Rebecca is noting the time."

"I'm telling you she doesn't care about me like that, but I'm not going to argue with you about it. So yeah, let me pay the bill, and we can go back to the ship."

Jaoel got up and found the waitress. He paid for their cups of coffee and left her a tip. He gestured toward Carolyn to get up and follow him out of the diner. They walked back to the ship not speaking to each other the entire time. When they boarded the ship, they went their separate ways. He had a lot to think about before his meeting with Rebecca, so he went to his bunk and lay down.

Jaoel couldn't help but wonder if Carolyn was indeed right about Rebecca. Did she love him? Could she be suppressing her feelings in the same way he was? Did he want to find out the truth? Even if she did love him, it didn't mean they had a future together. He decided to let it go because they were questions leading him nowhere. Jaoel had much more important things to think about and plan for. Wishing and hoping for her to love him didn't make it real.

Chapter Twenty-Nine

REBECCA GLANCED UP and watched as the stars twinkled against the dark sky. She left her quarters shortly after Carolyn came back, not wanting to get into another disagreement with her. Something about the look on her face made Rebecca want to smack her. She had a confident and oh so smug smile, as if she was in the possession of a piece of life changing information.

It took everything inside of her not to lash out when she entered their shared room. She gritted her teeth and breezed out of the room as quick as possible. So she had been sitting up on the deck for several hours. Joel said to meet him at midnight on the deck. She used the moonlight to glance at her watch. He should be up to join her soon, the time already being half past twenty three hundred hours.

"Have you been waiting long?"

Rebecca jerked her head to her left to see Joel leaning against the wall watching her, his arms folded across his chest and one leg bent with his foot resting on the wall. Part of his face in shadow and the other half illuminated by the light cascading down from the moon, one ancient aquamarine eye studied her, the other one obscured by the darkness.

"I haven't been waiting at all." Denial happened to be her best friend these days, and she leaned heavily on it when she needed to.

"And yet you're here. Appearances suggest you're anxiously waiting for someone to arrive. Unless you are expecting someone else, I'd say it's me you keep searching for."

Rebecca raised an eyebrow and glared at him with distain. "So sure of yourself, aren't you?"

He pushed himself off the wall with is foot and walked over to her side. "Not at all. Just stating the facts as I see them."

"So the world in the point of view of Jaoel, the guardian know it all?"

"Don't use that name," he demanded.

"Oh, Why not?" she asked, raising an eyebrow again..

"It would raise too many questions. Ones I don't particularly want to deal with."

"Which brings us to why we're here doesn't it." Rebecca placed her hands on her hips and took a step back. She studied him as she waited for him to start speaking.

"What do you want to know?"

Rebecca tilted her head and thought about what she wanted to know. She decided to test him and see how much information he would divulge. If she understood him and the little he already revealed, he wouldn't be forthcoming with any further information.

"Everything is a good start."

He shook his head and replied, "I can't tell you everything."

"So why are we bothering with conversation at all? This is a complete waste of my time." Rebecca turned to leave and

Joel grabbed her arm preventing her from storming away. "Let go of me."

"No, we're not done." Anger shot out of his eyes, barely visible under the night sky.

"That isn't for you to decide," her reply scathing.

"No, it's for both of us to go over and come to an agreement on. We haven't even begun to discuss everything we need to."

"So you're saying you're going to tell me what I want to know," Rebecca replied with disbelief laced through her voice.

"Not exactly. I am going to explain what I can." His eyes pleaded with her to understand.

Rebecca jerked her arm from his grasp and took a step back. "All right, I'm listening."

"I told you about being a guardian. You know what I am. Michael is a level higher than that. It's why he leads us."

"So what you're saying is your leader is like an Archangel," she replied.

Joel turned his back to her and stared up at the sky. He stared at it for several moments before he glanced over his shoulder at her. Resignation filled his eyes as he spoke, "Similar yes, definitely as powerful, but Michael is still a guardian."

"How is it different?" she asked.

Joel took a few steps eliminating the distance between them and gazed down into her eyes. "The best explanation I could give you so you understand is it's all about power. Who has it and how they wield it. Michael has enough power to rival any of them, but he chooses to use it to help others.

His fight is different, in some ways more noble. We are all given a choice, and only the ones truly special are given the opportunity to become a guardian."

"So this is your way of telling me you're extra special." A bemused smile fluttered across her face.

"So from everything I said all you got was I'm special?" Surprise filled his voice as he continued to stare into her eyes.

"Seems to reason you must be. I already know you can read people with gifts. It's what you meant by only the special ones get an invitation to be a guardian. How does one become one anyway? Who gets the choice? Is it just angels? Do people become angels after they die or are angels born? What I'm asking is how are you created?" Rebecca rattled off a bunch of questions at once hoping he would answer at least one of them.

He shrugged. "You're offered a choice. If Michael feels you've earned a place as a guardian, he approaches you. If you decide to join, you are a guardian. It's quite simple, and only angels ever are given the opportunity. General humans are not turned into angels...they are souls sent to Earth with individual purposes. Only the extraordinary can ever ascend to heaven as an angel."

Not really an answer, but she didn't care. She had other things on her mind. "How long have you been a guardian, Joel?"

"So long I don't remember a time I wasn't," his tone quiet, almost inaudible as he spoke.

"So you're ancient. It explains why your eyes appear so old when you stare at me."

Rebecca let everything absorb and fill her mind. Joel was so old he didn't remember a time when he wasn't a guardian. It explained a lot about him, and why he did some things she found confusing. She paced around the deck staring out at the night sky. Everyone, except necessary personal, slept in their beds. It left the deck almost eerily quiet. Any sound would be easily heard so it surprised her Joel sneaked up on her without a sound. He spun her around and wrapped his arms around her.

"Becs, you need to fix your shield. If you don't, I may not be able to help you."

"Why do you keep coming back to that? My shield is fine. I don't need to fix anything," she exclaimed.

He studied her for several seconds as if trying to decide what to do next. Joel wanted something from her, but she was at a loss to what it could be. "Why are you so stubborn?"

"I'm not. I don't see everything the way you do," her voice quiet with a touch of huskiness intertwined. Being so close to him, with his arms wrapped around her, made her heart flutter with a need she couldn't explain. He always made her feel a little unsteady and nothing had changed in his absence.

"You don't have to agree with me on everything, Becs. Life would get too boring if you did." He raised his hand and glided it over her hair. "Just this once, open yourself up to the possibility you could be wrong."

As he continued to stroke his hand down the length of her hair, she began to feel her lungs start to seize up. Her breaths came out in short ragged gasps while her heart pounded rapidly in her chest. Why was her body reacting this way to him? She shouldn't be feeling this way about another man, and especially not Joel. An angel send down to be her guardian. Clearly something went wrong inside of her on the day the she met him. She always had a peculiar reaction to him. Maybe it went deeper than that. It could be inherent within her waiting to come out and spark to life each time she neared him.

"What are you doing?" she asked and tried to pull away from him.

"I'm testing a theory."

"What theory?" She gazed up at him with a puzzled look, crinkling her eyebrows as she studied him.

"This one," he replied as he leaned down and placed his lips on hers. A soft and gentle kiss, as he coaxed with each roll of his lips over hers. She raised her hand and pulled his head down closer to hers, wrapping both of her hands on his head holding him in place. Her eyes closed as she allowed herself to feel every emotion rolling through her.

He deepened the kiss when she opened her mouth, a small gasp escaped before he took control. As the passion floated through her, she could feel her shell beginning to disintegrate. It allowed more emotions, many she denied herself over the past several months.

Joy, ecstasy, and a wave of pure happiness filled her to the brim, on the brink of overflowing. Rebecca reveled in each sensation as she welcomed them once again within her heart and soul. They were like old friends she sorely missed.

How could she have denied herself the wonderment of emotions?

Joel's kiss gave her the opportunity to once again enjoy the luxury of every emotion available. If he hadn't wanted to test this theory of his, she would still be a bitter shell of the person she turned herself into. She let her hands roam through his ebony hair and tugged his head closer. She wanted to be as close to him as she could possibly be. The touch of his lips on hers would never be enough. She wanted so much more.

The kiss went on for a long time; so long it lost all meaning and meant everything at the same time. Their tongues dueled for control, each of them trying to put all of their passion into the kiss. His hands roamed across her back as they both tried to crawl inside each other with each roll of their tongues together. Their kiss became one shared breath as they consumed each other. Rebecca wanted more, so much more, and she intended to get it. Unfortunately, Joel had other ideas. Just as suddenly as it started, it stopped. He took a step back and stared at her with a tiny amount of confusion deep inside his ancient aquamarine eyes.

"What?" she asked as her head tilted to the side. "Why did you stop?"

"I don't know what just happened there."

Joel appeared disturbed, as if their kiss something he found distressing. Rebecca didn't know what to make of it. She did know one thing; he was not going to apologize for it. They both wanted it or it wouldn't have gone as far as it did.

"I believe you kissed me."

He scrubbed his hands over his face. "No, I mean, I know I did. It shouldn't have happened."

"Really? Well then you shouldn't have instigated it."

"I know." He gazed down as he spoke, his tone soft and barely audible.

"So did you get your answer?"

"What?" His head shot up to stare at her, surprise filled his eyes.

"You're theory," she replied, reminding him of why the kiss had started.

He nodded his head a small smile forming on his face. "Oh, I believe I did."

"Are you going to share?'

"No, I don't think I will." Joel turned around and walked away.

Shock filled her as she watched his retreating back. How could he stroll away as if nothing happened? Their kiss changed something inside of her and gave her a reason to feel again. Didn't he feel the shift inside of her? He wanted her to adjust her barrier, and surely he realized she had. Maybe that was why he believed he could disappear again? He got what he wanted out of her and now he could just go on his merry way.

"You're going to leave?"

He glanced over his shoulder and replied, "Yes, I think we're done here."

How dare he leave after kissing her? Wasn't it just like a man to get what he wanted and leave the girl alone and confused. See if she ever let him kiss her again. Who did she think she was kidding? If he kissed her again, she would jump at the chance. The man knew how to kiss, and he invoked feeling she buried deep inside of her. Now that they found new life she refused to let them go. Let him run they could have a battle of wills later. She strolled away once she could no longer see him. Time to go to bed and think about everything that happened over the last several hours. Everything changed and hopefully for the better.

Once she got to her room, she saw Carolyn pretending to be asleep on the top bunk. Out of nowhere, a wave of energy hit her, and she couldn't breathe. All the emotions she had been suppressing hit her at once. Agony and despair all rolled into one; filling her with so much pain she couldn't push it away. The grief she suppressed after losing David and her two friends became so poignant, she could feel tiny shards stabbing her whole body, but especially her heart. Tears fell from her eyes and trailed down her face. The wetness streamed down her neck. If she could wipe them away, she would have. She stood frozen as each emotion found a way to burst out of her, not allowing her control over her own body. She tried to reach up to her throat, her hands remained dead weights next to her. A scream filled her mouth, but no noise could actually be released. A silent scream ricocheted through her mind, her mouth gaping open with nothing audible to warn Carolyn of what would happen next. As the emotions disintegrated, her strength followed suit.

She could feel every amount of energy leave her body and knew she was completely helpless to stop any of it. Rebecca dropped to the floor in a loud *thud*, her head banging on the hard surface. She could see Carolyn jumping down from her bunk and kneeling beside her. Everything had an abstract feeling to it. It almost seemed like it was happening to someone else and she only observed it.

While she could see Carolyn next to her, she could not feel her hand brushing against her cheek. Carolyn's mouth moved, but she could barely make out the words she spoke. It seemed like she asked her if she was all right. Rebecca wished she could tell her no. She didn't know if she would ever be all right again. Her mind went blank and soon after that the world went black, finally giving her an escape from it all.

Chapter Thirty

JAOEL MADE SURE TO wander off at a nice slow pace until he knew for certain Rebecca couldn't see him. He glanced back, glad to see he was no longer visible to her. His pace became much more rapid and purposeful. He still doubted Carolyn's assumption about Rebecca loving him. He did believe she desired him. The kiss they shared couldn't be faked. On some small level, she wanted to kiss him as much as he wanted her. For a brief moment, he had everything he wanted. The feelings rolling through him were oh so wonderful. A tinge of lust topped off with a whole lot of love.

His emotions began to swim through him and they became both powerful and overwhelming. The longer he kissed her, the more he wanted. When he got the intense feeling to push for more, he knew he needed to stop. In those moments, he realized pushing her too soon would only be detrimental to any future they might have. So he pulled back, making the decision to wait and pursue her another time. If he backed off and wooed her properly, she might fall in love with him. He didn't believe she did yet, but with enough time she could. Before he rounded the corner to his shared quarters he heard his name echoing through the corridor.

"Joel, wait stop." He turned to see Carolyn waving at him as she ran down the hall. She reached him and leaned over trying to catch her breath. Her nightgown billowing at her ankles, no robe to speak of. "Thank you. I thought you hadn't heard me."

"What's going on?" he asked, puzzled why she sought him out. Her state of undress bothered him, but he assumed she would have a reason for running around in her nightgown. "Why are you yelling for me to stop?"

"Rebecca." A short breath. "Collapsed." Another short breath. "Floor." She pointed down the corridor she just came running down.

"Where?" he asked, realizing what she tried to get out. Rebecca needed him and nothing else mattered.

"In room. On floor, can't move her myself." Carolyn's breathing tapered out as she once again regained control. "She's barely breathing, I don't know what happened. One minute she was standing there fine, and the next, she fell to the floor in one big heap."

He raced by to get to Rebecca. Something must have happened to cause her to collapse, but what, he didn't know. It worried him... Mere moments ago, he'd kissed her and left her standing on the deck alone. What if him pushing her—kissing her—caused her unexpected fall. When he got to their room, she lay sprawled on the floor with a pillow under her head. No doubt Carolyn's effort in making her comfortable.

Rebecca's eyes were open and glassy. He waved his hand over them and received no response. She stared off into nothingness. No movements as if she had checked out when she fell to the ground. Something didn't sit right with him. Her response and the fall were not normal. He needed to look deeper to see what could have caused this to happen. With his gift, he checked her to see what could have happened. Her aura shattered into a million pieces. She must have taken down the protective barrier on her own emotions and couldn't handle the chaos that ensued. If he didn't act quickly, she would be lost. He could almost feel her hold on life slipping away, and Jaoel would not allow her to leave him. She had become too important to him, and he didn't know if he could remain whole if he lost her.

"Is she all right?" Carolyn asked as she entered the room. Concern etched over every one of her features. She stood next to them, wringing her hands in front of her.

Jaoel shook his head and replied, "No, far from it. She took down her shield. It's going to take everything I have to repair it, and she's likely to be out for days, healing." His heart grew heavy with worry. He had to save her; Jaoel couldn't lose her now, just when he decided to fight for her. He brushed away any thoughts of her possible death, because he refused to believe it could happen. Faith, he trusted his ability to help her get through this horrific event. He closed his eyes and let it flow through him. After several seconds, he opened them again and glanced over at Carolyn, anxiously awaiting him to get control of himself.

"I will help with whatever you need. Tell me what to do." A new determination took hold of Carolyn. Her face showed how much she would do to fight for her friend. Her eyes, still filled with worry, also had a different edge to them. They spoke of loss edged with strength. Carolyn would fight until her last breath to never lose a loved one again. "I can't lose anyone else. Not after losing Ginny and Maxi in the bombing."

Jaoel nodded and barked orders. "First, I'm going to have to repair her aura. It's scattered all over the place. Her grief probably descended on her all at once, and she couldn't control it."

Carolyn nodded her head. "Yeah, she stood there with her mouth gaping open. I didn't know why until she hit the floor hard. It's like she isn't there anymore. Her stare is completely blank."

"She's there, and she is probably still screaming inside her head. Once I'm done, I am going to need you to help me back to my bunk. It's going to drain a lot of my energy, and I don't know if I will make it. Staying in this room isn't proper, so I need to try. Do you think you can do that?" Jaoel stared directly into her eyes willing her to understand everything he told her.

"Yes, absolutely. Is that all you need from me?"

Jaoel inclined his head, and said, "For the most part, yes. Before we begin, help me get her settled in her bunk. I won't have the strength afterwards, and I want her to be comfortable. Pull her blankets back, and when I lift her, put the pillow back so I can rest her head on it."

Carolyn leaped forward and did as Jaoel instructed. She pulled the blanket down in one full sweep. Once she completed the task, she turned to watch Jaoel as he scooped his arms underneath Rebecca. When Jaoel lifted Rebecca up into his arms, she grabbed the pillow and placed it on the bed. He took small easy steps as he made his way over to the bed with her safely ensconced in his arms. As he reached the bed he lowered her, slow and gentle, until her head touched down on the pillow. He set her down as gently as he could, trying not to jar her too much. He straightened out legs and arms and took a step back.

"This is where it's going to get tricky. I might not speak for a while because I need to concentrate. Do not interrupt me. It could cause her to go into a permanent state of shock. If you have any questions, ask them now before I begin."

"No. I'm good with everything. I'm going to stand over here out of the way. Let me know when you're done so I don't make the mistake of interrupting." Carolyn backed up and stood still against the wall.

Jaoel turned away from her and put all of his attention toward helping Rebecca. He kneeled down beside her bunk and place one hand on her head, the other over her heart. With his eyes closed, he began to feel the shattered pieces and started the slow process of piecing them back together. It was like a jagged jig-saw puzzle with over a million separate pieces all begging to be connected. They radiated power, and he could tell which pieces went together by their polarity. The connected like magnets, opposites repelling each other. One by one, he dragged them together until he had a bunch of large pieces needing to be put together as one large picture. He slid them together, clicking them into place. As he slipped the last piece in, he could see all the pain Rebecca suffered from letting the shield over her heart drop.

She agonized over David's death. He meant so much to her, and she loved him like she had never loved anyone before him. Jaoel understood why she didn't want to feel the loss. It devastated her, and the pain had been too much for her to bear. It also made him feel like a first rate jerk for kissing her earlier. This whole mess was probably the result of him mauling her earlier. It forced her to think about her loss and helped to bring down the shield. If she had said something, he would have helped her to remove it slower and at a much less dangerous pace. Instead, she dropped it suddenly and caused chaos to ensue.

He would give her some space to come to terms with her loss and what happened between them. Jaoel believed he owed it to her after the trauma she went through because of him. Even if Carolyn was right and Rebecca loved him, it didn't negate the feelings she had for her husband. He died, and she would need time to grieve him properly. He mentally backed away, her aura once again whole and strong. She would sleep for a while, but when she woke, she wouldn't remember the pain. She would remember David and the grief, but it wouldn't devastate her. She would be in a better place to handle it.

He opened his eyes and glanced over his shoulder. "It's done."

"She's going to be all right?"

"Definitely. Now if you don't mind, I need to get back to my bunk before I pass out myself."

Carolyn leaped forward and helped him to his feet. He leaned on her as they exited the room and with slow steps, walked to his quarters. Once they got there, she helped him over to his bunk. He stumbled falling forward onto the bed his knees and feet hitting the floor.

"You really are drained. Here, let me help you get into bed." Carolyn helped him pull himself up on the bed and rolled him over. His blankets were already at the foot of his bed from him resting earlier in the day. She grabbed them and pulled them over his body and tucked him in. "Thank you for helping Rebecca. I can see how hard it was for you and how much it took out of you. I appreciate it."

"My job, protect. Didn't mind." Jaoel could barely get the words out.

Carolyn shook her head. "You can't protect her from everything. Although I appreciate your willingness to try. See, I knew you were in love with her."

Jaoel shook his head in denial.

Carolyn interrupted him, "No don't try to make me believe you don't. I have all the evidence I need. You put yourself out there to help her. Not too many people would do that for someone they didn't at least care for. No matter what you say, I won't believe anything other than you are madly, deeply in love with Rebecca. Don't worry, though. I will keep your secret for now."

"Thank you. Don't want to..."

"Get some sleep. Rest assured, when the time is right, Rebecca will know how you feel. It isn't now. I don't think she's in the right place to know it yet."

"Not your place."

Carolyn raised her eyebrow and replied, "Not my place to tell her? No you're right it isn't. It should be you telling her, but if you stall and take too long, I might have to push you both in the right direction. Just be warned, I will do anything for my friends. Don't you feel lucky I include you on that list now? I'm sure you do. All right, I'm leaving. I will check in on you tomorrow."

Carolyn got up and walked out of the room, but not before Jaoel saw the smug look on her face. Nothing he could do about it. He'd have to sit back and wait to see what she would do. In the meantime, he would pray she didn't run off and tell Rebecca before he was ready to deal with it. They both needed time. She needed to grieve and let go of her husband. Jaoel needed time to gather a proper plan of wooing her. He gave up trying to get over her, now that he saw her so clearly he intended to win her.

No more denying himself and refusing to admit how much he loved her. No one would ever care about her the way he did. He planned on devoting himself to her completely. Once he started he wouldn't give up until she admitted she wanted to be with him just as much. Nothing and no one would stand in his way. Rebecca O'Shea was the one person who held his heart, and he didn't give it away easily.

Chapter Thirty-One

"CAN YOU BELIEVE HOW unbelievably dreary this tour has turned into?" Carolyn asked.

Rebecca grinned and replied, "Not what you imagined is it?"

One thing remained clear the longer the war went on. Time flew by quicker than any soul on board liked. Each individual was distinctly aware it could end for them at any moment, whether by death or a cease fire. The latter of course was the way everyone preferred things to go. The Japanese had launched an attack spanning across many islands in the Pacific. If they were going to gain some measure of control back from them, they would have to counter attack them. A plan to achieve their goal, to get the Japanese to fall back in retreat happened to be under advisement by General MacArthur. So the *Solace* followed the Pacific fleet, scooping up any wounded in battle and hauled them back to this ship. If the Japanese attacked, they would need a hospital ship to house any injured.

Rebecca decided she needed to launch a battle plan of her own. Ever since the one night a few months ago, when Joel kissed her, he made sure he was never alone with her. She didn't know what to make of his attitude. What did he learn by kissing her? Whatever he deciphered from their one and only kiss it appeared to scare him enough to put a wall up between them. At least she got one thing out of their lip lock, her emotions returned in full force along with her friendship with Carolyn.

She woke up the next morning feeling refreshed and whole. The whole night a complete blank, all she recalled after Joel's heart stopping kiss was walking to her room. She must have been extremely tired to fall asleep so quickly and not remember going to bed. Carolyn seemed to instinctively know she'd changed. Her friend hovered over her with worry framing her face. In an effort to reassure her, Rebecca wrapped her arms around her in a fierce hug, one which Carolyn returned with tears falling down her face. After a long talk, they agreed never to go a day without talking about what bothered them.

"Are you ever going to tell me what happened with you and Joel?"

They were in the middle of organizing the supply room. They were running out of busy work with only a limited amount of patients on board the ship. They took some on the *Solace* and others they transported to a base hospital for extended care as soon as possible. Something they were both thankful for and annoyed with at the same time. No one wanted anyone injured, but boredom could be rather tedious.

"Nothing to tell," Rebecca replied, brushing off the question again. Carolyn kept bringing it up at random times.

"Well if you want my opinion..."

"I don't," Rebecca said, cutting her off.

"You're getting it anyway. I think he's avoiding both of us because of how he feels about you."

What nonsense did she have going through her head now? Carolyn, somewhere along the way, had turned into a hopeless idealist. What happened to her organizational control freak of a friend?

"I don't know what you're talking about, and I don't want to either. However, I do agree with you on one point."

"Oh really, which one?" Carolyn asked, raising her eyebrow.

"He is avoiding us. Me at least, the only reason you are getting the same treatment is because we are friends and share a room."

Carolyn laughed and replied," Have I told you how glad I am you are acting semi-normal?"

Rebecca rolled her eyes and muttered, "I wish *you* were."

"What did you say?"

She needed to distract Carolyn from her latest obsession, Joel's mythical feelings. Maybe she should give her something else to focus on. If she had another outlet, she might leave Rebecca be. If she believed Joel truly loved her, she could use it to her advantage. She wanted to get him alone so they could finally talk. Carolyn always devised the best plans, and Rebecca was desperate enough to use her skills to get what she wanted.

"You know if Joel's avoidance bothers you so much, you should come up with some kind of plan to rectify it."

"Why would I bother? He isn't my friend, and I'm not in love with him."

Rebecca stopped and stared at her. "You didn't seem to let that bother you before we joined the Pacific fleet. In fact, I remember you joining him for a dinner the night before."

"You're still jealous about that? I am not nor have I ever been interested in dating Joel Remak."

"Good, neither am I."

"Liar."

Rebecca dropped a box of bandages on the floor and spun around to face her. "What's that supposed to mean?"

"You can deny how you feel about it all you want, but I know you. I also got a small glimpse into what he's feeling. Neither one of you is very good at hiding it." Carolyn's lips tilted into a knowing smile.

"Well you're wrong. I'm not in love with Joel. He certainly isn't with me either. Two people who care about each other do not avoid each other at all costs."

"They do when they don't want to feel the emotion. I'm guessing you both have your reasons for denying it, but it's plain to anyone with eyes."

"You're wrong."

Carolyn walked over and placed her hand on Rebecca's shoulder. "No, I'm not. I get it, you love David, but he's gone. It's all right to move on."

"You're right. I do love David. Nothing is going to change it, even if he will never be here with me again. Quit trying to force me into another man's arms," Rebecca replied with a scathing look on her face.

"I'm not forcing you anywhere," Carolyn said, her tone as soft as a whisper.

Rebecca stared into her warm brown eyes and studied her. She took it one step further and opened herself up to her friend's emotions. If she wanted to know what Carolyn believed, she could see for herself. She closed her eyes and reached deep down into the abyss and got swept away in concern wrapped around love. Carolyn wanted her to be happy and truly believed Joel could be the way to finding it.

"Did you like what you discovered?" Carolyn asked, a bemused expression on her face.

Rebecca shook her head and frowned. "Have I ever told you how peculiar you are?"

"Awe, I love you too." She pulled her into a fierce hug. "I'm serious though, you and Joel would make a great couple."

"I'm not ready for anything like that right now, Caro. If you are asking if I'm attracted to him, then yes I am. He is very nice to stare at—what woman wouldn't appreciate his broad shoulders and thick-muscled arms along with his exquisite face. Ask any of the nurses here, and the first thing they will mention is his unusual aquamarine eyes."

"I think you are ignoring something that could be very good for you. You should reach out and grab what is right in front of you before it's too late."

Rebecca shrugged and replied, "I can't help how I feel."

"Now there is my point exactly. You stopped acting so mean and angry. It's time to let yourself love again."

"Did it once, not doing it again."

"You were married for one day, less than that, actually, before disaster rained down on us. David would want you to move on. If you're being honest, these feelings you are denying inside of you have been there all along."

"I may have been married for a day, but we were together longer than that. It doesn't negate how much I loved and cared for him."

With a sympathetic look on her face, Carolyn reached over and squeezed her hand. "I know, you were together for several months. You have years ahead of you, too young and beautiful to remain a widow."

"You may be right, but I'm not rushing into anything," Rebecca replied with a shake of her head. "Besides, even if I did feel something for Joel, it's useless to attempt any kind of relationship with him."

"Really why?"

"He, well, doesn't do relationships."

Carolyn tilted her head with a puzzled expression on her face. "Again why?"

"His job wrecks havoc on them. I'm guessing he's never had a serious connection ever."

"I fail to see how his job is any different than anyone else's. We are all in danger daily."

Rebecca bit her lip and replied, "It's different. Trust me on this please."

"All right, I will let it go for now." She took a step back away from Rebecca and resumed filling the cabinet with bandages. "But if you want my help, just ask. I'm willing to help form a plan to gain his attention."

Rebecca admitted to herself the idea held a lot of appeal. She did want to gain his attention. If she could get him alone for a little while, she might be able to get some answers out of him. She was sick and tired of him avoiding her. He needed to stop before she resorted to drastic measures to gain his attention.

"I don't want anything like that with him."

"Suit yourself." Carolyn shrugged and continued working.

"I do want to talk to him though, alone."

Carolyn stopped filling the shelf and stared her over her shoulder. "Alone? Who are you trying to fool? You want to do more than talk to him."

"I swear I just want to talk to him, nothing else. He has a lot to answer for, and his avoiding me is driving me crazy."

"I can attest to the crazy part," Carolyn uttered, a wry grin on her face.

"Very funny." Rebecca glared at her. "Are you going to help me?"

Carolyn studied her as if trying to gauge her determination. After several seconds ticked by, she nodded her head and replied, "Yes I will help you."

"Good. We need to come up with a plan then."

"I happened to check the schedule before we came in. I know he's on duty as we are going off. I think I know how we can make sure you have some alone time."

He probably arranged it so they would see less of each other. If they were not on duty together, they would be less likely to have any time together. You couldn't talk to someone or see them much if you weren't forced into each other's company. No doubt he called on Michael's special skills to make it happen. Didn't that go against the guardian code somehow? Seems like if he was meant to protect her he would want to be with her at all times. Well, he would have to make some adjustments, because Rebecca would soon be needing to see him a lot. She may refuse to believe in love again, but she still had a deep desire for him and him alone.

"Really? How?"

"Well, you are suddenly very eager. It's easy enough. We have slacked a bit in stocking these here shelves. If you stay here, I can arrange for him to carry in a heavy box, and once he is inside I will lock you two in together. As he happens to be on the skeleton crew for the night shift, no one will think to check in here. I can let you both out in the morning."

Rebecca bit her lip and replied, "You truly think it will work?"

"Oh yes, I'm good at manipulating people. Joel is going to be easy to lure over here in the guise of helping poor weak little me."

"You're wicked. Don't worry I still love you. In fact, I think I do even more because of it."

Carolyn glanced down at her watch to check the time. "He should be arriving any minute. I'm going to leave. You stay here and do not step out of the room. I'd hate to lock Joel inside for nothing."

Rebecca inclined her head in agreement as her stomach rumbled. "I'm not going anywhere. Though if you slipped some food inside the box before you made him carry it, I'd be grateful."

"I'll see what I can do."

Carolyn left the room leaving Rebecca alone. She wasted so much time in bitterness over her loss and should never have pushed her away. Her blindness almost cost her one of her best friends. She refused to make the same mistake again. Now she had to wait for her friend to lure Joel into the room with her. Once she had him in her grasp, she planned on making sure he didn't pull the avoidance technique on her ever again. They needed to have a full on discussion about whatever they each had going on inside of them. After months of the silent treatment, she was ready to burst out and do some serious damage. Not to mention the unbridled passion she kept hidden deep inside of her. Something she hadn't known existed until he kissed her. Joel Remak had a lot to answer for and it was time to pay up.

Chapter Thirty-Two

JAOEL SCRUBBED HIS hands over his face in frustration. He scanned the ward to see where Rebecca lingered so he could avoid a conversation with her. If he ever believed he needed to check on her, he made himself invisible. Sometimes he thought this hide and seek game he played with her a bit ridiculous. Then he remembered why he did it.

She needed his protection, and it didn't include dealing with any of his unadulterated feelings, no matter how real or pure they flowed through him. He'd almost lost her when she shattered apart. Jaoel made a decision to keep their relationship chaste. Their lives would always be intertwined, but some things had to be a certain way. Never would he be far from her side. When you loved someone, you did what was best for them, something Jaoel fought to do each day watching her from a distance. His desire for more—had to be sidelined for the greater good. His selfishness nearly destroyed Rebecca once. He'd not be responsible for her unraveling again.

"Hello, Mr. Remak."

Jaoel turned to find Carolyn dancing around him anxiously, terror filling him at the sight of her. Rebecca must be near if she stood before him. "What do you want?" His eyes never resting on her as he searched through the whole room to locate Rebecca.

"Why must you be so rude?"

He gave her a cold look. "You only talk to me when you need something. What is it?"

"It's just a little thing."

He pinched the bridge of his nose and reined in his displeasure. "Tell me so we can get it out of the way." Jaoel needed her gone, so he could continue his plan of avoiding his charge.

"There's this heavy box I can't seem to lift. I need to put it in the supply room. Do you think you can carry it in there for me?" she said, her voice so sugary sweet it made him pause with concern. She laid it on so thick, he couldn't help thinking she had some ulterior motive, but he couldn't imagine what it might be.

"What are you up to?"

"Nothing, I need help with this box. After you carry it inside the supply room, I promise I'll leave you alone, well at least for tonight."

Honesty spilled out of her eyes, begging him to trust her. What could it hurt to humor her and take a box into the supply room? It shouldn't take more than five minutes to accomplish it, and then he could push her along and deal with his own duties. "Fine. Show me where this box is." The sooner he got it done, the quicker he could be rid of her.

"It's right over there," she replied, pointing to a box almost as big as her.

All right, maybe he exaggerated a little bit. The box's actual size the equivalent of a hope chest. He marched over to the box, bent down, and lifted it up into his arms. "Good grief this thing's heavy. What do you have in it?"

"Some items that will be needed in the supply closet for immediate use. I promise everything in there is absolutely necessary."

"If you say so. Lead the way so we can deposit it inside. I have a lot to do."

Carolyn walked ahead of him, the top of her head barely visible above height of the box. She stopped at the door to the supply room and glanced back at his progress. Once he neared the door, she opened it and held it open for him to enter.

"Where do you want me to set it down at?" He turned to see her closing the door with her on the opposite side of it. "Hey what are you doing?"

He heard the lock click into place. He glanced down and swore when he realized it locked on the outside, effectively leaving him stuck. He set the box down on the floor near the door and accessed his options. If she didn't let him out, he could use his powers to shift out, but he only wanted to use them as a last resort. One, he didn't have a huge hold on moving from place to place, and two, normal people didn't disappear out of locked rooms.

"This is for your own good. You two need to talk. Use this time wisely. I will be back in the morning to let you out." He heard her footsteps as she walked away, ignoring his pounding on the door demanding her to come back.

Her words sunk in. Wait a minute; she said you two need to talk. Which meant someone else shared the room with him. He closed his eyes and turned around hoping the one person he didn't want to see didn't suddenly appear before him. When he opened them, his biggest fear came crashing down on him. Rebecca stared back at him, emerald-green eyes searching him for answers.

"Fancy meeting you here." She acknowledged his presence with a gamine smile.

"This is a bad idea."

"I guess that depends on your outlook. Now, the way I see it, this is an opportunity, one I've been looking forward to."

Disbelief filled him at her words. "You got her to arrange this?"

"Of course. You wouldn't talk to me. I had to resort to drastic measures."

He shook his head in an attempt to reason with her. "You do realize I could leave anytime I wanted too?"

"I do, but I also know you don't want to draw attention to yourself in that way. You did tell me to not use your real name." Her lips tilted into a knowing smile.

Aggravation filled him when he glanced over at her, so smug and sure of herself. Of course she had him cornered; exactly what she wanted and it irritated him. He scrubbed his hands over his face in an attempt to regain his composure. She forced his hand, and he had no choice but to deal with the situation. Time to lay everything out and deal with it once and for all. Once he did, he could move on and continue as if he never met her. As if he could ever do that, she would always be a part of him. His heart beat only for her and nothing would change it.

"All right, you have me here, what do you want?" His voice brusque, stressing his level of annoyance with each word he spoke.

"Hmm, I'm starting to see why Carolyn says you're so rude."

"Get to the point, Becs. I want out of this room."

"So you do have a problem with me?" Her eyebrow rose as she spoke.

"Of course not, but I honestly don't have time for any histrionics."

Her laugher floated through the room causing his heart to tighten in his chest. He missed her laugh and seeing such pure joy spreading across her face. Jaoel wanted to reach for her and pull her into his arms. Instead, he took a step back putting as much distance between them as he could. Rebecca's eyes narrowed on him assessing him with a concentration that alarmed him. After several seconds, she smirked at him and traipsed over to him, stopping directly in front of him. She lifted her hand and trailed it down his chest, and stopped at the edge of his shirt, resting on his lower belly. Her hand slipped into his belt buckle and tugged him closer to her.

"I think you're afraid of me."

She didn't know how close to being right her statement was. Not terrified of her, but for her. His body tingled with joy as her hands roamed across his body, but he needed to put a stop to it before it went beyond his control. As things stood, he was on the brink of shattering his composure.

"Not at all, this is quite boring actually. Is this all you want to do? Rub your hands all over me? If you bothered to ask, I'd have let you. It's best to get it out of your system though. This is not going anywhere."

He watched as the smile on her face fell, his words hitting their mark. Jaoel hated hurting her. It was an unfortunate necessity. Maybe this little tête-à-tête would prove to be a good thing. It would ensure she understood nothing could ever happen between them.

"So explain something to me."

He nodded and replied, "I'll try."

"If you don't like this." Her hands grazed his belly and moved up skimming his chest, circling around his neck pulling his face close to hers. "Why do I feel your pulse racing when I touch you? But more importantly, why do you keep staring at my lips as if you would like to kiss me?"

Jaoel couldn't take it anymore, every ounce of his control snapped as his arms flew around her, tilting her head to give him better access. He gave in to his deepest desire and lowered his head until his lips grazed hers in a gentle kiss. As soon as their lips touched sparks flew around them, electric and full of energy. Rebecca gasped when he pulled back and stared into her emerald-green eyes, his hands intertwined with her red gold hair. Needing to taste her again, he ravished her with his mouth, deepening the kiss as their tongues fought each other for dominance. Jaoel needed her in ways he couldn't explain. He wanted all she had to offer, and she presented herself for the taking. He moaned and yanked himself backward, putting some distance between them. This altercation had not gone as he wanted. He gave into his baser instincts and almost went too far.

"I knew you wanted me."

His head whipped around and pinned her in place. "What I don't understand is why you want me?"

"Why wouldn't I want you?" Rebecca stared at him, confusion filling her gaze.

"Your husband died six months ago. You declared on several occasions how much you loved him. Have you forgotten him already?" he asked with a scathing look on his face.

"How dare you." She reached up and slapped him, the sound echoing through the room. "I'll never forget him. He was an honorable, decent man who never would have spoken to me as you just did."

"And yet you still can't bring yourself to say his name."

"Of course I can..."

But she couldn't. He could see the worry on her face. "It's all right, Becs. You should grieve him."

"I'll always grieve him, don't you understand? He'll always be a part of me because he was my first love. I didn't understand what it meant. He showered me with attention and made me feel good about myself. Looking back, I see it for what it was. David made me happy, and if he lived, I'd still be overjoyed to be his wife. You see there, I said his name, are you glad? What you don't get is, as much as I loved him, I didn't feel an all-consuming passion for him. It doesn't even come close to the emotions rolling through me when I'm around you."

Jaoel stood stunned at her words, and yet he couldn't take anything she said into consideration. Passion did not equate love. If he let this go and pursued her, she would regret it, and over time, so would he. He didn't want to be her rebound guy, and he sure as hell needed a whole lot more from her than an intense love affair.

"This is not going to happen, Becs. Passion isn't enough, and you know it. Let it go, please. I'm begging you."

Rebecca studied him for several moments before she nodded her head in agreement. "On one condition."

"Anything"

"You quit avoiding me. I miss you, and I don't like this distance."

He would have liked to continue on without the constant reminders of what he could never have, but he would concede to her demand if it got her to drop her newfound infatuation with him. "I can agree to that provision as long as you concur this kind of thing will never happen again."

"I won't ever force you to acknowledge what we feel for each other. I don't believe in making a fool of myself more than once. If you want me, you will need to pursue me."

"I won't."

"Still, so you understand, I don't beg. If you change your mind, you know what to do." Rebecca crossed her arms and stared at him, her pride gleaming in her eyes.

"I can live with that," he whispered. "What do we do in the meantime? Carolyn isn't going to let us out of here for hours."

"The box you carried in should have some food in it. I say let's eat because I'm starving. After that, I'm going to try to get some sleep. Not that anything in here appears comfortable, but I can feel fatigue starting to settle in."

Jaoel walked over to the box and opened it up. It was filled with everything they might need, food, pillows, and a blanket. He had to raise his eyebrow at that. Did she think they would only need one? Carolyn probably believed she did them a favor by forcing them to share one blanket. Jaoel could live without it and let Rebecca use it. Her comfort would always be his top priority.

They settled in and had a cold dinner, their backs resting against the wall. They ate in silence, having spoken everything they could manage. After a while, Rebecca's eyes drifted closed and her he body fell sideways with her head landing in his lap. He couldn't help but laugh at the situation he found himself in. In another time or place, having her in his lap would have been more advantageous.

Now all he could do was enjoy having her near and caress the soft strands of her golden red curls. So beautiful and at peace, he couldn't help watching as her chest rose and fell with each breath she took. Not wanting to wake her, he pulled the nearby blanket over her and settled in for a long night of discomfort. When she woke, there would be hell to pay for allowing her to sleep in his lap all night.

Chapter Thirty-Three

REBECCA WOKE UP IN slow degrees. She pulled the blanket up to her chin and sighed with pleasure. Her body wrapped up snuggly in its warmth; if only the pillow beneath her offered an equal amount of softness her life would be complete. As soon as those thoughts rolled through her head, she immediately remembered she was not in her bed. Her eyes flew open, and she scanned her surroundings. Directly in front of her rested the box Joel carried in full of supplies. Not the supplies he thought they were, but ones very necessary for spending the night locked in a room together. Which meant the semi-comfy pillow below her could only be Joel himself, as she didn't see him anywhere near her.

"You can get up now. I know you're awake."

Damn him and his perceptiveness. She could have enjoyed being close to him for a little while longer. With a sigh, she lifted her head and stared over at him. His ancient aquamarine eyes were filled with misery, and he appeared exhausted. "Did you sleep at all?"

"Not so much. It's all right. I don't need a lot of sleep."

Rebecca couldn't help the waves of guilt beginning to flow through her. She didn't want to be the one responsible for his discomfort. Maybe Carolyn would be by soon to release them from the locked room. She glanced down at her watch. Carolyn should be by any minute according to their agreed upon time.

"Well you're in luck. Carolyn should be here soon, and you can go get some much needed rest without me disturbing you." Rebecca stood up, smoothed down her skirt, and ran her fingers through her hair to make herself more presentable.

"I'm fine, Becs. Quit worrying about me."

"I can't help it. It's what I do."

His lips tilted up into a soft reassuring smile, "I can take care of myself, and I know better than you do what I can and cannot handle."

"Yeah, but..."

Before she could get the words out, the door opened, and Carolyn's head peeked through. Her hand covered her eyes, a tiny open slit between her fingers so she could get a tiny glance of her surroundings. "Are you two ready to get out of here or do you need more time?"

Rebecca shook her head in amusement. "You can uncover your eyes, Caro. You're not going to see anything interesting."

"Oh, I hoped you both would be able to work things out."

"Who said we didn't," Joel asked raising his eyebrow.

Carolyn frowned. "I somehow doubt this went the way I envisioned it."

"Sometimes things don't always go the way you want them to. I know this is not how I saw my life playing out. We have to take what we get and make the best of it." Rebecca didn't want to admit her own disappointment of how the situation unfolded. She had to put the best spin possible on it to alleviate Carolyn's questions. Otherwise he friend would nag her until she exploded.

Concern filled Carolyn's eyes as she strolled over to Rebecca's side. "Oh honey…"

"I'm going to leave you two alone. It's been a long night." Joel nodded to the two of them and raced out of the room.

"He left in a hurry," Carolyn remarked.

"I suppose he is getting tired of always protecting me. I'm sure spending the whole night in my presence was very taxing on his self control."

"What do you mean? What happened?"

Rebecca sighed as tears pooled in the corner of her eyes. She turned around as she wiped the wetness away before it streamed down her cheeks. "I don't know. I'm not sure I can explain it."

Carolyn wrapped her arms around her and rested her head on Rebecca's back. "I'm here for you, no matter what. Explain it to me as best as you can."

Rebecca patted her friends arm and pulled herself from the embrace. She turned to face her and responded, "I think it has something to do with David."

"I'm confused. What does he have to do with what happened with Joel?"

"He doesn't think I've grieved enough."

"Ah, I guess I can see his point." Carolyn's eyes clouded with something Rebecca didn't understand.

"What are you not telling me?"

"He told me you wouldn't remember."

"Remember what?" When Carolyn bit her lips and didn't say anything more Rebecca demanded, "Tell me now."

"What do you recall from the night we left port?"

"Not much. You went to dinner with Joel. I talked to him on the deck later that night. He um...." Rebecca blushed at the memory of their first shared kiss.

"He what?"

"He said he needed to test a theory. It was the first time he kissed me."

"Ah..." Carolyn stared at her with a knowing smirk on her face.

Puzzled by her reaction, Rebecca stomped her foot and ordered, "Tell me what it means."

"I told him you had feelings for him at dinner that night. You had a look in your eyes, and I just knew it. He didn't believe me. I still don't think he does. "

"So this is the theory he tested out?" Rebecca folded her arms across her chest as an ache filled her heart.

"Maybe, I'm not sure. I did suggest he kiss you. I'm glad he took a chance, although in light of this information, what happened later makes so much sense now." Carolyn bit her lip as she stared at Rebecca.

"Finish telling me everything."

"You had—I'm not sure what to call it. An episode? Scared me to pieces. I didn't know what to do. I knew about your gift, and you weren't right after David died. You lost so much, but I didn't understand what you did to yourself. I didn't think a doctor would do any good, so I went and got Joel. Of course he reacted immediately. If not for him, you would have died."

Humph.

As her words spilled out, everything came back to her in flashes. She remembered her emotions cascading through her. The grief, anger, and loss all culminating into one huge tragic event, if she hadn't closed herself off, it wouldn't have devastated her. Joel brought her back from the brink of emotional overload. If not for Carolyn and Joel's fast actions, she would have been lost in a sea of nothingness. Why did she forget it all? They were her emotions, and not something she should have failed to remember. Which meant Joel did something to make her forget.

"It's not right..." Anger filling Rebecca as she thought about his high-handed behavior, Joel should not have erased her memory. Of course, he didn't erase it so much as suppress it, but still, he had no right.

"What are you going to do?"

Rebecca thought about the question. What did she plan on doing? Joel made it clear what he wanted. He did feel something for her, but it wasn't enough to make a difference. In retrospect she could see everything clear. He kept his distance for a reason, not wanting to give into temptation. Joel believed he acted in her best interests, not once taking the time to find out what she wanted. He assumed he made the right decision. Well no more, she would not beg anyone to be a part of her life.

"Nothing. He made his choice, and it isn't me."

"Don't be so rash. He loves you. I know it," Carolyn pleaded with her.

"He as much said I'm not enough for him, Caro. I'm not going to keep throwing myself at him. He's got a hang up about David. When I'm rational, I can see why. I married him and planned on living out the rest of my life with him. Well fate had other plans for us. It's time I accepted it and moved on. I told him I'd always grieve for the husband I lost too soon, but I'm all right now. David will always be my first love, but I don't think he will be my last. He didn't want to hear about it. Joel has his mind set and nothing is going to change it."

"So you're going to give up?" A baffled expression came across Carolyn's face.

"Yeah, it's time I took care of myself without Joel. He's looked out for me long enough."

"But..."

Rebecca raised her hand and interrupted her. "Enough. I'm done with it. We have other things to worry about. You know where this ship is heading. A huge battle which means a lot of injured men. We should be nearing Midway, and once the fight begins, we won't have time to worry about trivial things. I'm going to go take a shower while I still can. I'll see you in the ward in a couple hours when we are on duty."

Rebecca left Carolyn in the supply room. She meant what she said. If Joel wanted her, if he truly loved her, he would fight for the right to be in her life. He needed to stop protecting her and instead do whatever was necessary to win her forever. If he couldn't or wouldn't do that, she had better things to do with her life. She would not waste one moment of it longing for a man who didn't actually want her.

Chapter Thirty-Four

JAOEL STOOD OUTSIDE of the room and listened to them talk for a few moments. He wanted to make sure Rebecca would be all right. He couldn't help himself; her well-being would always be a priority to him. After listening long enough to ascertain she'd be fine in the care of her friend, he left. A small pain stabbed his chest at the thought of leaving her. He didn't think he would need to hover quite as close much longer. Rebecca had a good handle on things and would only grow stronger with each passing day. He would continue to help out during the battle at Midway, but after it ended, he'd talk to Michael about pulling out. He didn't want to cause Rebecca anymore undo pain. If he stayed any longer, he would only add to it, not alleviate it as he wanted to. He couldn't give her what she wanted.

"Oh good. I'm glad I ran into you. The battle is in full swing, and we are going to need some men to go out and retrieve injured soon. Be up on deck in an hour to go to shore."

Jaoel glanced at Doctor Thorne and nodded his head. "I'm ready to go now if you need me to."

"No, the aircraft carriers launched their bombers a half hour ago. We don't want to send you out too soon. Just in case, you can go up now and wait."

"I think I will. I'm in need of something to do. It's been a restless morning so far."

"I know how you feel. This is huge. It's been six months since the Japanese attacked Pearl Harbor. If the navy can win this, it could be a turning point for us in this awful war." The doctor shook his head, sadness filling his eyes. "I have some things to do. I hope to see you later."

Jaoel watched as he walked off in the direction of one of the ship's hospital wards. He could hear buzzing overhead as he made his way up to the top deck. His immortal existence may be headed in the direction of perpetual misery, but at least he could do one good thing with it. If he managed to help save some poor soul's life he would consider the price he paid well spent.

Once he got on deck, he could see Navy bombers flying overhead. In the distance, some of the planes dropped out of the sky as fast as they reached the Japanese ships. So much loss with each bomb that reached its target, an orange glow filled the skyline.

"Are you going to Midway?"

Jaoel turned to see Carolyn standing behind him. "As soon as the bombing is done. I doubt any of them are on Midway though. More likely an unlucky fellow is lying injured in the water from being shot down, that is if they were fortunate enough to not die from the crash. I'm going with the first wave to retrieve any possible injured."

"You're making a mistake."

"It's my job..."

"Not about your job, though it's dangerous enough. I mean about Rebecca. You shouldn't be pushing her away."

Jaoel turned and pierced her with his stare. "This doesn't concern you."

"You know sometimes a look comes over you that's truly frightening." Carolyn shivered and wrapped her arms around herself.

"I made up my mind, and I'm not going to discuss it further with you. I explained everything to Rebecca. I'm not about to rehash it all with you." Jaoel stared out again at the fires spreading in the distance. Some ships were slowly sinking. "If you're done, I'm sure you have better things to do than harass me."

Carolyn stuck her tongue out at him. He didn't know what to make of it as never had he seen someone do such a thing before. "You're an idiot. I'll leave, but not before I tell you one more thing."

Afraid of what her answer might be, he almost didn't ask. He couldn't stop the words from falling out of his mouth though. "What's that?"

"I already told you how big of an idiot you are. Here's something to think about as you are out there risking your life. Rebecca already lost one man she loves. Don't be a fool and get yourself killed so she has to start mourning all over again. She's been through enough. I don't want to see her crash all over again."

"Rebecca doesn't love me."

"There you go again, proving how big of an idiot you are." Carolyn shook her head with disgust all over her face. "And to think, I once believed you an intelligent man. Just goes to show I have a lot to learn."

"You're right about one thing. You have plenty to learn. Go do something more productive now. I'm sure the bombing will end soon, and I'll have better things to do than teach you a few life lessons."

"I'm going, but think about what I said. It's not too late to rectify your mistake. She may have decided loving you isn't worth crying over anymore, but she does still care. I saw it in her eyes when she wiped the tears away. She's resolved to move on and live her life." Carolyn paused to take a breath and stared into his eyes. "Without you. You do understand what that means right. She's going to be the one pushing you away now."

"It's for the best." Jaoel meant it too. He believed Rebecca would be better off without him mucking up her life. He loved her enough to let her go.

Carolyn walked away shaking her head. He could hear her muttering the word fool as she marched away. She could think of him what she wanted. Rebecca never once said she loved him. Passion ignited when she was in his presence, but he would never settle for it alone. If he were to risk it all, he needed more from her than some fleeting emotions. Passion flared fast, but ultimately died as rapid as it rose up. His heart wouldn't be able to handle having her and only losing her once her desires were sated.

"Are you going to be on one of the rescue boats?"

He turned to find one of the seaman who worked on board the *Solace*. Jaoel didn't recall his name even though he worked with him often enough. He tried not to get to know any of them. If he did, he might begin to get to close. A war led to a lot of deaths, and he didn't want to find himself mourning more than he already was.

"I am. Are you my partner on this expedition?"

"Yeah, they radioed in the bombers are heading back to their carriers. We're going to get in a boat and check out the waters first. From the sounds of it they don't expect us to find anyone alive."

"I hope they're wrong." Jaoel folded his arms across his chest and closed his eyes. "When do we leave?"

"I believe now. You want to walk over to the boat with me?"

"Yeah might as well get started. The sooner we get to anyone, the better their chances of survival.

They rushed over to where the boats were being launched. Only three were going out, besides the boat Jaoel and his partner got in. As they lowered them, someone from up above tossed a medical bag down. Jaoel caught it, placing it in a secure place on the boat. The process of lowering the boat didn't take long, but at the same time, it seemed to take forever before it hit the water. They reached over and undid the ties holding the boat onto the crank high above on the ship. Jaoel and his partner rowed through the waves toward the area where some planes had gone down.

They searched and searched the waters, not finding any survivors amongst the wreckage. Jaoel didn't want to give up. He hoped to find someone, anyone, who survived the early stream of planes shot down. In the distance, he saw something floating on the water and it almost appeared as if someone floated on a piece of wreckage.

He pointed over to it and asked, "Do you see someone over there?"

"Yeah, someone's floating on that piece of plane. Don't know if he's breathing. We'll have to go over and check."

The problem with going to retrieve the injured man was he happened to be beyond the line they were allowed to go. It got a little too close to the enemy line. Invisible it might be, but it existed. They were in shooting distance of some of the Japanese heavy cruisers. They could fire at them, possibly killing them. Jaoel assessed the risk and decided he was willing to take it.

"I'm good with checking, but if you don't feel comfortable with it, I won't push you," Jaoel explained to his partner.

"No, if he's alive, I don't want to leave him out here. I think we'll be fine. They are probably licking their wounds and won't bother with us."

Jaoel certainly hoped so. He didn't particularly feel like getting shot at. They rowed over to the wreckage. When they got over there Jaoel leaned over and checked the man's pulse. It still beat, however it was very faint. "He's alive. Quick, help me pull him into the boat."

They both worked together and finally got him securely in the boat. Jaoel wanted to check his injuries, but knew they needed to get clear of the danger area. "Does he appear like he has any injuries in need of immediate attention?"

When they rolled him over, Jaoel got a good look at him and he stared, stunned at who lay in the boat with them. His old roommate Kenneth Blackman, his brown hair plastered to his head. Out of nowhere, they heard a loud boom. It rattled through his eardrums, deafening him to all sound around him. They turned as a blast hit the water, pushing the boat back a little bit. Jaoel fell back and hit his head on the back of the boat. Pain shot through his skull. He didn't have time to think about it. He ordered his partner to help him start rowing and fast.

The Japanese apparently didn't care who or what they were. They needed to get out of firing range and fast. So much for them licking their wounds and retreating to fight another day. It took everything they had in them, but they managed to get the boat back to the ship. The pounding in Jaoel's head worsened with each stroke of the oar through the water. For a moment, he thought he wouldn't make it back to the ship before he passed out. He sent a silent thank you out to the powers that be that he made it back. Just as the ropes were hooked back onto the ship to be raised he fell backward again, blacking out.

Chapter Thirty-Five

REBECCA TURNED AS TWO injured men were brought into the ward. One of them soaked to the skin, the other one bleeding from a head wound. She didn't stop to think about who the two men were. There wasn't any time to ponder it. She jumped forward and checked their vitals. The man with the wet clothes was closest to her; she checked him first. When she saw his face, she gasped. Carolyn rushed forward to see why.

"It's Kenneth," she exclaimed, her hand flying to cover her gaping mouth.

"I know. Quick, go get something to cut these wet clothes off of him. He's barely breathing, and he's going to die of hypothermia if we don't get him warm."

Carolyn rushed off to do as Rebecca asked. When she got back, they cut off all of his wet clothes and wrapped him in a blanket. He didn't appear to have any outside injuries. He must've hit his head when his plane crashed.

"Do you think he will be all right?" Carolyn asked, worry etching over her face.

Rebecca studied her for several moments before saying, "I didn't think you knew him well."

"We spent some time together after Thanksgiving. I didn't say anything because it was all so new, and well, I didn't know in what direction it might head. He's so sweet and caring. Did you know his best friend died in a plane crash?" Rebecca shook her head, but Carolyn kept rambling on. "No, you wouldn't have known that. You didn't talk to him much. When he shipped off again, he promised to keep in touch. I got some letters from him, but they were few and far between. Once I got on board the *Solace*, I didn't hear a word from him. I suppose they could have gotten lost somewhere."

"I'm sure they did. You care about him a lot don't you?" Rebecca pulled her into her arms and gave her a fierce hug.

"I guess I do. I didn't realize how much until I saw him lying here."

"Then he's going to be all right. He has to be. I refuse to watch someone else we care about die, not if I can do something about it." With a determined look, Rebecca scanned the room for the nearest doctor. She saw Doctor Thorne off to the side talking with one of the nurses and marched over to his side.

"Excuse me, Doctor Thorne, can you examine Kenneth Blackman? Carolyn and I have him stabilized, but we are not seeing any actual wounds other than some superficial cuts and scrapes."

"I'll get to him when I get a chance. There are some patients in more critical condition than he is." The doctor walked away, ignoring her presence as he reached another injured man.

Rebecca wanted to scream at him to come back, but she knew it would be a futile effort. The doctor was stubborn and wouldn't listen to a word she said. She never really liked working with him, especially after he made her stay almost a week in isolation with Kenneth and Joel. A stab of pain hit her chest, and she spun around to find its source. Something about those two men and their previous hospital stay bothered her.

Kenneth still lay on his bed, pale and unmoving. Carolyn held his hand in hers as she wept over him. Rebecca glanced across the room, and her eyes landed on the source of her discomfort. Something about the patient in that particular bed drew her to him. Before she knew what she was doing, she strolled over to his side. He was perhaps two feet away from Kenneth as they worked on him.

A loud moan could be heard from the man, so Rebecca tried to see what was going on with him. A couple nurses surrounded him on both sides, blocking her view of his face. She walked over to get a look at him and gasped when she saw who lay in the bed. With a head wound dripping blood down his face and neck, Joel's complexion lost all color—his skin a pale white. If he didn't get help, death would probably pay him a visit soon. Rebecca rushed over to his side just as his eyes flew open. His ancient, all knowing, aquamarine eyes she'd grown to love so much stared back at her, filled with pain.

"Hey, Becs. I think I might be dying." His voice a whisper on her ears as he struggled to speak.

"No, you're not. Don't say things like that! I thought you couldn't die anyway. You have a job to do." A lump formed in her throat as she fought back tears.

"I never said I couldn't die. Anything with life in them can have it snuffed out. It must be my time. Made no promises. Just because one can live forever, doesn't mean they have the right." His eyes closed once again, and his breathing burst out in short shallow pants.

"No!" Rebecca screamed.

Carolyn rushed over to her side to see what she was so upset over. When her eyes fell on Joel, she wrapped her arms around Rebecca attempting to reassure her. "I'm sure he'll be fine. Just like Kenneth."

"No, it's not the same. You don't understand. He's actually dying. He's not supposed to die ever. He's not like us." Panic filled Rebecca's voice with each word. She wrenched herself out of Carolyn's grasp and kneeled by his bed.

"You don't know what you're talking about. Of course he'll be fine. I know how special he is to you."

Tears streamed down Rebecca's face. When she found out about David, she thought the world ended with his death. The thought of losing Joel was a million times worse. Her heart dropped right out of her as grief pooled inside of her. She couldn't live if he no longer existed in this world. She would give up anything; do whatever it took to make sure he survived.

"Joel's suppose to outlive us all. Don't you get it? What he does is important. He saves people."

"So do we, Becca. Everyone here does. If he can be saved, every person on board this ship will work to make it a reality." Carolyn rested her hand on her shoulder. "Let them do their job."

Rebecca pulled away from Carolyn. She didn't get it because she didn't know about Joel's real job. A guardian sent to protect people. He would do anything to save someone even if they were not one of his charges. Why did he have to push her away? Why did she allow it? She never once told him how much she loved him. She laid her head on his stomach and wept for all she lost. As her head lay on his chest, a warmth began to spread throughout her. Something new began to grow and take root.

She closed her eyes and investigated what it meant. Her shield still held even though she wanted to fortify it and block all emotions once again. She resisted her first impulse and explored this new development. The noise behind her lowered to a dull roar. She lifted her head, keeping her eyes closed and placed her hands on Joel's stomach. Something inside him called out to her.

The warmth spread through her hands and flared out of her, filling him. In her mind, she could see it glow a brilliant yellow. The powers inside of her expanded, snapped, and grew beyond her imagination into something much more beautiful. She understood what she was capable of for the first time. Rebecca could do far more than feel emotions. Her gift also allowed her to reach deep inside of someone and heal them from within. Joel's case a bit more extensive because of his longevity, but Rebecca didn't mind the risk.

She'd give up her own life to save his. As she held her hands over him, she began to lift the injury out and restore him to his former self. She opened her eyes and watched as her gift brought him back to her. No longer did he lie before her dying a slow painful death, but filled with a youthful vigor. With each push of energy into him, she could feel hers draining. His eyes flew open once again, clouded in confusion.

"Becs..."

"Sshhh, you're going to be all right."

"What are you doing?" He sat up as she the last of her energy left her. "No, please stop. If you keep going, it could kill you."

"It's worth it." Her eyes drooped down as she fought against passing out. Soon, her eyes closed completely, and she fell forward against him.

"No, nothing is worth losing you." Joel leaned forward and pulled her into his arms. "Becs, can you hear me."

"Of course I can, silly." She forced her eyes open to gaze into his beautiful aquamarine eyes one last time. "So happy to see you."

Her eyes closed once again. Rebecca couldn't fight it anymore. She could hear Joel screaming her name, begging her to come back to him. It seemed so far away, like an echo bouncing back to her. She tried to tell him she was still there, but he couldn't hear her. Rebecca could still hear and feel him though. He rocked her back and forth sobbing. The wetness drenched her cheeks and trailed down her hair. She wished she could reach out and reassure him, but knew she might never be able to talk to him again. Worth it—Joel lived—nothing else mattered.

Chapter Thirty-Six

BIG WHITE FLUFFY CLOUDS traveled across the cerulean sky. Waves crashed on the beach in a brilliant blue and white foam mist. The breeze a nice warm balm wrapping around her, making her feel loved.

"I thought you might enjoy this scene."

"Michael?" Rebecca turned surprised to see him next to her. "What are you doing here?"

"I'm surprised you are not asking where here is."

She tilted her head and replied, "I know where I am."

"Do you?" Ancient eyes filled with amusement as his golden blond hair blew in the breeze.

In some ways, he reminded her of Joel. They both held their otherworldliness inside of them, only seen in the depths of their eyes. "Can I see Joel here too?" she asked, ignoring his question.

"No, I'm the only one you can see. You never answered my question."

"Because you already know the answer," she retorted.

"I'd still like to know where you believe we are."

"Isn't this heaven? Or at least my version of it. My favorite place in Hawaii. The little lagoon where I met Joel to train each day." Rebecca closed her eyes and let the warmth of all those memories seep into her soul.

"We're not in heaven," Michael retorted.

"What?" Her eyes flew to his as surprise filled her. "Of course we are."

"Trust me, this is not where your soul has gone to rest. You are deep inside your own mind."

"Then how are you here," she asked.

Maybe this whole thing was one big nightmare, and she'd wake up soon to find Joel next to her, whole and alive. Ah, only if wishing made it so...

"It's one of my gifts—as you refer to it. I can project myself into someone's subconscious. I don't do it often as it disturbs people."

Rebecca snorted, that's the simple way of looking at it. She glanced at him and rolled her eyes. "Gee, I wonder why."

"Don't get sarcastic with me. I'm here for a reason."

"Oh and what is it, oh great and powerful one." Rebecca couldn't rein in her scorn. She decided against holding anything inside ever again. It only led to heartache.

"Mocking me won't get you the answers you seek." Michael's piercing gaze pinned her in place.

"All right, you have my full attention. Why are you here?"

"I came to give you a choice."

A choice? Maybe he could help her get back to Joel. Eager to find out what her choices were she asked him, "You have my full attention. What is my choice."

"More than one actually."

She wanted to roll her eyes, but suppressed the impulse. "Tell me them all."

"Your first choice is to allow me to heal you, and send you back to your world."

She eyed him wearily. Something about his tone told her that choice lacked something she wanted. "What's the catch?"

"Your memory will be erased. Joel won't ever be a part of your life again."

"Will he remember me?"

"Yes, but he won't be allowed to contact you ever. You will be forbidden to him."

What kind of choice was that? She'd live, and Joel would go on suffering. She understood his reason for pushing her away now that she had time to reflect on them. He loved her enough to give her space and grieve. Joel believed she needed more time, but she had no doubt one day he would have given in and told her how much he needed her.

"I don't think I like that choice. What's the other one?"

"I can leave you as is and let Joel visit you whenever he wants, always grieving for you because you will never wake up."

These choices were getting worse and worse. Why did he even bother to visit her if he was only going to torture her? She wouldn't pick either one, because in both choices, Joel suffered. Rebecca didn't want to ever see him endure pain again.

"I see, well then, I choose neither."

"But you must choose," Michael demanded.

"I refuse to pick between Joel in pain and Joel in more misery. That's no choice. It's torture. Just leave. I like it here, and you bothered my serenity."

"You don't think it would be easier on him if he knew you lived and led a fulfilling life."

Michael seriously ruined her peace and quiet. She turned to him, her eyes filled with revulsion. "No, I'm sure if he were given the choice, he would pick me to live. He would want me to have a wonderful life, but no matter what happens to me, his pain will be acute. I refuse to allow you to have that kind of control. I'll find another way." She turned away from him again, ignoring his presence for the irritation it held.

"You love him, don't you?"

"Why does it matter to you?" she asked, but didn't actually expect an answer.

"What if I were to offer you a third choice?"

Rebecca spun on her heals and faced him. "Depends. The other two were a complete waste of my time. Is this one going to be one I'm willing to consider?"

Michael studied her for several moments before he spoke. "Do you know where you are?"

"I thought we already established that. I'm in dream land, and you're visiting." Why did he keep wasting her time?

"No, I mean physically. Where your body is?"

"No, I believe I lost track of it." Hello, dream world, idiot. She fought again to roll her eyes at him. She wanted to figure out where he was going with this line of questioning. Maybe he could give her something to work with.

"You're body is in the base hospital near Pearl Harbor. Joel is now, as we speak, watching over you."

Oh why did he have to tell her that? She wanted to reach out to him so much. If only she could tell him she loved him and wanted him to let her go. If she couldn't hammer out a deal worth her time with Michael, she'd find a way to make him know what lay inside her heart.

"You should make him leave."

"No, I don't think I will."

If she thought she could hurt him, she'd have done it as soon as she laid eyes on him. How did Joel deal with him all the time? "Do you have a point to all of this?" she demanded, her frustration getting the better of her.

"I can send you back to him now, if you'd like."

"Why? So we can say our goodbyes? Is that your final offer?"

He shook his head and replied, "It would be more than that. If you accept what I'm offering, you could live a very long life with him."

"What's the catch? There's always one."

"You would come to work with me as a guardian. There is a reason Joel was sent to watch over you, Rebecca. Your gift is a powerful one we haven't seen in centuries. Something had to bring it out of you, and the seers among us saw Joel was the key to unlocking it."

"So if I sign up to be a guardian, you will allow me to be with Joel forever?"

She didn't want to sound too eager, but couldn't help it from spreading through her. He offered her the one thing she wanted. All she had to do was reach out and take it and never let go, but she couldn't take it blindly without knowing everything first.

"Yes."

"What would you expect of me?" she asked.

"To do your duty as a guardian. I'd even be willing to let you and Joel work as a team. Sometimes the best works are done with more than one person." A hint of a smile twitched on his lips.

"You still haven't explained the catch." Rebecca eyed him wearily.

"You would cease to exist to your friends and family. Instead, you would be welcomed into our fold and become one of us."

"So Carolyn would never remember me?"

"No one would."

Rebecca weighed it over and thought she could live with it. She'd have Joel and no one would suffer. "All right. How do we go about this?"

"You agree?" he asked once again.

"Yes, I do. I'm willing to be a guardian if it means spending eternity with Joel."

"You realize you will have to follow my orders?"

Did he think she was incapable of doing so? "Yes, I am fully aware of that, and I'm even willing to concede to your every demand."

Michael smiled. "Good, then go home, little one. I'm going to force you to wake up now."

Rebecca didn't have time to respond to him. Her body slipped away, fading against the backdrop of the lagoon. The next thing she knew, her eyes were flying open to see Joel sitting by her bedside. His head leaned forward resting in his intertwined fingers. She studied him for several minutes, trying to think of what to say to him now that she had the chance. Suddenly, his eyes flew to hers, widening in surprise.

"You're awake," he nearly shouted with joy.

"Yeah. I guess I am."

He pulled her into his arms so tight it made it almost impossible to breathe. "Joel" She pounded his back with her hand. "Can't breathe."

Releasing his grip on her he pulled back enough to stare into her eyes. "Don't ever scare me like that again."

"Well, no worries. You're stuck with me for the unforeseeable future."

"Nothing could make me happier. I want you to be with me forever." His eyes warmed, happiness overflowing out of him. She could feel each increase of joy as it built up inside of him. All of her powers at full strength.

"Be careful what you wish for. You might get it." A gamine smile appeared on her face.

His features grew dark as he continued to caress her. "Don't ever do something so foolish again. If you'd died..."

"I didn't, and I won't," she reassured him. "Besides, I doubt something like that could happen again considering."

"Considering what?" His eyebrows rose, questioning her response.

She couldn't wait to break the news to him. "My newly minted guardian status."

"Pardon me?"

"Michael offered me a choice, I could remain in a coma for the rest of my life, or I could be a guardian and use my powers for good."

"He would have left you in that state when he was capable of helping you?" Joel pulled away as anger filled him.

"Easy, now. I think he wanted to test me a bit. See how much I'd be willing to put up with and what I'd give up for someone I loved. The, uh, meeting was a bit more complicated than the summary I gave you. Just be glad I can now be with you forever. You still want that right?"

"More than anything—Becs I need to tell you."

"That you love me?" she teased.

"More than you'll ever know." His eyes searched hers as he spoke, "I shouldn't have pushed you away. I promise I never will again. Even if I wanted to, I couldn't. I need you too much to ever let you go again."

"Good, because I don't plan on ever letting you go either. I love you, too, you fool."

Joel pulled her into his arms and kissed her breath away. Rebecca wrapped her arms around him and pulled him closer to her. She couldn't get enough of him. Joel's hands roamed across her back. He pulled away and showered her cheeks with tiny light kiss, finally settling on her lips again for one more scorching, mind melding, lip lock. Their tongues danced together as they tasted every inch of each other's mouths. Joel pulled back and helped her to her feet.

Rebecca observed her surroundings, surveying the contents inside the room. In the distance, she could see Carolyn sitting next to Kenneth's bed. He had her hand firmly in his grasp as he stared back at her. They were lost in their own world, not noticing anything or anyone around them. Somehow Rebecca doubted they would have seen her or Joel anyway. If they did, neither one of them would know who she was. She would miss her friend, but she knew the cost when she agreed to Michael's deal. It made her happy to see joy on her friend's face. Kenneth appeared to be all right, and they would be free to build a life together if they chose to.

Rebecca turned her attention back to Joel. He didn't say a word while she studied Carolyn and Kenneth. He must have known what rolled through her mind. Michael's rules were set in stone. You had to let go and move on. Her lips tilted into a pleased smile as she wrapped her arm through his, gazing into his gorgeous aquamarine eyes, radiating his inner happiness.

"Well, sexy Becs, you ready to leave and start our lives together?" Joel asked, his lips tilting into an audacious grin.

"I am. Can we visit our private lagoon before we go? I'd like to spend one more day there with you before we start a whole new adventure."

"Anything for you." He leaned down and kissed her forehead before leading her out of the room. They walked out of the hospital hand in hand, no one giving them a second glance. Their smiles bright as the sun. Pure bliss poured out of them, love an overwhelming part of each of their souls.

About the Author

DAWN BROWER HOLDS A Bachelor of Arts in Psychology, a Master of Arts in Education, and a Master of Arts in Liberal Arts with concentrations in Literature, History, and Sociology. She works as a substitute teacher and enjoys the flexibility it gives her to concentrate on her other endeavors.

Growing up she was the only girl out of six children. She is a single mother of two teenage boys; there is never a dull moment in her life. Reading books is her favorite hobby. While she loves all genres she focuses most of her writing on historical and contemporary romance.

There are always stories inside her head; she just never thought she could make them come to life. That creativity has finally found an outlet.

For more information visit her website at: http://www.authordawnbrower.com/

Books by Dawn Brower

Broken Pearl
Deadly Benevolence
Don't Happen Twice
A Wallflower's Christmas Kiss
Marsden Romances
A Flawed Jewel
A Crystal Angel
A Treasured Lily
A Sanguine Gem
A Hidden Ruby
A Discarded Pearl
Novak Springs
Cowgirl Fever
Dirty Proof
Unbridled Pursuit
Sensual Games
Christmas Temptation
Linked Across Time
Saved by My Blackguard
Searching for My Rogue
Seduction of My Rake
Surrendering to My Spy
Spellbound by My Charmer
Coming Soon
Stolen by My Knave

DAWN BROWER

Heart's Intent
One Heart to Give
Unveiled Hearts
Coming Soon
Heart of the Moment